"I've been hiding behind my work for a long time.

"You're the only woman who's ever made me want to change that."

"Thank you," she said, so moved by the depth of that compliment she couldn't think of any more to say to it than that.

"So now what?"

She sighed. "We're both too old to go blundering into this blindly, pretending we don't know the consequences."

"So I guess we have two choices. We walk away from this and go on as before, or we…"

"Keep our eyes open and jump into the fire?"

He closed his eyes and leaned his head back. "It is that, isn't it? Pure fire…"

The simple admission that he felt as she did, hot and intense and urgent, caused a rush of reaction in Kit unlike anything she'd ever felt. This was a hunger that was new to her, a hunger she'd never known herself capable of.

Until Miguel de los Reyes had kissed her and changed her world.

Dear Reader,

Summer's in full sizzle, and so are the romances in this month's Intimate Moments selections, starting with *Badge of Honor*, the latest in Justine Davis's TRINITY STREET WEST miniseries. For everyone who's been waiting for Chief Miguel de los Reyes to finally fall in love, I have good news. The wait is over! Hurry out to buy this one—but don't drive so fast you get stopped for speeding. Unless, of course, you're pulled over by an officer like Miguel!

Suzanne Brockmann is continuing her TALL, DARK AND DANGEROUS miniseries—featuring irresistible navy SEALs as heroes—with *Everyday, Average Jones*. Of course, there's nothing everyday about this guy. I only wish there were, because then I might meet a man like him myself. Margaret Watson takes us to CAMERON, UTAH, for a new miniseries, beginning with *Rodeo Man*. The title alone should draw you to this one. And we round out the month with new books by Marcia Evanick, who offers the very moving *A Father's Promise*, and two books bearing some of our new thematic flashes. Ingrid Weaver's *Engaging Sam* is a MEN IN BLUE title, and brand-new author Shelley Cooper's *Major Dad* is a CONVENIENTLY WED book.

Enjoy all six—then come back next month, because we've got some of the best romance around *every* month, right here in Silhouette Intimate Moments.

Yours,

Leslie J. Wainger
Executive Senior Editor

Please address questions and book requests to:
Silhouette Reader Service
U.S.: 3010 Walden Ave., P.O. Box 1325, Buffalo, NY 14269
Canadian: P.O. Box 609, Fort Erie, Ont. L2A 5X3

JUSTINE DAVIS

BADGE OF HONOR

Published by Silhouette Books
America's Publisher of Contemporary Romance

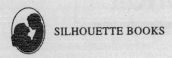

SILHOUETTE BOOKS

ISBN 0-373-07871-4

BADGE OF HONOR

This edition published by arrangement with Harlequin Books S.A.

® and TM are trademarks of Harlequin Books S.A., used under license.
Trademarks indicated with ® are registered in the United States Patent
and Trademark Office, the Canadian Trade Marks Office and in other
countries.

Printed in U.S.A.

Books by Justine Davis

JUSTINE DAVIS

lives in San Clemente, California. Her interests outside of writing are sailing, doing needlework, horseback riding and driving her restored 1967 Corvette roadster— top down, of course.

A policewoman, Justine says that years ago, a young man she worked with encouraged her to try for a promotion to a position that was, at that time, occupied only by men. "I succeeded, became wrapped up in my new job, and that man moved away, never, I thought, to be heard from again. Ten years later he appeared out of the woods of Washington State, saying he'd never forgotten me and would I please marry him? With that history, how could I write anything but romance?"

Chapter 1

"Why are you writing a stupid parking ticket when there are killers running around loose?"

Kit Walker almost missed a step at the screamed accusation. She turned and saw a young, uniformed man standing in the street next to a yellow sedan. He looked harried and was being confronted by a clearly irate woman.

Kit backed off the sidewalk into the doorway of the Marina Heights dry cleaners she'd just exited, to get out of the way of the pedestrians who were watching the display with varying degrees of interest and paying little attention to where they were going.

A parking ticket, she thought in mild amusement. Sometimes it seemed as if nothing made people angrier.

Normally she would have left him to handle it, knowing he had the lesson to learn. Every cop had heard what the woman was screaming at one time or another from citizens who didn't know or care that a parking control officer had nothing to do with murderers and criminals, and was a civil-

ian just like they were. The comment was right up there with
doughnut shop jokes, and usually issued by someone who
would scream even louder if a similar stereotype-based comment was aimed at them.

It was part of the job, part of being professional, learning
to deal with verbal abuse without retaliating. But Kit stayed,
hanging back, just in case. The instinct to back up another
uniform ran deep in her, as it did in any cop. And violence
had erupted out of lesser situations than a dispute over a parking ticket.

"I understand you're upset, ma'am," the young man said
patiently. "But the meter is expired, and I have no choice but
to write a citation."

"That's all you cops know how to do, harass innocent people—"

Kit only half listened to the familiar tirade. She glanced at
her watch. She'd been so nervous about the detail Captain
Mallery had given her last night that she'd left her house extra
early this morning. Her stop at the cleaners hadn't taken long,
so she had some time to spare. She'd stay, just to be sure the
young man—barely more than a boy, really—didn't get in
over his head.

"Writing parking tickets when the murderer of my son
walks the streets freely!"

Kit's attention snapped to the woman. The young man
holding the cite book was gaping, clearly startled by this unexpected turn.

"But you don't care about that, do you?" the woman exclaimed. "You don't care that an innocent boy was beaten to
death. You just want to write your little ticket."

Uh-oh, Kit thought. She moved out of the doorway toward
the pair, threading her way through passersby who were slowing as the scenario before them grew more interesting with
the mention of murder. The last thing the poor kid needed
was a crowd, she thought. He would end up having to call

for armed backup, and this could escalate unnecessarily into something even more unpleasant than it already was.

The parking control officer spotted her then, and the look of relief that crossed his face told her he'd recognized her— and expected her to solve the problem. She flicked a glance at the woman, who was still ranting, and gave a quick shake of her head. The boy looked puzzled, then seemed to realize that she didn't want the woman to know who she was. It would be better if she thought Kit was just a passing citizen rather than another cop. Feeling outnumbered might only make things worse.

Kit came to a halt beside the woman. She was Hispanic and petite—about six inches shorter than Kit's five-eight. Her hair was coiled in a tidy bun at the back of her head, and Kit guessed it would be almost as long as the woman was tall. She was suddenly very conscious of her short, tousled blond locks. They had once been nearly as long, but had long ago been sacrificed to the practicalities of 3:00 a.m. call outs.

The woman's face was lined and worn, and her expression told Kit it was as much from sadness as from time. She wore a thin gold wedding band that Kit guessed from its wear had not been off her hand in decades. Her eyes were a rich, warm brown, although right now they were more hot than warm. She was glaring at the young man before her in a way that belied her diminutive stature. Dignity fairly radiated from her despite—or perhaps because of—her anger, and Kit made sure there was respect in her tone when she spoke.

"It certainly doesn't seem fair, does it?" Kit said sympathetically. The woman glanced at her, clearly startled at her intrusion. "Seems like all the taxes we pay ought to allow us to park on our own streets without having to pay all over again."

"It most certainly does," the woman agreed.

"It's not like this is Marina del Mar," Kit went on, "where you have to pay to park at the beach. That's a choice. But in

Marina Heights you have to come here to get your business done, don't you?''

Her tone was gentle, empathetic, and invited the woman to join in her commiseration. The woman studied her, then finally responded.

"That's right. We have no choice. We must come here to go to the bank, to the shoe repair.''

"And there are no shopping malls here where the parking is free. You must park on the street. It just doesn't seem fair, does it, Mrs....?''

"Rivas. Carmela Rivas,'' the woman said, and Kit gave an inward sigh of relief. It was a tiny bit harder for people to be angry if you were on a first-name basis. "And no, it is not fair,'' the woman added emphatically.

"I'm Kit Walker,'' Kit said, holding out her hand. After a moment's hesitation, the woman took it. Her grasp was firm but brief, and Kit sensed she was diverted enough. Kit glanced at the young officer.

"You must hate your job sometimes, to have to give nice people like Mrs. Rivas citations.''

"Yes, ma'am,'' the boy said fervently, his gratitude at Kit's intervention obvious. "Sometimes I do.''

"Are you in school?''

"Yes, Sarg—I mean ma'am,'' the boy corrected at the quick shake of her head. "I take classes out at the junior college. I'm in my fourth year. It's taking longer because I can only afford to go part-time.''

"So this job is to pay your school expenses?''

"That's one reason. I want to—''

"Good for you,'' Kit said, cutting him off. She guessed he'd been about to say the other reason was that he wanted to join the cops of Trinity West, as the Marina Heights police station was called because of its location on Trinity Street West. Many young men took the PCO job thinking it would get them a foot in the door. And Kit could tell from Mrs.

Rivas's expression that she was for the first time seeing the young man as a person, not just a uniform, and Kit didn't want to lose that bit of progress.

"You should find some other work," Mrs. Rivas said with audible disdain. But, Kit thought thankfully, no anger. And the passing pedestrians had returned to their normal pace. The situation had been defused. And, she thought with another glance at her watch, she still had time to spare before she had to be at the airport. This distraction had killed several minutes, and she had to admit she was grateful.

"I will pay this, I suppose," Mrs. Rivas said grudgingly. "It is not really his fault." She watched the young officer move on, and a remorseful expression came across her face. "My Jaime would have been nearly his age now," she whispered. "His twenty-second birthday is...would have been next week."

The woman's earlier words, the ones that had spurred Kit to action, came back to her now. "Jaime is...your son you spoke of?"

Grief haunted the woman's eyes as she looked at Kit. "Yes. He was murdered, not far from here, five years ago."

He would have been seventeen, Kit thought. "So young," she said. "How awful for you."

"It would have made no difference if he was older. He was still my son. And he was a good boy, a smart boy. He belonged to no gang, I don't care what they say."

"Is that what they say?"

"Of course it is. They say that about all young Hispanic boys, that they are all in gangs. It is not true. It was not a rival gang who did it. My Jaime was never in a gang."

Kit had heard this from lying, denying or honestly unknowing parents nearly as often as she'd heard the parking ticket complaint. But she wasn't about to point that out to the woman she'd managed to calm down.

"I gather," she asked delicately, "they never caught who did it?"

Anger flashed in Carmela's face again. "Caught him? You mean the police? Of course they have not. Why would they?"

Her tone said everything, and Kit stifled a sigh. Blaming the police for everything from traffic to the weather had become commonplace. She knew she should have walked away once the immediate situation had been controlled. But something about this woman's vehemence, the pain beneath her grief and anger, reached Kit in a way she'd come to recognize. Whatever this woman was feeling, it was very, very real.

"The police will never *catch* the man who killed my Jaime," the woman said with bitter emphasis.

"I'm sure it feels that way, Mrs. Rivas," Kit said gently. "But sometimes it takes time."

The woman laughed, a harsh, bleak sound. And suddenly Kit realized what had kept her here, why she had stayed. The woman sounded just like she had after Bobby had died, and then Anna. As if there was no hope left in the world. Or for it.

"He will get away with it," Mrs. Rivas insisted. "They won't touch him."

She sounded so positive Kit couldn't stop herself from asking, "Why do you say that?"

"Because—" the woman fairly spat the words "—it was a *cop.*"

Well, Kit thought as she pulled onto the loop that circled the airport parking areas, she'd been looking for a distraction, and she'd certainly found it.

And in the process, she'd cut her time margin to almost nothing. If she didn't find a parking place in the lot close to the terminal, she was going to be in trouble. Being late to pick up the chief of police was not a good career move.

She wished the captain had sent somebody else on this run.

But she had no good reason to avoid the task, none that she wanted to use, anyway. She could hardly tell Captain Mallery she didn't want to pick up the chief because she was never quite comfortable in his presence. That would be an unwise career move, as well. She'd picked him up before, and every time found herself babbling like a fool or not talking at all, and either one made for an uncomfortable ride in a car with just the two of them.

It wasn't his position as chief that made her uneasy. Miguel de los Reyes wasn't the kind of man who used his rank to intimidate. Nor was it his demeanor. While he could project command presence with the best of them, he was also unfailingly courteous, gentlemanly in an old-world kind of way that suited him unexpectedly well and sometimes made him seem older than his forty-four years. She supposed that was why he was able to bridge the gap between the youth of the city and the older residents—he looked young enough to understand the former, but his demeanor helped him relate to the latter.

No, there was no reason for her to feel so uncomfortable, other than the simple fact that his aristocratic good looks would make any breathing woman…twitchy. But she did feel that way. She always had in the fourteen years she'd been at Trinity West, back when he'd been just a sergeant, and his wife her friend, long before tragic circumstances had made him chief. She supposed she always would.

Her outlook brightened slightly when she saw that the parking lot adjacent to the terminal wasn't yet full and closed off.

That's half the battle, she thought. *Now to find an empty spot.*

For a moment she wished the chief was the kind of man to take advantage of his rank. Then she could have parked right in front of the doors, badged the sheriff's deputy and marched on in. But Miguel de los Reyes had strict rules, and not invoking professional courtesy for small things like this was one of them. Save it for when it will help you do the job, he said. Nothing was more important.

She admired him for it, really. She admired him for many things. But right now she would have settled for a little less admiration and a visible parking space.

Of course, she could have kept circling and let him walk to the curb to meet her—that was always his suggestion—but her deeply ingrained respect for the man and his rank made that seem wrong. He deserved to be met at the gate, she thought. But if she didn't find that elusive spot in the next couple of minutes, it was going to be academic.

She turned down yet another aisle of the big lot, her mind going to Mrs. Rivas and her claim about her son's death. Kit found it difficult to believe a cop had killed the boy and nothing had come of it, but the woman's passionate declaration, issued to a woman she had no way of knowing was a cop, stayed vividly in Kit's mind.

She tried to set aside her instinctive reaction, that gut-deep bond she felt with all cops, built over years of dealing with the ugliness, the kind of bond no one on the outside ever quite understood. She wasn't about to say that it never happened, that things never got out of hand, but this...it just didn't seem likely.

On the surface, it was simple, an open and shut case. Rival gangsters, taking each other out in the tradition of the streets. True, a personal beating, one on one, as Mrs. Rivas said this had been, was rare. Gangs weren't called gangs because they worked alone. Their strength was in their numbers and the willingness of every member to die for the honor of his gang and his "homies." And what they saw as bravery many saw as cowardice—shooting from racing vehicles, sniping from hidden positions, heedless of innocent bystanders who got caught in the crossfire.

"Give me an old-fashioned gang rumble any day," then Lieutenant Mallery had once said years ago, after a night filled with particularly ugly carnage and a body count in the double digits. "Make 'em kill each other in a real personal way. It'd save a lot of innocent lives."

"Maybe we should give them weapons training," Clay Yeager had said rather fiercely as he'd stared at the body of a beautiful, tiny little girl who would never grow up. "If they were better shots, maybe they'd hit who they meant to hit instead of...babies."

A chill swept over her at a sudden storm of memories. She hadn't thought of Clay in a while, but as always when she did, she sent up a little prayer that, wherever he'd gone after his life had crumbled, he was all right. He'd been a cop's cop and a people's cop. He'd been a miracle worker in the simplest of ways—he cared. He cared for his fellow cops, he cared for the people he served, he cared for the job. He cared for everybody, and they'd let him, never once wondering if he might need a little care himself.

Guilt welled inside her. She had to blink back the moisture that brimmed stingingly behind her eyelids, and almost missed an available parking place. Maneuvering into it enabled her to shove aside her emotions, and by the time she was walking into the terminal she was in control once more. The chief was a very perceptive man, and she didn't want him asking her questions that would only bring back a time that was painful for him, as well.

She got to the gate before the passengers had begun to deplane and took a moment to steady herself.

It's just because he's your chief, she told herself. *You've known him for years, but now he's got all the power, and it makes you edgy.*

But she knew that wasn't true. He wasn't that kind of man. He didn't rule by coercion, as his predecessor had been known to do. And there wasn't the slightest hint of any misuse of his considerable authority on any front. He was scrupulously fair, sometimes painfully honest, and he genuinely

cared about his people. As Gage Butler had once said, de los
Reyes had taken a bunch of cops who didn't give a damn
anymore and turned them into the toughest, best run police
department in the county, if not the state.

And most of them would follow him into hell if he led the
charge.

None of which explained why she was standing here talking to herself, trying to convince herself she wasn't really
nervous at all. That she wasn't feeling an odd sort of unease
in her stomach, that she wasn't—

She saw him before he saw her. He was dressed in a black
suit—he almost always wore black or gray, she'd noticed—
was carrying a briefcase and had a dark gray overcoat tossed
over his arm. He certainly didn't need it here. Even in Oc-
tober the southern California days were pleasantly warm, so
it must have been cold wherever he'd been.

Chicago, she realized suddenly, glancing at the flight des-
ignation that glowed in red letters over the gate. The captain
had mentioned that, but it had slipped her mind. That explained the coat, she thought. It had been cold there of late.

Among other things, she added inwardly with a frown, he
looked exhausted. Even his golden skin couldn't hide the
traces of it, the dark circles beneath his eyes, the fine lines
around his eyes that seemed more pronounced, too pronounced to write it off to the unflattering lighting in the terminal.

But nothing, not even the weariness etched in his face, not
the slight effort that showed in his long strides, could rob him
of that innate dignity.

And, she admitted wryly, that undeniable attractiveness.
Even tired, Miguel de los Reyes was a beautiful man. Tall,
at least six-two, lean and fit, and with patrician features that
made her think of kings of ancient cultures, thick dark hair
touched with a becoming silver at the temples and pale gray

eyes that seemed to see far beyond the surface, he turned more than one head in the crowded terminal.

And most of them were female, Kit noted with what she told herself was amusement.

He saw her then, and when their gazes met, Kit felt the odd little jolt she'd almost grown used to. But then he smiled, as if he was glad to see her, as if he was glad it was her waiting for him, and she felt a warmth blossoming inside her unlike anything she'd ever known—except when this same man had praised her work or her judgment or her handling of a difficult situation.

"Kit," he said as he separated from the stream of passengers. "You got the taxi duty? How are you?"

"Fine, sir." She thought his mouth twitched slightly, but couldn't be sure. "How was your trip?"

His mouth did twist then, into a wry grimace. "It was... tiring."

"I—" She bit off the rest, horrified that she'd almost said, "I can see that." This was the chief, for crying out loud, she told herself. "I'm sorry to hear that," she said instead. "Captain Mallery said it was a vacation, so I—we all hoped you were relaxing."

If he noticed the choppiness of her conversation, it didn't show. But then, the chief was a gentleman to the core and would never comment on her nervousness. Sometimes it was hard to remember that he was the same man who could take charge with complete authority in a crisis or could be as tough as necessary on the street. But she'd seen him do it, and more than once.

He glanced at her, then said quietly, "I went to visit Anna's parents."

Kit's breath caught. "I...didn't know—that you...kept in touch."

"They're still my family." She knew his parents had died, as had hers, in a car accident when he'd been in his twenties, and he was, also as she was, an only child, so she wasn't surprised when he added, "About all I have, now." He shrugged, as if it didn't matter.

And you're all they have left of Anna, too, Kit thought sadly.

He rarely spoke of Anna, and she'd had no idea he was still close to her parents. But it wasn't surprising. He'd deeply loved his wife, and he was the kind of man who would take ties like that very seriously. She was a little surprised that she was so sure of that, but she was. And it didn't mean anything, not really. It only made sense to try and know a little bit about him, since he was the chief.

There was a great deal of safety in that title. It was easier to distance herself from the rank than the man, the man she'd worked alongside for fourteen years now, the man she'd laughed with when they were both on the street, the man whose promotions she'd celebrated, the man who, she suspected, had been behind her assignment to detective, the man she'd watched quickly advance through the ranks without losing the trust of those who became subordinates, the man any one of the Trinity West cops would trust with their lives.

And then the probable reason for the trip struck her, and she said the words without thinking.

"Her birthday…"

"Yes. It's very hard for them."

And it's easy for you? Kit knew the answer and felt a tightness in her throat. She had known and liked Anna de los Reyes. They had met when Miguel was still a sergeant. Kit had come to consider her a valued friend and had felt welcome in their home. When Anna died, a gaunt, hollow-eyed shadow of the vital, intelligent, loving, beautiful woman she'd been, Kit had railed against God, fate, medicine and anyone or anything she could think of. And at all of them all over again for doing this to Miguel de los Reyes, one of the finest men she'd ever met.

And suddenly she was incapable of seeing him as only a rank, only the chief. He was a man, a man who had been hurt deeply but had somehow found the courage to go on. A man she had admired for years. A man she admired even more now.

"I'm sorry." It was all she could manage to get out.

The chief looked at her—he was one of the few men she knew who made her five foot eight seem a nice, petite height—with an oddly intent expression.

"I know," he said softly.

Flustered by his tone and the way he was looking at her, Kit turned hastily away and gestured toward the escalator that led to the baggage claim. "The car isn't too far," she said. "When they start unloading your flight's bags, I'll go bring it around front."

He seemed to hesitate for a moment, then nodded, and they started to walk. Kit was conscious of the faintly spicy scent of his after-shave, the same one he'd used for years, that always made her think of him. She was conscious as well of his long-legged stride and knew from experience he would have shortened it had she not been able to keep up. But her legs were long enough to cover nearly as much ground. They fit well together—

She recoiled from that thought as if it was an already agitated hornet's nest. *He's the chief, for God's sake,* she told herself fiercely.

But he was right there, too close, and she was always so darned edgy around him. She tried to think of something else, anything else, but the only thing that came to mind was Carmela Rivas's passionate accusation.

Fine thing, she thought, *when the idea of a killer cop is the only thing powerful enough to keep your mind where it belongs.*

It was going to be a long ride to Trinity West.

Chapter 2

Miguel de los Reyes liked the way he didn't have to shorten his stride for Kit to keep up with him. It didn't happen often. Not that he minded when he had to do it with other people—it was a matter of simple courtesy, and he knew his above-average height made it necessary with some men as well as women. But Kit stayed with him easily with those long legs of hers.

He remembered when Trinity West had challenged the up-scale Marina del Mar cops to that charity softball game in the spring, to raise money for Kelsey Gregerson's halfway house. For most of the players, the most memorable moments had been when Quisto Romero had squared off at the plate against his old partner, now Marina del Mar sergeant Chance Buckner, who, it turned out, had a wicked curveball, or when Chance's songwriter wife, Shea, had sung the national anthem in her clear, lovely voice.

But to him, the most memorable moment had been Kit Walker, clad in shorts and the team's white baseball jersey, diving across the infield to make a one-handed catch of a line drive that should have driven home at least a couple of runs. She had flown, her long, slim body stretched out as she reached for the ball...and he had realized her legs went on forever.

God. He grimaced, rubbing a hand over his face. He must be tired when he gave in to that kind of thinking. He had no business even noticing Kit's legs. Not only was she an old and valued friend, she worked for him, and that way lay trouble of a kind he never wanted to deal with.

"Are you all right...sir?" she asked as they came to a halt beside the large, oval baggage carousel.

That tentative "sir" shook him out of that lingering reverie. "Fine," he said, glancing at her. He'd always liked long hair on a woman, but there was something exceptionally appealing about her short, tousled blond hair, perhaps the way it seemed to play up lovely hazel eyes that seemed as changeable as the sea, sometimes green, sometimes gold.

Something in her expression made him realize he was staring at her, and he said quickly, "I was just thinking about...Cruz. And how he badgered everybody into that softball game."

She laughed lightly, with no trace of reluctance or resignation. "He'd do worse than that for Kelsey. He's crazy about her."

"She's a dynamic woman. That halfway house of hers is piling up an enviable success rate with runaways already."

"Yes," Kit agreed, and Miguel wondered if she was agreeing to both. He knew she and Cruz were close, and he had even suspected it might have once gone beyond friendship, but there was no sign in her demeanor or in those expressive eyes that she was anything less than delighted for the happiness Cruz Gregerson had found.

"Tell me, what's happened in the last week?"

She gave him a startled look. "I...I'm sure the captain kept you filled in better than I could."

He smiled at her. "He kept me posted. But in keeping with the rolling downhill theory, I know there are things that never filter up that high."

She smiled at him and finally seemed to relax, to look at him as she had when there hadn't been this gulf between them. Sometimes he hated this part of his job, where people he liked and admired were stiff and uneasy around him because of those four gold stars on his uniform collar. *You'd think I'd be used to it,* he thought. Cops were always set apart, and he'd had twenty-three years of being one.

"Really, nothing unusual," she said. Her brow furrowed for a moment, as if something contrary to her words had just occurred to her, but she went on without explaining. "Cruz wrapped up that counterfeiting case he was helping the feds on, Ryan popped that bar owner who was running underage hookers, and patrol made a good drug bust, a couple of keys of coke." She gave him a sideways look. "Max hit on it."

Miguel smiled in satisfaction. Sending their single canine for drug-sniffing training had been his idea, and he'd had to do some fancy number-crunching to come up with the funds. "I'm very glad to hear that."

She grinned, and his breath caught. "It almost got by the humans," she said. "It was hidden in a fancy birthday cake, and the field sergeant thought Max was just hungry. But Joe insisted Max knew better, so they finally made a little cut through the top of the cake, and there it was."

He chuckled, unable to resist the humor of the story—or her cheer. And suddenly the weariness of the past week seemed to retreat a little.

"And what about you, Kit?"

"Me?" She seemed startled.

"How are you doing? I know you need help in there, but we're so short-staffed right now—"

"I'm okay. Things have been relatively quiet. I miss Gage, of course—he did the work of three—but I'm staying even."

They all missed Gage, Miguel thought. The detective had been an integral part of the team. They'd known how hard he worked, how many hours he put in, that he'd lived, breathed and slept the job, but until he'd gone they hadn't realized just how big a hole he'd leave behind. But Miguel knew there wasn't anybody who had begrudged him. Gage had been teetering on a precipice, obsessed beyond reason with the job, and all of them had been dreading the inevitable crash. And then Laurey Templeton had come along and pulled him from the edge of the abyss, changing the haunted, driven cop they'd known into a happy, contented man. As much as they missed him, they all welcomed his salvation as if it was their own. Gage was more than well-liked at Trinity West.

"Have you heard from him lately?" he asked.

"I talked to Laurey last week." She grinned again, and Miguel thought what a lovely expression it was, lighting up her eyes like that. "She said he's so busy exploring up there around Seattle she's afraid he's never going to get a job. She's going to suggest he open a sporting goods store or something."

Miguel laughed again. "I'm glad to hear he's taking a long vacation. He needed it. Deserved it."

"Yes," Kit said softly.

"You were worried about him."

"I think I knew he was on the edge, but not how close."

"I remember when you came to me about him."

She smiled rather shyly. "And you backed me up, made him take that time off. Did I ever thank you for that?"

"You did, but it wasn't necessary. You were right. It had to be done. And I thought all the more of you for your concern."

Something in the way she looked at him then made him

restless somehow. But the clank of the baggage carousel starting to move, indicating his bags were about to arrive, served as a distraction.

"I'll go bring the car around," she said. "I presume you're going home first?"

He shook his head. "To the station first. My car is there, and I'll take it home from there—after I see what has piled up while I was gone."

She looked at him as if she was thinking he should go straight home and to sleep but didn't dare say so. And he wasn't sure he would disagree with that, but as tired as he was, he was also feeling a bit unsettled.

"I'm hoping the pile will be so huge it will make me want to avoid it," he said wryly. "Then I'll go home and sleep for about twelve hours."

She looked startled, then, as if unwillingly, that grin spread across her face again. "I think that's an excellent idea."

He watched her walk away, forgetting entirely to look for his bag as the luggage from the flight thumped steadily onto the rotating carousel. She was wearing neat, white linen slacks and a crisp, pale yellow blouse. She wore a lot of yellow, he'd noticed, and it made her look like the quintessential California golden girl. Except that there was none of the vapidness about her that had given rise to countless jokes about the species. No one would ever mistake Kit Walker for a brainless blonde. There was too much life, too much vivid, snapping intelligence in those hazel eyes. He was lucky to have her.

Trinity West was lucky to have her, he amended quickly, feeling a bit uneasy with the way his mind had formed the thought.

He turned to look for his battered black suitcase and tried to put the golden image out of his mind.

Kit sneezed. It was dusty down here in the file morgue, and they didn't have enough clerks to staff the big, dreary room, so she had been hunting on her own for several minutes. Naturally, what she was looking for had been before the cutoff date for microfilming. They were eventually going to do everything, but it was a slow process, and they'd begun with cases that were still open, then gone back in chronological order. And Trinity West was so far behind in this kind of modernization that most of them took what there was gratefully, glad of any help at all in modernizing the process.

It was a wonder they were even as far as they were, she thought. There had been no money in the budget for new computer equipment, the patrol units were starting to fall apart and had to be a priority, but still the chief had managed to find, somewhere, enough to at least get them started on archiving the old cases. He'd wangled an old system no longer in use out of the city library, and sweet-talked the head librarian into loaning them someone to teach several clerks how to run it, so at least the huge project was begun.

He really ought to run for mayor, as he joked on occasion, Kit thought as she dug through more files and sneezed again at the dust. He got things done. But she couldn't help but hope he wouldn't. Trinity West couldn't afford to lose him. He'd worked miracles here, at a time when nothing less would have held this place together.

She thought again of the exhaustion that had shown when he'd gotten off the plane this morning and of the strain she was sure he'd been under, sharing Anna's birthday with her parents, dredging up memories that had to be so very painful. For all that Anna had died nearly six years ago, he mourned her still. He'd loved her so much the consensus around Trinity West was that he'd never remarry, and Kit couldn't help thinking that was very sad. That she had no room to talk was a fact she chose to ignore for the moment.

This time when she sneezed, it was on dust stirred up from the right file. She double-checked the report number and then

pulled the file off the long shelf crammed full of manila folders.

Her first thought was that it was awfully thin for a murder
investigation file. Her second was an audible groan as, after
flipping it open and confirming it was the Rivas file, she noticed the signature of the investigating officer.

Robards. *Didn't it just need that?* she thought.

She almost put the file back. She wasn't quite sure why
she'd looked it up, anyway. It couldn't be to keep from thinking about those moments when she'd been forced to look at
Miguel de los Reyes and see the man instead of the rank. And
she didn't believe Carmela Rivas's story that it had been a
cop who had beaten her son to death. She believed the woman
believed it, but she knew how desperate people were, in the
throes of grief, to blame someone or something for their loss.
And of late, because of a couple of high-profile cases representing such a small percentage of the overall number of cops
that it would be dismissed as insignificant if it was any other
group, it seemed the police had become a too likely and too
frequent target.

At the same time, she knew cops were held to a higher
standard than almost any other professionals. Whether or not
that was fair had been discussed at great length, she knew,
and each side had valid points. Kit hadn't dwelt on it—it
made little difference to her if it was fair or not, it *was,* and
she thought her energy better spent dealing with it. Of course,
she often thought wryly, being a female in a traditionally male
job—for that matter, being female, period—had taught her
much about dealing with unfairness.

And Robards, she thought, looking once more at the signature on the report, was the dean of the school. Unfortunately, the swaggering blowhard was also her boss, the lieutenant in charge of the detective division. And again she
almost put the file back.

She didn't want to deal with him on this. She knew what

his reaction would be. He was nothing if not predictable when it came to anyone—let alone a woman—questioning him. About anything. He did his best to make life miserable for them all—even the men of Trinity West called him a dinosaur, and Kit thought it a generous term for a man living so far in the past. He'd been a cop for thirty years and saw no reason to change his tactics just because law enforcement had moved into the twentieth century. He was immovably certain that a change to the old days when cops could, as he put it "kick ass and take no names," would solve every problem in society today.

That, and getting women and all the other groups he didn't approve of back where they belonged, of course. He'd only made lieutenant because he'd been tight with the former chief, who'd been careful to get as many of his old boys as he could into ranking positions. It certainly wasn't because of his modern ideas and approach.

She slapped the file folder shut and lifted her hand to shove it on the shelf. It really was awfully skimpy for a murder case, she thought. That made her curious. As did the fact that Robards had done the investigation at all. It was unusual for a patrol sergeant, which he had been at that time, to do paperwork on a crime. That was usually passed off to a street cop, with the sergeant in charge doing at most a supplemental report if he was involved in the investigation.

She opened the folder again and flipped through the pages. Crime report, supplemental info, property report—Robards's name appeared on the bottom of each as the sole reporting officer. And even more oddly, they had been read and approved not by the watch commander but by the former chief himself. It gave her an odd feeling to see the signature of the man now dead. She'd never liked him much—he'd seemed to her cut from the same cloth as Robards—but he was a cop and he'd been gunned down in the street in a nightmare drive-by shooting.

It was, in the end, the oddities—and the curiosity they aroused—that made her hang onto the file. Occupational hazard, she told herself as she dutifully signed the file out on the log before leaving the room for the thankfully less musty air of the rest of the building.

In her office, she closed the door and sat at the desk with the file. She glanced at the two phone messages that had come in while she'd been in the file storage room, trying to decipher Betty Serrano's handwriting. Trinity West's budget hadn't run to voice mail yet, either. If you wanted those perks, you went to work for Marina del Mar PD.

Determining that neither of the messages was urgent timewise, she set them aside and opened the folder. The initial report was embarrassingly brief. Robards wrote that just after going on duty for the graveyard shift at one in the morning, he'd heard the call go out of a man down, and since he happened to be close to the scene at the time he had responded. That alone made Kit's mouth twist. Robards had never been known for volunteering for actual work.

The report said he'd found a man lying in the alley in the three hundred block of Trinity Street East behind a tavern. He'd thought him drunk at first, but quickly determined he was dead. Curious, she flipped to the autopsy report and found that there had been no evidence of drugs or alcohol in the victim's system.

Interesting, Kit thought, the implications of that phrase about thinking the man drunk. And why, since it had been proven he hadn't been drunk, would Robards even mention it, unless it was to plant the idea? Especially since, according to the records check, Jaime Rivas had been clean except for a couple of traffic tickets and one petty theft years ago. She went back to the report.

Something else caught her eye, and she thumbed through the rest of the report. There was no copy of the dispatch log attached, but she wasn't exactly sure when they'd started including that in files. She tapped her fingers on her desk, thinking. It would take their records section hours to track down a case this old. However, there was another option here....

She looked up a number and picked up her phone. It took her a couple of transfers, but she finally got to somebody at County Fire who said they could find what she wanted.

"It'll take a few minutes, since it's so long ago," the woman warned. "Do you want me to call you back?"

She considered that, but decided she'd prefer the slight extra pressure of having a caller on hold. "I'll wait," she said. "I'll just put you on my speakerphone."

She went on reading as she waited, wondering in the back of her mind how quickly the system would grind to a halt if the civilians ever went on strike. Cops needed to think about that more often, she thought.

The phone was still silent as she finished reading. Not that it had taken long. This had to be the shortest major felony report she'd ever seen. And the most...uncaring, she supposed—it was the only word that seemed to fit. The overall impression she got was that this victim was a nobody, his murder not worth investigating thoroughly. There was no evidence, no witnesses, nothing. A boy had been beaten to death, and it was reduced to a couple of pages of useless information.

Even the autopsy said only that the cause of death was blunt force trauma and speculated on numerous possible instruments that could have caused it. And the detective follow-up was practically nonexistent, completed by Darrel Brennan, she noted, who had retired shortly afterward. He had been one of Robards's cronies, and the two of them had often been heard bemoaning the loss of the good old days when cops were real men, not the pansies of today.

If Robards could have gotten away with writing what he had often said, "Good riddance to one more Mexican," she supposed that would be in here, too. Lord, she despised that man. She wondered why the chief put up with him. He had more reason than most to want to be rid of him. It had been Robards who had made the biggest stink when de los Reyes had been chosen first as interim, then permanent chief after Chief Lipton had been killed, ironically in retaliation for a drug bust Trinity West hadn't even made.

She'd heard Robards had publicly vowed he would never take orders from any greaser. She hadn't been there, but she had no trouble believing it. She had too much personal experience with the man's vitriol. He hated women as much as he hated minorities. Although to her surprise, unless she had to approach him, he left her pretty much alone. She'd never realized why until Gage Butler had explained it to her one day.

"You confuse him," he'd said. "You're a woman in a man's job, which he hates, but you've got rank, which he respects, and you have the right skin color."

She knew with grim certainty it was true. Not only did the man openly despise Chief de los Reyes, she'd seen Cruz Gregerson and Ryan Buckhart have to deal with Robards's other prejudices more than once, as well. Although he'd backed off Ryan considerably—she didn't think she'd heard Robards call him "Indian" or "chief" for a long time. Rumor had it that Lacey Buckhart, Ryan's wife, had somehow managed it. Kit didn't know how, but she wouldn't put it past Lacey. The woman was a tiger when it came to Ryan. And now little Amanda, Kit thought, picturing the little charmer who in less than a year had turned the solitary, taciturn Ryan into a doting, enraptured father.

With a smothered sigh, she turned to the report. Really, she knew why Robards was still here. You didn't dump a cop with thirty years on, especially one like Robards, who would fight you ugly every step of the way, without having everything you could possibly have on the man. She could only hope the chief was building a file on him.

"Hello?"

Kit grabbed the receiver and turned off the speaker. She hated talking on them herself, and didn't know anybody who didn't, so she tried to avoid it.

"Hi," she said. "Were you able to find it, Jenny?"

"Yes," the woman said, sounding instantly more amenable, one of the reasons Kit always made sure to remember names when she asked someone to do something for her. "What times did you want?"

Kit told her, wrote down the answers, thanked her profusely, then hung up. And stared at her notepad.

Robards had never even called the paramedics. They didn't have that exact detail at the fire department, but they had the times, and their records showed that the paramedics were only called when the second unit, a patrol officer, had arrived on the scene. Knowing Robards, there was little question in her mind what had happened.

That the paramedics had confirmed Jamie Rivas was dead and that the coroner's report stated he could have been dead as long as a couple of hours before he'd been found didn't really matter. What mattered was that Robards hadn't known that, and he hadn't even tried to help the boy.

And that made her just mad enough to confront him.

Kit knew that bearding the lion in his den would rob her of the protection she seemed to have outside it. He might not bother her much where he could be heard, but in private he unleashed the ugly beast of his attitude a little. But sometimes there just wasn't any other choice.

She walked out of her office toward the larger office in the corner. Then, thoughtfully, she slowed.

Cover every contingency, even when it doesn't seem necessary.

Clay had taught her that years ago. He'd been her first training officer, her mentor and her friend, a man determined to give her an even chance at a time when there were less than a dozen women at Trinity West, and most of those were civilians. She owed her career to him, and quite possibly her sanity, as well. He'd never held back but told her exactly what to expect and what she'd have to do if she was going to make it in this job.

And one of the things he'd taught her was to recognize enemies disguised as your own.

With a silent thank-you, only the latest of many, to the sadly absent Clay, she made a detour into the records section for a few minutes, stopped by her own office, then once more headed for the corner office.

She nearly gagged at the smell of the man's cigar. The chief had thankfully decreed the building smoke-free, but since Robards had a private office he was allowed to smoke inside it. And the repulsive, half-chewed, wet stub sat in an ashtray, as if he kept it there to assure himself he could still control his own office. Fortunately the sight was partially blocked by the ornate name plaque that proclaimed him, in polished gold letters, Lieutenant Ken Robards, Commander, Detective Division.

Her mouth twisted. Plain white letters with rank and name were enough for everyone else, but not this man. If he could have gotten away with a coat of arms above the door, he probably would have done it. Funny, she thought, she'd bet Miguel de los Reyes probably had more right to a family crest than this man. She'd heard his family line was unbroken for centuries. Maybe all the way back to those original Aztecs. Of course, that would mean nothing to Robards; "A greaser's a greaser," was one of his favorite phrases.

Robards was on the phone, finishing a crude joke with a belly laugh at his own wit. He hung up and looked at her with narrow-eyed curiosity; he had to know she would never approach him unless it was unavoidable. But she thought of Jaime Rivas dying in an alley and Robards not making even a token effort to help him, and her determination solidified.

"What is it, girl?" he said.

Kit controlled her irritation at the appellation. Instead of reacting as she'd like to, she sat down without invitation, knowing that would irritate him more than anything she could say yet save her from any official discipline for being insubordinate. Even Robards wouldn't write her up for simply sitting down.

The entire detective division spent far too much time thinking about such things, she thought in irritation, and it detracted from their job.

But her ploy worked—he scowled at her. On his heavily jowled face, emphasized by his buzz-cut blond hair, it was a fearsome expression. She could see another remark, more inappropriate and insulting words, she was sure, perking behind the man's muddy brown eyes, and she spoke quickly to forestall it.

"Do you remember this case?"

She held out the folder to him. She kept her eyes on his face as he took it. He glanced at the case number on the tab as he flipped it open, and she saw his small eyes narrow even further.

She knew she hadn't mistaken the expression that flitted quickly across his heavy, square face. And her breath caught at the idea of what it would take to produce that expression in this man.

Ken Robards was afraid.

Chapter 3

"Haven't got enough to keep you busy, Walker? I can change that, easy," Robards said, dropping the case file on his desk.

"I ran into the victim's mother today," she said.

"And she's still spouting off her crap, right?"

She was beginning to think she'd imagined that instant when the man had looked at the file and fear had flickered in his eyes. He was certainly back to his usual bluster.

"She had...some things to say."

"And you listened to the old bitch and decided to ignore your current caseload and go back and dig into a case that's been closed for five years?"

"She said—"

"I know what she said. She's lying, like they all do. You know how those people are. They won't even tell you the truth about their names, let alone anything else."

Kit opened her mouth to point out that many Anglos—including some cops—simply didn't understand the way Hispanic names were structured and thought they were lying when they gave more than one variation. Not that the real criminal element didn't use that to their advantage and use that ignorance to hide their real identity, but often it was just a matter of culture clash. But she stopped herself. There was no point in explaining to a closed door.

"She didn't seem to me to be lying. I think she genuinely believes what she's saying."

Robards snorted. "That's why women shouldn't be in this work. Too soft, believe anybody with a sob story."

Kit clenched her jaw, fighting for control. You'd think she'd be numb to it by now, but she wasn't. "I didn't say I believed her," she corrected tightly. "Just that *she* believes what she's saying."

That seemed to throw him. "What difference does that make? Look, precious, it was an obvious gang retaliation. He pissed some rival homies off, and they thumped him. Somebody found the body, I took the report, that was it. They did the world a favor, saved us putting the kid in the slam someday. We should just let those gang punks keep killing each other off until there's no one left."

The patronizing tone of his first words gave way to a vehemence that made her want to back away from him. She held her ground with an effort. She knew his sentiment was shared by many, cop and citizen alike, and she understood the disgust and outrage that led to it. Sometimes she felt that way herself, when gang gunfire took out innocent bystanders, women and children who had never done anything except be in the wrong place at the wrong time.

But she had also broken the news of death to too many parents, seen the grief, the anger and then the resignation in their eyes, as if they'd expected it all along, that they would do what any parent dreaded—outlive their own child. She was too haunted by those eyes to ever really wish for more death and destruction, to wish for the end of the violence by way of annihilation.

"She insists Jaime wasn't in a gang."

Robards stood up abruptly, slamming his fist hard on his desk. "They *all* insist that! According to them, none of their kids are in gangs. So where do you suppose those gang bangers come from? Don't you get it? Those people all lie to the police, it's one of their favorite things to do."

She didn't point out that he was by implication slandering his own chief. She knew he knew that perfectly well. It was the only way he could strike at the man he hated for having achieved what he never would despite a heritage Robards thought should have kept him down. And if she did call him on it, he would simply deny he'd meant Chief de los Reyes, or Cruz, or Ryan, or any of the others he held in such low esteem because they were different from him.

"Why didn't you call the paramedics?" she asked abruptly, knowing she'd pay for phrasing it in an almost accusatory way but hoping she could rattle an answer out of him.

"What the hell for? He was dead."

"Isn't that for someone with medical training to decide?"

"Listen, sweetheart," he said with a sneer, "I've seen more dead bodies than most of this department put together, and I don't need some wannabe doctor to tell me when a guy's dead." He grabbed the folder and gestured rather wildly with it. "This case is closed, and it's staying closed. There was no evidence, no witnesses, no leads…and no point! Bury it, Walker. It's none of your business."

His vehemence seemed odd, even from him. It really was an old case, and she didn't quite understand why he was getting so wound up about it after all this time.

"I'm a cop," she said, her voice controlled and even. In a perverse way, she found it easier to do when he was ranting. "That makes it my business."

"Don't give me that righteous crap," Robards snapped. "You're here to deal with sex cases and juveniles, not real police work. And that's the only reason I've let you stay here, taking up a detective slot that could go to somebody who deserves it. And if you didn't have great legs, you'd be out of here, anyway."

He sat down with a smug expression, watching her expectantly. But Kit refused to rise to the bait. She hadn't gotten where she was in this man's world without having developed a very thick skin. And she knew men like Robards were becoming the exception instead of the rule. They might still be around, but they were learning to keep their prejudices to themselves. Thankfully there wasn't another like him at Trinity West, at least.

So instead of responding, she stood and reached for the report folder. Robards pulled it away.

"I'll keep this so you're not tempted to waste any more of the department's time and money on a closed case. Get to work on what you should be doing—chasing down runaway brats."

Without a word, she turned and walked out of his office. Even when the door shut behind her she could still smell the stench of his cigar, and she felt the urge to go home and change clothes and wash her hair.

She walked to her office, pulled the door closed behind her and sat. She sat there for a long time, wondering. Wondering at the vehemence of his reaction. Wondering at her suspicion that he'd recognized the case number before he'd even opened the file. Wondering what it would take to engrave a five-year-old case number on Robards's mind so clearly. Wondering why he'd been so determined to divert her that he'd used sexual harassment blatant enough even for him to recognize. Wondering why he'd been so determined to keep her from looking at that file again when there was so little in it.

And then she smiled. She opened her center desk drawer. And sent out yet another thanks to Clay Yeager, wherever he might be, for his thorough training, as she looked at the copies she'd made of the Jaime Rivas murder report.

It was after eight when Kit walked down the hall toward the chief's office. This end of Trinity West was quiet now. The administrative staff had long since gone home. To her surprise the chief's door was open and the desk lamp on, although the chair was empty. The door to his anteroom was also open, although the room was dark. She wondered if, in his jet-lagged, exhausted state, he'd simply forgotten to lock up. She'd do it after she dropped off the monthly stats, she thought.

She dropped the pages she held into his in tray and glanced at the empty office. She knew Rosa Douglas, his dynamic, energetic secretary, had done the decorating. If she'd left it to the chief, the walls would have been bare, she'd joked. It was Rosa who had framed his many certificates and commendations, his master's degree in public administration, and after a fight had put up his Medal of Valor plaque, although he'd ordered her, Rosa had said, to forgo hanging the photograph. He was not, he told her, going to sit there looking at himself all day.

"Working late?"

Kit spun around, startled, as his voice came out of the dark anteroom at her.

"Sorry," he said. "I didn't mean to startle you, but I thought it only fair to let you know I was here."

And that, she thought, was Miguel de los Reyes to a T. "I...was just turning in the monthly stats," she said.

"Thank you."

She knew it was unusual for a chief to look over each section's statistics reports personally, but he said he preferred it that way rather than to wait for the compilation report that wouldn't hit his desk for another week or so. That it gave him a better handle on what was happening. Kit made sure her reports were thorough and on time, and she often included comments on trends and potential problems, which he had told her he found both insightful and observant.

"That was a good call last month, on that mobile night-club."

She smiled, genuinely pleased with the compliment. She'd taken a chance with that suggestion of a team to stake out possible locations for the wild, rolling parties, enhanced with illegal substances, taking place at a different location every night, but it had worked. They'd hit pay dirt at a vacant warehouse and made several arrests.

"Thank you," she replied, meaning it. It was odd, talking to a shadowy figure she could barely see. It made her feel almost spotlighted, standing in his lit office.

"You earned it. They've packed up for greener pastures, thanks to your foresight."

"Thank you," she said again.

Kit hesitated, looking toward the darkened room. She could see him now that her eyes had adjusted, could see his face, cast in light and shadow by the faint glow from his desk lamp. He truly did look like one of his aristocratic ancestors come to life, she thought. He could have been cast in some bronze metal, lovely in its sheen and color, its strength masked by the rugged beauty of his features. He sat in the dark, alone. It struck her then how alone he really was. How alone the job made him.

They're…still my family. About all I have, now…

His words at the airport came back to her, and she realized he was alone in his life, as well. He went to official functions alone, and from what she'd heard, rarely if ever dated. She remembered what he'd said at the time he was being considered for the interim chief position, after Lipton had been killed in the attack that had nearly killed him, as well. He'd said there was nothing else that mattered to him, so the work ahead would get his all. And in that time of chaos, that was exactly what Trinity West had needed. And it was exactly what Miguel de los Reyes had given.

Kit wondered if Anna had meant to take his heart with her to the grave.

She knew she needed to get out of here when she started thinking like that, so she muttered an apology for disturbing him and turned to go.

"You didn't," he said, and to her surprise he got up, flipped on the anteroom lights and gestured an invitation at her. "I was just...thinking."

She questioned the wisdom of this but didn't feel she could turn him down. As she stepped into the room, she saw him look at the plaques and photos that lined the walls honoring Trinity West's Medal of Valor winners, men who had risked their lives, even died to carry out the credo, "To protect and serve."

Miguel's plaque hung in his office, but the others were here—Cruz, Ryan and a long line of others who had given above and beyond the call. Including Bobby, her Bobby, who hadn't survived to receive his honor. It was an old pain for her, more of a distant sadness than anything else.

"About them?" she asked softly.

He nodded. "And others. Sometimes I think every cop should be up there, just for taking on the job."

The silence that fell seemed right somehow, in this place that was a shrine of sorts. And eventually—inevitably, she supposed—they ended up looking at the same place on that wall of honor. The place where three separate plaques commemorated the heroics of one man, the man who had become a legend, not just at Trinity West but throughout the state.

Clay Yeager would have received a statewide commendation the very next year—if he had been here. If they'd been able to find him to give it to him. But by then he was gone, vanished as if he'd never been, leaving behind his gear, his house, his life and a stunned Trinity West. His name was spoken in hushed tones, laced with awe or sadness, depending on if the speaker had known the man or just the legend he'd become.

And for a few, Kit knew, those hushed tones were laced with guilt. She was one of them. And it was never worse than here, standing before the undeniable proof that the man they had all failed was something very, very special.

"I'm sorry," she whispered to the man whose heroics, commemorated here, had been only one facet of his giving. "We are all sorry."

Her breath caught as the chief responded to words she hadn't been aware of speaking aloud. When she looked at him, his expression was so empathetic that she couldn't stop the rest from pouring out.

"But I am, especially. I knew Linda. I saw her fairly regularly. I should have known, should have sensed how close she was—"

"No, Kit," he said softly. "You can't bear the burden of this alone. We *all* should have known. Should have realized how bad things had gotten. We failed Clay, we failed Linda, and most especially we failed their little girl. And I doubt any of us will ever forgive ourselves for that."

She was utterly disarmed by his quiet, gentle understanding, and for the first time she felt a little of that guilt ease. She had to look away for fear he would see the moisture stinging her eyes.

"I...we'd have heard, wouldn't we? If anything had... happened to him?"

She knew she was voicing the fear they all carried, all of the many who owed Clay Yeager. The fear that the memories, the guilt, the pain had become too much and that somewhere, wherever he'd run to, trying to escape the agony, he'd found relief in the way too many cops did. That, broken and alone,

the man who had helped so many had found himself beyond
help and had ended the pain in the most final of ways. The
unspoken knowledge that Clay might have eaten a bullet was
in all their minds but never admitted.

But here, now, with the chief's quiet, compassionate and
understanding words in her mind, she hadn't been able to hold
it back any longer.

"I don't know, Kit," he said softly. "He cut his ties so
thoroughly, even from his family, that I don't know if anyone
would know to notify us. I pray he was not reduced to that.
I pray that if he ever got to that point, he would come back
to those who would give anything to help him as he helped
us."

She didn't care if he saw the tears as she looked at him.
"I know you send out requests to agencies across the country,
asking about any contact with him."

"Quarterly, for all the good it does," he said. He met her
gaze, and she had that feeling she'd had before with him, that
he was somehow seeing her soul. "And you organized that
massive effort to find him."

When a year had gone by with no contact from Clay, when
all their inquiries and requests of other police agencies had
come up with nothing, Kit had gathered those he'd meant the
most to and suggested they dedicate a year to finding him.
Each had taken one of their vacation slots and used the time—
and money from the pool to which they'd all contributed—
to search for him, beginning with what the person before them
had discovered, and handing off what they'd learned to the
next.

Despite false leads and dead ends, they'd traced him halfway across the country before the trail petered out entirely.
When the last three searchers had turned up the same dead
end, they had had to face the fact that either Clay did not
want to be found or there was no trail left to find.

"I have always felt badly that I couldn't give the time," he said.

"No!" she exclaimed. "You couldn't. You had to be here for Anna."

She had been diagnosed by then, and the long, hard battle for her life had begun, the battle she eventually lost. There was no way this man would have left his wife at a time like that. And that had made Kit respect him all the more.

His expression didn't change, but Kit fancied she saw the clear gray eyes darken for a moment. She wondered if the time would ever come that he could remember without pain. She doubted it. He had cared too much, felt too deeply. And she felt a flash of envy for Anna de los Reyes, a flash that made her feel the biggest of fools. Anna was dead. There was nothing to envy, except perhaps the way she had died, with more courage than Kit would ever have.

And her husband at her side until the very end.

"We all knew how much you wanted to help," she said quickly, retreating to a less volatile subject. "No one ever doubted that. And you put in more money than you should have, with all the medical bills...."

Her voice trailed away, and she hated that she'd brought them back to the subject that caused him pain.

"It's all right, Kit," he said gently. "It's been a long time. And it's not a forbidden subject. Not to you."

She shivered. He'd used her first name before. He always did, treating her no differently than any of his sergeants. But somehow it sounded different now, here, alone with him, in the quiet end of Trinity West. And the way he'd said that. *Not to you.*

He meant because she'd been Anna's friend, of course, but it still made her feel... She wasn't sure how it made her feel, but her throat was so tight she couldn't have spoken even had she dared.

"So," he said briskly, giving her the change of subject she

couldn't manage, "why are you here so late? You didn't stay just to do those stats, did you?"

It took her a moment to shake off her emotional reaction and make the shift to business. In a way it was a relief. The quiet moments of deep emotion had created a bond of sorts, or seemed to, and she knew in that direction lay trouble.

"No," she said. "There was...an old case I wanted to look into."

"An old case? What kind of case?"

She hesitated. This was jumping the chain of command. Any complaint she had about Robards should go to Captain Mallery first. But the chief had made it clear his door, his ear and his mind were always open to his people.

Besides, he had asked her a direct question, and although she could probably evade giving a direct answer, she knew he would recognize what she was doing, and she didn't like the feeling that gave her.

"Some reason you can't tell me?"

He was looking at her steadily, and she knew if she said yes, he would probably accept it. Miguel de los Reyes put a lot of trust in his people.

And it was that—plus, she admitted, that she was still steamed to a high heat at Robards—that decided her.

"It's an old murder case."

"Murder?" He lifted a brow at her.

"I know, it's not my business."

"You're a police officer," he said. "Of course it's your business." She gave him a startled look, and his mouth quirked. "Not all of us subscribe to the Robards division of labor, you know." She couldn't stop herself from smiling, and he winced. "Sorry. I shouldn't have said that. Chalk it up to jet lag."

He was right, it wasn't appropriate for him to make negative comments about one subordinate to another, especially one lower in rank, but still, it warmed Kit to know he wasn't blind to Robards's faults. Not that he could be, having been the target of the man's bigotry so often himself.

"So what about this old murder case?"

She hesitated, then plunged ahead. She told him the whole story from the time she'd spoken to Carmela Rivas to Robards's reaction to her questions, although she left out the nastier things he'd said to her and the implied threat to her position. She had never bemoaned prejudice and the glass ceiling or the fact that women too often had to work twice as hard to stay even. It would get her nowhere in this man's world.

The chief listened intently. When she was focused on this single thing, she was almost able to forget how shaky she usually was around him. When she'd finished, he hesitated before speaking.

"Do you feel there may be any validity to her claim?"

"I don't know," she said honestly. "There are some incongruities in how the case was handled, things I'd like to pursue, but I don't know if that means what she's saying is true. All I know is that *she* honestly believes it. She wasn't just looking for somebody to blame."

He was silent, considering. Kit waited. She couldn't read his expression and was terrified that she'd made a huge mistake. As offensive as Robards was, he was still a lieutenant and she a mere sergeant—

"Go ahead," he said.

"Sir?" she said, startled.

"I trust your judgment. Look into it."

Warmth flooded her, and she wanted to hug him for those words, however inappropriate the action would be, and it would be in the extreme. But after Robards's abuse, his solid faith was balm to wounds she hadn't let herself acknowledge.

Miguel de los Reyes was indeed quite a man.

Chapter 4

Kit yawned. It had been a twelve-hour day, her third in a row. Figuring it was best to err on the side of caution, she had been waiting until Robards left for the day to turn her attention to the Rivas case. It wasn't so much that she didn't want to get caught ignoring his order to drop it, but if he did catch her and write her up, it would go to the chief, and she knew he would come to her defense and tell Robards he'd given her the okay. It would put the chief in the line of Robards's fire, and she didn't want that to happen, especially not because of her. So she'd do this on her own time, and Robards could go whistle.

Not, she thought, that she was finding anything. She'd gone over the reports line by line. She'd had the coroner fax the complete autopsy on Jaime Rivas, not simply the cover sheet they'd been sent five years ago. She'd called the fire department back and gotten their complete record of the case. And so far, everything matched.

The disturbance of trash in the alley and the presence of

blood indicated the altercation had taken place where the victim had been found. The businesses on either side of the bar had been closed—no possibility of witnesses there. There were short, individual statements from the people who had been in the bar at the time, all saying none of them had seen or heard anything.

Interviews with the victim's friends had put him last seen at a local gas station two hours before he'd been found, but no one knew—or was saying—where he'd been going. Further interviews had been inconclusive, and there was nothing that proved or disproved his gang status, despite Robards's heavy-handed insinuations that the victim being Hispanic was all the proof that was needed. Carmela Rivas was said to have been hysterical and irrational, with no real idea who had killed her son.

It was short. Far too short, it seemed to Kit, to document the loss of a young life. But it was, if not thorough, at least complete. Robards hadn't, perhaps, gone the extra mile, but he'd done the job. True, there was his failure to call for paramedics, but in his surly way he had explained—although Kit didn't doubt his reaction might have been a little different had the victim been Caucasian. And it was hard to argue with him when the autopsy showed he had probably been right. The boy had been dead when he'd found him.

And then there was the fact that Robards had apparently done all the reports himself. Odd, she thought, that the patrol unit that had gone to the scene, the officer who had belatedly called for the paramedics, hadn't done a supplemental report. In fact, he wasn't even mentioned in Robards's report, only in the fire department log, by his unit number. She made a mental note to have records check and see who the officer working that beat had been that night. Not that he would remember much, after all this time, if he was even still here. Although having Robards write all the reports, apparently voluntarily, might be enough to make it stick in his mind.

With another yawn, she shoved the reports into a large envelope and put them in the right-hand bottom drawer of her desk. She would lock it, but she knew that meant little in Robards's domain. He had a master key and no compunction at all about using it if he was on someone's back—which was most of the time. Some maintained he was in violation of the police bill of rights section that protected officers from unwarranted searches in their absence or without their permission, but until it was settled whether a desk containing information on active cases fell under that section of the California government code, Kit guessed he would continue his covert searches.

So in line with that expectation, and with a small smile curving her lips, she covered the envelope in the bottom of the drawer with her favorite, extremely personal feminine camouflage—a loose pile of tampons. She figured just the sight of them would make Robards run screaming. She could take the file home with her, but she didn't really think it was necessary. She was reasonably sure Robards would think she was sufficiently cowed and would follow his order to drop it.

And if you had a brain stem, you probably would, Kit muttered to herself, knowing she'd be buying herself a world of misery if Robards did snare her.

A third yawn told her it was time to get out of here and get some sleep. She'd been working a lot of extra hours since Gage had left, and it was starting to catch up with her.

The thought of the former detective made her smile despite his absence. Laurey was so good for him, she thought as she stood up and stretched. Kit had had her doubts that they'd ever work it out. The fact that they'd first met years ago when he'd arrested her in a high school undercover operation hadn't made things easy on them, but Laurey had finally forced Gage to look at himself, to see what his obsession with the job was costing him. Kit had little doubt that Laurey had saved his sanity, perhaps even his life. He'd been a man on the edge for too long.

She missed him like crazy, and not just for the massive amounts of work he'd done. He'd been her friend, her sounding board and on occasion her whining partner.

She picked up her purse and her sunglasses. She obviously didn't need them now, but she'd be sorry if her weary eyes had to face the sun in the morning without them. She considered locking her office door, but knew that would be enough to put Robards on guard. She'd seen him show up early just to see who was locking what. It was part of what he called his "management technique."

She turned her thoughts back to Gage as she headed down the hall. He was so darned happy she couldn't help but smile at the changes in him. Laurey Templeton Butler was a miracle worker. In place of the driven, haunted cop she'd known for years was a joyously happy man, and it would take a pretty selfish soul to begrudge him that.

"You look awfully happy to be here so late again."

The familiar voice yanked her out of her thoughts and made her realize she'd walked past the chief's office as he was leaving. She stopped and, looking at him, knowing he would understand, said, "I was thinking about Gage."

The smile that instantly curved his mouth warmed her. "That is enough to warrant a smile," he agreed.

"Seems almost epidemic around here lately, doesn't it?" she said, then looked away from him as she realized with some shock that she'd sounded almost wistful.

"Yes," he agreed, his voice even, as if he had not noticed her tone. "With the Butlers, and with Ryan and Lacey getting back together, and Cruz and Kelsey…"

"It's funny," she said when he paused, "Cruz and I went to dinner once at Kelsey's restaurant. You know, the Sunset Grill in Marina del Mar, the place she ran before she opened the inn? Who would have thought that five years later he'd be madly in love and married to her?''

"You're all right with that?"

She realized he was watching her speculatively, and she hoped she wasn't blushing. There had been a time, when she'd been a young twenty-two and new on the force, that it hadn't taken much to rattle her. But after years in this world of frequently rough language, gallows humor and sometimes off-color jokes, she'd learned to control it. But somehow, with this man, all her normal safeguards seemed to malfunction.

And she wondered suddenly if he knew of her short—very short—involvement with Cruz. They'd tried a couple of dates, but it had been awkward, and they'd very quickly called it off. Neither felt at all badly about it, and both of them knew it had been the right decision, the only decision.

"We make much better friends than we ever would have a couple," she said quietly. "And we both knew it right away."

He seemed to relax, and she wondered if he thought she would be jealous that Cruz—and his adorable daughter, Sam—had found precisely what they needed in the steady, generous heart of Kelsey Hall.

"Kelsey is perfect for them," she said. "And besides, I get to baby-sit Sam and the critters more often, to give them some time alone now and then."

He laughed. Sam's menagerie of wounded animals, all watched over with the girl's tender, intuitive care, was a well-known story around Trinity West, as was the tale of how the most unlikely of the creatures, a king snake named Slither, had wound up helping Cruz rescue his beloved daughter from a crazed intruder last year.

"How old is she now?" he asked as they began, seemingly in accord, to walk toward the building's exit.

"Samantha? Eleven. She'll be twelve in a few months."

He shook his head. "Eleven. God, I remember when Cruz

started at Trinity West, and she was just a baby, a year or so old."

"Me, too," Kit said. "She's growing up so fast."

"And now there are new babies," he said softly.

She nodded. "Amanda Buckhart, and Quisto and Caitlin's little Celeste."

"The cycle goes on," he said, and for a moment he looked so infinitely sad that Kit felt her stomach knot. Was he thinking of Anna and the children they'd never had or simply of life going on without the woman he'd so loved? Again she felt that flash of unwanted envy for the woman who had had this man so in love with her that he had almost given up when she died.

And it seemed he had given up on that part of himself. He wasn't simply alone, he was apart, as if the fire he'd gone through had somehow made it impossible for him to regain a normal life, as if the grim reality he'd suffered had made any kind of happiness seem impossible. Or undeserved. She knew Anna would hate that, but Kit also knew she could hardly tell him that. She might have, once, as a friend, but not now, given who he was. As her chief he wouldn't appreciate her probing into his personal life, however spare it might be.

And she was getting fanciful, speculating on things she had no right to, things she really had no way of knowing.

"You're here late yourself," she said as they neared the door, even though she knew he rarely went home when everyone else did.

"Budget report," he said with a grimace. "Trying to convince the city council we can't run this place on a 1980s budget."

She shook her head. "I don't know how you deal with that stuff," she said frankly. "Or how you get as much done as you do, given what you have to work with."

He'd been reaching for the door but stopped suddenly, giving her a lopsided grin that made her pulse take a little leap. "I'll take that as a compliment."

Startled, she looked at him. "Of course it was. We all think you're a miracle worker."

To her amazement, a slow, pleased smile spread across his face. "Thank you. That's…nice to know."

Realization struck her. "I guess we all thought you knew. How we felt, I mean."

It was a moment before he said, "One of the things I hate about this job is the barrier the title of chief puts around you. With a bit of work, I can keep on top of what's happening on a statistical level. But it's a lot more work to get the truth of what people are thinking and feeling. And since I'm the chief, it's hard to be sure what I do get really is the truth."

She'd never thought of it quite that way. But it didn't surprise her that he had. He was that kind of man. And when another thought struck her, she couldn't help wanting to tell him. It was too important that he know. She tried to form the words in her mind, tried to remember that this was the man who had been her friend and colleague long before he'd become her chief.

He turned the knob and pushed the door open. It was a warm evening and there was the familiar shock of heated air after the air-conditioning of the station. Kit spoke quickly, before she could chicken out.

"I hope you know the truth about how much respect and support you have."

He stopped dead, his hand clutching the edge of the door. She saw his knuckles whiten, realized his hand had clenched tightly. He stared at her, his expression more than a little stunned. Had he really not known? Was he that surprised to hear it?

Or, she thought with a sudden qualm, was it simply that *she* had said it? It was, she supposed, hardly her place as a lowly sergeant to tell the chief how he was doing. But she couldn't quite believe he would take offense at such a thing, couldn't believe he would even if it had been criticism rather than support. He just wasn't that kind of man. And again she was a little startled at how certain she was of that. She'd always admired and respected him, but she'd never really realized how positive she was of his character until the past few days.

"I... Thank you," he said, his voice sounding tight. "That means a great deal to me."

She was suddenly flustered in the face of the honest emotion in his voice. "I just thought if you didn't know already, you should."

"And that," he said quietly, "means a great deal to me, too."

As they walked to the parking lot, she told herself not to misinterpret what he had meant by that.

Indecisiveness was not a condition Kit was familiar with, but she felt like she was wallowing in it now.

She leaned back in her chair, staring at the envelope on her desk. The division was full of industry this morning, the voices of detectives using one of their primary tools—the telephone—blended together in a familiar hum. Robards was gone, signed out until noon, and there had been rejoicing in the ranks. After going through all her officially active cases, Kit had dragged the Rivas case file out yet again.

She still had nothing to go on. There was nothing to indicate anything out of the ordinary, nothing to indicate it had happened any way other than how Robards had described it. Except Carmela Rivas's passionate insistence.

And there it was. The logical thing to do—if this was a normal investigation—would be to talk to Mrs. Rivas again. But this was not a normal investigation. It was a case five years old, and she was poking around in it against the orders of her sergeant but with the okay of the chief. She had no justification except her certainty that Jaime Rivas's mother believed absolutely that her son had been murdered by a police officer.

Kit knew if she talked to the woman again, she'd be committing herself to pursuing this to the end, whatever it might be. And if Carmela Rivas was right, Kit might not care much for what that end was.

But if she walked away, she didn't think she'd care much for herself.

She looked at the address on the report, wondering if the victim had still been living at home and if his mother still lived there. She turned in her office chair and grabbed the telephone book from the credenza behind her. There was a full column of Rivases, but she found the address toward the top in this year's book. Apparently she still lived in the same place.

Kit was still in the same quandary. Knowing that the woman was findable didn't make the decision any easier. It would be beyond cruel to raise the woman's hopes if there was nothing here, if she was simply a loving but misguided parent protecting the memory of her child.

And if she wasn't, if there was something to her story, Kit knew she'd be opening a can of snakes, not merely worms. Exposing a bad cop didn't make anybody feel good, most especially other cops. Although most of the cops she knew would welcome it, knowing that such officers only made a tough job tougher by making the public distrustful of all cops.

But those who felt that the kinship of the uniform should be stronger than anything, including right or wrong, would despise her for violating that tenet. But then, most of that type probably despised her already for the simple sin of being female, she thought wearily. And still she sat staring at the file. Finally she put it away, out of sight.

But she couldn't manage to get it out of her mind.

And she knew she wasn't going to be able to. She was

honest enough to admit she wouldn't mind if she could prove Robards had fluffed an investigation, but that couldn't be her goal. There was too much else to consider, including the woman who already felt betrayed by the system. Robards would say it was one of her failings, this seeing all sides, this relating to the victim, but Gage had told her it was why he loved working with her.

Once she had gotten a handwritten commendation from Chief de los Reyes on her handling of the victim of a brutal rape who had been too traumatized to speak when they'd found her. Robards hadn't helped any with his innuendo-laden questions, trying to find out what she'd done or worn that had brought on the attack and stopping just short of saying she'd asked for it.

By the time of the trial the victim had nailed her attacker to the wall with her furious, impassioned testimony, unassailable even in the face of his defense attorney's borderline tactics. And the change, de los Reyes had said, had been in a large part due to Kit's efforts.

Kit had been flattered and greatly touched that he'd been aware, let alone taken the time to write the commendation himself. She had worked hard on the case. She had spent hours of her own time with Margaret, empathizing, supporting and coaching. But in the end it had been Margaret's strength and determination that had put her attacker where he belonged. It was one of those rare times when everything worked as it should, when one man who had smugly gloated about his power over one woman had found she had the power of the system behind her.

Kit only wished it would work that way all the time, that the system would always be strong enough for the victims who didn't have Margaret's strength, for the ones who most needed it to be strong for them. But it wasn't. There were too many ways for it to be manipulated, and if there was anything that made Kit despair about her work, it was that.

She figured it was some idea of fixing a possible wrong done by the system that was supposed to insure justice that made her, with a sigh, pick up her keys and purse, grab the small dog-eared notebook she carried on investigations and sign herself out of the office.

As always when driving through Trinity West, the neighborhood of Marina Heights that was closest to the ocean and the wealthy, neighboring town of Marina del Mar, Kit noticed the gradual changes. The farther east she went, the more the area changed, going from new, expensive homes and tidy shopping centers to older, less well-kept examples of each, to the center of the city, where decay was more evident, with empty buildings boarded up and festooned with graffiti—a far cry from even the worst of Trinity West.

But there were signs of change even here, she thought as she drove past where Trinity Street West changed to Trinity Street East. And she smiled as she passed Caitlin Romero's Neutral Zone, the club for kids Caitlin had started in the worst block of the worst area, determined to give the kids who had to live on these streets an alternative to gang life. No one at Trinity West had given her a snowball's chance in hell of succeeding, but she'd done it.

And in the process, she'd been the spark that had revitalized the block. Mr. Cordero's corner grocery had been completely refurbished and freshly painted. The old gentleman had only to put out a call and Trinity West came running. They were happy to help after he'd helped them vanquish the Pack, the vicious adult street gang Ryan Buckhart had broken up last year. Other storefronts were showing signs of care, with new businesses getting ready to open. Next to Caitlin's club, another old building was gleaming with new paint and bustling with activity. Kelsey Gregerson's youth shelter was in full operation.

Yes, Caitlin had been good for this place, and Kit admired as well as liked the gutsy woman for what she'd accomplished. She liked and admired all of them, Caitlin Romero, Kelsey Gregerson, Lacey Buckhart, Laurey Butler.

And thinking of them did *not* make her feel empty inside, she told herself firmly. She was glad her friends had found women strong enough to deal with their powerful personalities, strong enough to deal with spouses in one of the most difficult jobs in the world.

And kind enough to go out of their way to include Kit in many of their activities. She even went, sometimes, when she thought she wouldn't feel too much like an extra wheel. At least Gage's departure had given her a valid excuse for not having a social life—she didn't have time. She was buried in cases, and now this one on top of it.

"Darn," she muttered. She'd meant to bring a photo of the missing Carlisle boy to show to Caitlin and Kelsey, to see if they'd seen him, but she kept forgetting to grab it when she was headed this way.

She dug into her purse with her right hand, fishing for the small tape recorder she always carried. When face to face with someone, she preferred her notebook. She'd found people were less intimidated by it, perhaps conditioned by years of images in movies and on television. But while driving, she always kept the recorder handy for thoughts like this one as they occurred to her.

She dictated the note, put the recorder in her purse, then pulled her thoughts to her surroundings as she neared the neighborhood she'd been looking for. These residences were old and small but showed signs of care, neatly mowed if tiny lawns and flowers planted near the walls or in pots on the covered porches.

She found the number she was looking for on the front of a weathered but sturdy-looking brown house with an array of flowers—asters, maybe, Kit thought—whose colorful touch was delightful this late in the year.

The yellow sedan she'd seen that first day sat in the driveway alongside the house, indicating Mrs. Rivas was probably at home. Kit took in a deep breath. She'd reached the point of no return. And if she continued she could soon be, in the words of one of her favorite songs, past the point of rescue. She felt a little like Pandora looking at the box, contemplating opening it despite the warnings. Her life, she thought with a sigh, would be so much easier if she didn't have this darned abhorrence for injustice.

She got out of her car, walked swiftly up to the front door of the house and knocked before she could change her mind.

Mrs. Rivas, clad in a crisp white uniform and shoes, answered. The woman recognized her, although Kit had to prompt her with her name. Her expression went quickly from surprise to wariness, and Kit knew Mrs. Rivas was wondering not only what she was doing on her doorstep but how she'd found that doorstep in the first place.

"Mrs. Rivas, I wanted to talk to you some more about what you said the other day. About your son."

"Why?" the woman asked, clearly—and rightfully, Kit thought—suspicious. She was going to have to work to make her as receptive as possible before she admitted who she was.

"I would like to know why you think what you think, about his death. And whether or not it's true, if there's some inequity about the way the case was handled, I want to look into it."

The woman still clutched her half-open door as if she was ready to slam it closed at the first sign of anything she didn't like. And Kit knew that right now, finding out she was a cop could well be one of those things.

"Why?" Mrs. Rivas repeated. "Are you some kind of nosy reporter or something?"

"I'm not a reporter," Kit said. "I just feel very strongly about injustices, Mrs. Rivas, and if one was done here, I'd like to find out."

"A *murder* was done," the woman said fiercely. "But why

should you care? You did not know my boy. It was so long ago even those who did know him have forgotten."

"You haven't," Kit said quietly.

"No," she said, and in the single syllable was a world of mother's grief. "I will never forget my Jaime."

"Please, Mrs. Rivas, I want to help. I want you to tell me everything. If there were things you said that were not listened to, I want to hear them."

For a moment something changed in the woman's eyes, and Kit dared to think it might be hope dawning. She went on before the woman could ask the inevitable question.

"If there were circumstances that were ignored, I want to know. If there is some kind of evidence that was overlooked, I want to know."

It *was* hope, Kit thought as the woman absorbed what she'd said.

"Mrs. Rivas," she said quickly, "I cannot promise you anything will change. I cannot promise you the killer will be found, especially after all this time. I can only promise you my complete honesty. Even if I don't like what I find. And whatever I find, I will tell you."

"Who are you?"

The question she'd been expecting, short and sharp, cut her off. And she knew the woman suspected, if she hadn't already guessed.

"I'm Detective Sergeant Kit Walker, of the Marina Heights police. And," she added quickly as she saw the woman's expression go cold, "I meant every word I said. I'm here to help."

"My family has had enough of your kind of help." Mrs. Rivas backed up, ready to shut the door.

"Mrs. Rivas, please. I know you have no reason to trust me, but think. Why would I have come if I didn't mean what I said? What reason could I possibly have for looking into an old case that's been classified as inactive?"

The woman hesitated, studying Kit's face. Kit took advantage of her hesitation, hoping she could convince the woman.

"I'd never heard of your son's case until that morning I met you. I wasn't in the detective division when it happened. So I have nothing to go on except what you're willing to tell me."

"I told them all before. No one listened."

"I'm sorry about that. But I can't change it. I can only listen now."

"Why should I believe you will do anything? You are a cop. You protect your own."

"Just as you protect yours, Mrs. Rivas," Kit said. "But I'm not blind to the fact that there are a few cops who aren't what they should be. The only blindness I believe in is that of justice. Give me something to tip her scales."

For a long moment there was silence. And then, reluctantly, Mrs. Rivas opened her door. "Come in," she said.

The room was as tidy as the yard, although a bit gloomy with the drapes closed and dark wood paneling on the walls.

"I was closing up the house, since I have to go to work soon," Mrs. Rivas said by way of explanation.

"You're a nurse?" Kit asked, indicating her white uniform.

The woman nodded. "I work for Dr. Kirk, in town." She gestured, still reluctantly, to the sofa, and Kit sat where she indicated.

"Do you wish something to drink?"

The offer was made more out of courtesy than anything else, Kit was sure, and she shook her head. "No, thank you. I know dragging up old, unpleasant memories will be difficult for you and that you'd like to get it over with quickly."

"Speaking to the police is what is difficult," the woman said, and Kit knew that while she'd consented, it didn't mean she'd thawed.

"If what you say is true, you have reason," Kit said.

The woman blinked as if surprised by the words. She studied Kit once more, intently.

"You have good eyes," she said after a moment. "I think you may be sincere."

Kit felt oddly warmed by the grudging assessment. "I told you, I can't promise you anything except that I will listen and be honest about what I find."

The woman nodded. "Ask your questions."

Kit wondered where to begin and how to do it without rekindling the woman's distrust. It suddenly seemed so cut-and-dried. The report had been short because there had been nothing else to document, nothing but a dead young man who had been this woman's son.

Finally she said simply, "I don't think reciting the facts of the case will serve any purpose. And in the end, only one thing really matters. Why do you think it was a police officer who killed your son?"

"I don't *think*," the woman said bitterly, "I *know*."

Kit sighed. Was this nothing but a desperate mother needing someone, something to blame for the horror of losing a son? Had she wasted her time and drawn attention needlessly? She grimaced inwardly at the thought and steeled herself for one last effort.

"How, Mrs. Rivas? The report says there was no evidence, no witnesses, no—"

The woman swore. Kit stopped. It was in Spanish, but she'd picked up enough here and there to know it was an oath she wouldn't have expected from the mouth of this woman.

"You said you would listen, but you're like all the others, like that man with the cigar and your other detective who hates my people. You don't want to listen."

"I *am* listening, Mrs. Rivas. Tell me."

"I will tell you," the woman said, nearly spitting the words out. "Your report is a lie!"

She was wasting her time, Kit thought. Robards had been

right, the woman wasn't rational about this. She had no real proof, she was just looking for someone to blame, perhaps unable to accept the truth about her son—

"You look just like they did now, those police who looked at my poor Jaime's body and did not care. But I tell you, one of them killed him! I know it. Just like I know your report is a lie."

"How?" Kit said wearily, not expecting any kind of sensible answer.

"Because there was a witness."

Chapter 5

Kit, Miguel thought when he saw her light still on, was putting in as many hours as he was lately. He knew she was working hard to keep up until they could get somebody qualified to replace Gage—as if they'd ever find anyone with his kind of dedication—but it was nearly nine, and that was a bit extreme. He'd always admired her dedication, along with her integrity and energy and more things than he could count, but she couldn't keep this up.

Telling himself it was purely out of concern for a valued employee, he stepped into the detective division and walked toward her office. He glanced through the window first and saw her studying something intently. He tapped lightly on the door before opening it and peering in.

She smiled, looking glad to see him. He felt pleased, more than he would have expected, then caught himself. That smile of hers could easily be simple gratitude that it was him and not Lieutenant Robards, he told himself. And he noticed that whatever she'd just been looking at had vanished. A legal pad with a few notes on it was the only thing on her desktop.

"Working late again?"

They both said it simultaneously, then both laughed, and he supposed he looked as sheepish as she did.

"Maybe we both work too hard," he said.

"No maybe about it in your case," she answered.

He looked pointedly at his watch, then at her. "At least I was about to leave."

She gave him a crooked smile that made him smile right back at her. He had always liked her smile.

"I guess we could both be charter members of the get-a-life club," she said. "Friday night, and here we both are."

The moment she said it, he could almost see her realize who she was joking with and wish the words back. He hated the intimidation factor of his rank. But he was finding he particularly hated it with Kit.

"You start showing up on weekends," he said lightly, "and you're in trouble."

She seemed to relax. "Not me," she said. "I learned from Gage that's the first step toward obsession."

"Good. Don't try and pick up all the slack yourself. We'll get you some help soon. As soon as we get those trainees out on the street, that will free us up for the transfer. Believe it or not, there are a few foolhardy souls willing to brave your lieutenant for the slot."

"That many?" she said dryly.

He had to stop this, he thought. It really wasn't right to say such things to her. But it seemed to remove the barrier between them, and he supposed there was a certain benefit to the detectives knowing the chief wasn't unaware of the problems they were having. Now if he could just do something about it. He might have to move Robards up on his priority list.

"Anybody you'd like to see in here?" he asked her. She looked startled, and he guessed she'd never been asked for her input before. "It's your unit, you should have a say on who comes in. You'll have to be working pretty closely with whoever it is. So if you had your preference, who would it be?''

"That's hard to say, without knowing who put in for it," she said cautiously.

"Ever tactful, aren't you?" he said with a grin. "Just take your pick."

It didn't take her long. "I'd say Romero, if he'd be willing to work the detail. He's got a lot of detective experience, even if it's not in Juvie and Sex Crimes. And he handles victims well, from what I've heard."

"He's still pretty new at Trinity West," Miguel said. "Putting a guy in with less than two years at the department might ruffle some feathers."

"It'll ruffle Robards, that's for sure," she said with a grimace. He knew exactly what she meant. Quisto Romero was everything that pushed Robards's buttons. He was young, smart, fit, up-to-date, handsome—and his skin was a shade too dark to earn him Robards's liking.

"Somehow," Miguel said, "I have a hard time seeing that as a bad thing."

Damn, he'd done it again. What was it about her that loosened his tongue like that? He was going to get them both in trouble if he didn't knock it off.

"I don't think anybody who knows Romero's record could be really upset. They've sort of been expecting it ever since he came over from Marina del Mar. And somehow I don't think Quisto would have any trouble handling it. Even...the lieutenant."

"Neither do I," he agreed. "And in fact, he did put in for it."

Kit smiled. "I hoped he might have."

"And suggested it?"

Her smile widened. "Well, maybe just a hint."

Miguel laughed. "So," he said as the thought occurred to

him, "whatever happened with that old murder case you were looking into?" Her eyes flicked to the legal pad on her desk, and he saw the barest edge of a white page protruding. "Was that what you were looking at?"

She hesitated, then nodded. Things were getting really bad in here if, knowing he'd given her the okay, she was still hesitant to admit she'd been doing it. Robards was definitely moving up on his list.

"Why don't we go get a cup of coffee, and you can tell me what you've found out?"

She glanced at the foam cup that sat to one side of her desk blotter. He could see it held maybe an inch of brown liquid, and he also saw her mouth quirk.

"I meant real coffee," he said dryly. "Not the stuff that passes for it around here."

"Oh," she said with a little laugh. He'd always liked her laugh, too, it was such a light, carefree sound. And she wasn't afraid to laugh, to really get into it until tears came. He'd seen it, in the days when he and Anna and she and Bobby had done things together.

And now Anna and Bobby were both dead, and it seemed neither he nor Kit had managed much of a life since, outside their work.

"The café?" he suggested, using the familiar term for the coffee shop that was just a few blocks away. "That way you can get something to eat, too. I'll bet you haven't even had dinner."

"I'll bet I had more than you did," she countered.

He smiled crookedly at her, glad for the return of the easy banter. "So where *are* the applications for that get-a-life club?"

She laughed, and after a moment's hesitation agreed to join him. "I am feeling the strongest urge for some of their extra-greasy fries," she said.

"Urp," he said descriptively, and she laughed again.

After a short walk, they turned down a narrow side street, both of them glancing in unison at the jewelry store as they passed. The glass had been replaced since Gage and Laurey had been shot at in the doorway, but nobody at Trinity West was likely to forget the incident very soon.

Kit actually ordered the fries, and Miguel had to admit they smelled wonderful. As if she'd read his mind, she nudged the plate toward him.

"Neither the calories nor the cholesterol counts if you steal them."

He chuckled and snaked one of the steaming strips of potato off the plate. "The salt, on the other hand," he said as he savored it, "won't help my blood pressure."

"Your *job* doesn't help your blood pressure," she pointed out.

He chuckled again. "There is that."

He had the passing thought that he liked this. They'd always gotten along well when Anna was alive and she would visit them. He'd enjoyed Kit's company.

And just how are you enjoying her company now?

His hand froze in the act of reaching for his napkin to wipe some of the extra grease from his fingers.

He knew the answer to that question by the speed with which the need to revert to business rose in him. And he knew he didn't dare ignore that need.

"So what about this case?" he asked, hoping he didn't sound too urgent.

She gave him a quick look but didn't seem to notice anything untoward. "I...talked to the mother today."

He lifted a brow at her. The way she said it indicated it hadn't been an easy decision for her, and he could guess why. Some cops wouldn't care that they'd be stirring up old, painful memories. If they wanted to talk to someone about a case, even five years old, they did it. But Kit wasn't one of those. She was always aware that they were dealing with people's feelings. She was very adept at reading those feelings, and whenever she could, she was careful of them.

And when she couldn't be, she did her job anyway. It was quite a balancing act, being as tough as she had to be when necessary yet never losing that caring sensitivity that in many other cops was hidden beneath a scarred facade they'd had to develop to survive. He admired and respected her tremendously for being able to do it.

He cleared his throat. "And did she explain why she believes a cop killed her son?"

Kit nodded. And hesitated. Miguel knew she was weighing what she'd learned against the wisdom of telling him, or rather, telling her chief. Or she was deciding how much to tell him.

"Would it help," he said casually, lifting the cup of decaffeinated coffee he'd ordered in deference to the hour—he had enough trouble sleeping without adding late doses of caffeine, "if this was unofficial?"

She looked startled, but then a slight smile curved her mouth, as if she was pleased by his perception. And she had such a lovely mouth, soft, full, tempting—

He nearly burned his own mouth as shock at what he'd just thought made him gulp instead of sip.

"She told me there was a witness. An eyewitness."

He was grateful for the distraction of what she'd said, enabling him to ignore what had just happened and concentrate on something safe. Like a possibly bungled murder investigation? The irony didn't escape him.

"A witness? I thought there hadn't been any."

Kit nodded. "According to the report, there weren't."

"Why didn't she say something then?"

Kit let out a compressed breath. "That's just it. She says she did."

He frowned. He wasn't liking the sound of this at all. Kit toyed with one of the remaining french fries—when not steaming hot, they lost a bit of their appeal—and he waited, giving her the chance to work it out, knowing Kit rarely spoke in haste. Anna had told him once that Kit spoke carefully because she expected to be held to her word. He'd known instantly Anna was right. It had fit with what he'd observed, and he'd thought all the more of Kit for it.

He admired her, it seemed, for a great deal, he thought warily. And he kept adding to the list.

"Stripped of the distortion of her anger," Kit said, "what it comes down to is that she says there was an eyewitness who had seen the beating and knew the suspect for a cop. She says she told the investigating officer—the man with the cigar, she called him—but he wouldn't listen to any accusation of a fellow officer."

His frown deepened. "Go on."

"She said it wouldn't have done any good anyway, because unlike her son, the witness *was* a gang member, and no cop would believe him."

Miguel knew, on a practical level, it was probably true. Any statement from an avowed gangster would be viewed with more than a little suspicion. Especially if that statement involved the actions of the police, the only enemy common to all street gangs.

"It's still a violation of procedure not to talk to a possible witness. If the information is questionable, then it's our job to sort it out."

She gave him a steady look from beneath thick lashes, soft brown tipped with the same gold as her hair. "It's a violation of written procedure and *your* policy. Under Lipton it was pretty standard."

She wasn't telling him anything he didn't already know. His predecessor had been of the old school, a product of the times before public outcries against the police, before civilian review boards, before political correctness, the times when police authority had been unquestioned and respected. He could see the attraction of those times and why some resented their loss. And not all of those who yearned for those days wore uniforms.

But if he had to choose between a lumbering dinosaur like Robards and a cop like Kit Walker, from either side, fellow cop or civilian, he knew which one he'd chose.

"So this witness told her he'd seen—"

He stopped when Kit shook her head. "He told her other son, Martin. Jaime's little brother."

"How little?" he asked, foreseeing another credibility problem.

Kit nodded in understanding. "He was only twelve at the time."

"So he's seventeen now?"

"Yes. Same age as Jaime was when he died."

"You talked to him?"

She shook her head. "There's the real credibility problem," she said, startling him with her use of the exact words he'd been thinking. "He's currently in the custody of the CYA." She grimaced at his expression. "I know. This whole thing is descending into farce. And it gets worse."

"Worse than the California Youth Authority?"

She nodded. "That gang witness nobody wanted to hear about or talk to?"

"Yes?"

"He's dead."

"Figures," he muttered.

"Want the clincher?"

Miguel grimaced. "No, but yes."

"He was killed in a drive-by shooting the night after Jaime Rivas was murdered."

He stared at her. "The *next* night?"

"Yeah, that's what I thought. A bit convenient. I've got records pulling the report, but from what she said, it sounds like just another typical rival gang hit."

He let out a long breath. "Were it anyone else, I would say I don't believe in that much coincidence."

She nodded. "Me, either. But with the life expectancy of the average gang member..." She ended with a shrug.

He pondered, then asked, "Do you want to continue?"

She gave him a surprised look. "I...yes, I do."

"Why?"

He agreed with her, there was enough about this case that bothered him to okay it, but he was curious to hear her reasons.

"I feel like we owe it to Mrs. Rivas. She's a good, honest woman. Whether she's right or wrong, she was treated badly, and her son's death was treated lightly. And she, if not he, deserves better than that."

"Yes," he agreed quietly, "they do."

It's a violation of written procedure and your procedure. Under Lipton it was pretty standard. Her words came back to him, and the compliment implicit in them warmed him. He hadn't liked Lipton's approach to most things, and he'd worked hard to change the written policies and the much harder to tackle unwritten policies.

"They tell me," he said slowly, "that I've turned Trinity West around for the better. I hope it's true."

"It is," she said earnestly. "You've set the tone, made the changes—"

He waved off her compliments, although he would have been happy to hear more. From her, anyway. But he had other intentions at the moment.

"If it is true, it's not me that's done it. It's the fact that I have people like you there to carry out the changes, people who know what's right and pursue it, who know that to protect is as big a part of police work as enforcement, people who can still manage to care when a normal human being would have given up on it long ago."

She stared at him, turning pale and blushing by turns.

"I…" She swallowed visibly. "Wow," she said, rather weakly.

He grinned. "You earned that wow."

"I…thank you."

"Now, I hope you're going to relax this weekend and not spend all your time thinking about work."

She looked suddenly guilty and stared at the lonely couple of fries left on the plate.

"Kit?" he asked, his tone ominous.

"I was thinking of driving up to the honor ranch north of L.A. tomorrow."

"Let me guess," he said, "Martin Rivas?"

She gave him a rather sheepish nod. "It'll be a nice drive."

"Certainly," he said dryly, "right through downtown Los Angeles." He paused, then added, "You realize even if he confirms his mother's story, we've only got hearsay."

"I know. But I still want to hear what he has to say."

And that, he thought, was Kit Walker in a nutshell. Some cops would drop a case the moment it became clear it could never be prosecuted. But Kit's goal wasn't a conviction, it was the truth. Even when the truth came in shades of gray not so easily categorized. He added another item to the rapidly growing list of reasons he admired her.

He was beginning to think perhaps he admired her a little too much.

Kit sat in Carmela Rivas's living room, sipping sweet, tangy tea and looking at the mementos a loving mother had saved. At all stages of his young life, Jaime Rivas looked at her, baby pictures that showed his ready grin, toddler shots full of wide-eyed wonder, childhood images of energy and enthusiasm, more serious adolescent photographs that nevertheless let that irrepressible grin peek through. And more, report cards showing a steady, stellar progress—hardly the sign of a boy caught up in the gang life. Jaime had been a good student, with teacher after teacher remarking on his potential. School papers marked with *A*s and *B*s, with a few *A* pluses on those dealing with his passion, which had been history.

"He used to say, 'We have to learn from the past, Mama, if we are going to change today.' He wanted to make the world a better place for his little brother."

Kit had to steady herself before she looked at this boy's mother. Mrs. Rivas had, this time, if not welcomed her, at least stirred herself to the hospitality of the tea without a grudging undertone. Considering what she believed about cops, it was more than many would do, Kit thought. She was beginning to see the strength of this woman, whose quiet dignity never deserted her even when she was furious.

She made herself look across the polished dining room table at the woman. "I am so very sorry, Mrs. Rivas. Jaime was clearly a wonderful boy. I believe that he was all you say he was and that he was not in a gang. I'm sorry for your loss. I'm sorry for the world's loss. We can't afford to keep losing young men like him. Or his brother."

Carmela Rivas stared at her. And Kit thought she saw the sheen of moisture in her eyes. "You can say this? After seeing Martin in that place today?"

Kit smiled gently. She had thought, at the last minute, to call Mrs. Rivas and ask if she would like to ride to the honor ranch with her. It was a long drive, and perhaps she was tired of making it alone. She'd told Kit she went every weekend to see her surviving son.

"It seems fairly clear to me that Martin is angry. Very angry."

She meant it. The boy was in custody for a string of joy-riding and minor vandalism offenses, relatively small things. And things that could easily be nothing more than a scream of rage, an announcement to the world that had taken his brother away that he would fulfill its grim expectations of him, as well.

"He loved his brother very much, didn't he?"

"The sun rose and set in Jaime, for Martin. He has never gotten over his death."

Nor have you, Kit thought. But then, how could she, when it was still a raw, open wound, exacerbated every time she saw a police officer?

Martin Rivas had indeed been an angry young man, even after all this time. And less disposed than his mother to speak to a cop. Only Mrs. Rivas's stern admonitions had gotten him to tell her what little he knew. The witness he knew only by his gang moniker of *El Tigre* had come to him, knowing he was Jaime's little brother, and told him he'd been in the alley that night, taking a leak. He'd seen it happen, all of it. If it had been one of his homies, of course, he would have come to his aid, cop or no cop. Since it hadn't been, he had dodged out of sight. But he had watched.

"He saw a cop beating up your brother?" Kit asked.

"Yeah." Martin had sneered defiantly. "Big ol' white pig. Beat him to death, for no reason at all. Pigs just like to beat on people, that's all, 'specially home boys. Beat 'em or rip 'em off."

"How did he know it was a cop? Was he in uniform?"

"No. But El Tigre knew him. Maybe he busted him once or something. Cops are always bustin' homies for nothin'. But Jaime, he wasn't no gangster. No reason to kill him. Bastard."

He'd clammed up, and Kit knew it was because angry tears were threatening and that the boy would die before he'd cry in front of a stranger, a woman and most especially a cop.

What she didn't know was how much of the description he'd snarled was literal and how much was typical street stereotyping of any and all cops. Martin insisted that was all he knew. That El Tigre had been going to tell him more, but he'd died before he could.

She also didn't know if there was any truth to what Martin said El Tigre had said. As she sat, in what had been Jaime's obviously loving home, looking at the sad memorabilia of a young life cut short, as she listened to Mrs. Rivas's impassioned declarations, as she remembered a brother's fierce anger, she found herself believing. Enough, at least, to continue digging.

"I think I'll go take a look at the scene, where it happened," Kit said, standing up. "Thank you for the tea, Mrs. Rivas. It was very good."

"I think," the woman said slowly, "that you must call me Carmela."

Kit left the tidy little house feeling as if she'd won a battle.

Chapter 6

"**B**itch," the young man muttered.

Kit tensed, then sighed. Maybe she'd been off the street too long. Stuff like that used to roll off her back like rain down a window.

"Yeah." Another male voice, heavy with pride and swagger chimed in. "This is our ground, you're trespassin'."

"Your ground," she said carefully, "is in my city."

"You gonna take over the racket now, that it, *puta?*"

She'd been called that before, and it didn't bother her much. She knew "whore" was the most common way these macho idiots referred to any female. She tried to consider the source and ignore it.

But the rumble increased, that blending of threatening voices that only a group of angry young males could produce. The fact that there were four of them against one lone female made them cocky, and that made Kit mad.

"Cops only come down here to hassle."

"Think a badge makes them God."

"Take your white ass back to—"

"Maybe we'll give you a little reminder of your visit."

Something about the tone of that last one set off an alarm in her head, and she turned just as a flick of the wrist opened a butterfly knife in the hands of the tallest of the four. She shifted her balance to the balls of her feet, almost welcoming the outlet for all the frustration that had been building in her for days.

She was taking a risk, gambling that nobody was going to pull a gun on her, and if they did that she could get to hers, tucked in her holster at the small of her back under her jacket, first, but she didn't see a choice if she wanted to have a chance to get something here.

The tall one jabbed the knife toward her, not really trying to stab her, just to scare her, she guessed. But it gave her what she needed. She grabbed his wrist and yanked. Caught off guard, he stumbled toward her. She stepped aside and let him go past. He twisted wildly, trying to free his wrist. Kit felt the sting as the blade sliced through her sleeve and caught her forearm, but she never let go. He was off balance, and she used his height against him, kicking his feet out from under him. In a split second he was down and she was kneeling on his back, his knife in her own hand, tickling his ear.

"You think this makes you tough? Four of you on one? And that one a woman?"

She wanted to tell him exactly what it made him—a coward—but knew if she did his pride would stop him from giving her what she wanted. This was the only one among all the street denizens she'd questioned or tried to question today who had dodged her gaze when she'd mentioned the Rivas murder. He knew something, and she wanted it.

His three companions moved restlessly, unsure what to do while she held the weapon at their friend's neck. They were looking at her in surprise, with a touch of respect.

"I suggest we all just back it up a notch," she said. "Now

maybe you don't care that somebody got murdered on your ground without your say. Maybe you don't care that you and your homies are being blamed for it while the real killer laughs. But that boy who was killed, his mother cares. And so do I."

The three looked at each other, then at her warily. But she'd stake her detective badge on her guess they didn't know anything. It was this one who'd reacted, this one who'd been so eager to scare her off he'd risked a charge of assault with a deadly weapon on a police officer. And he was maybe twenty, old enough to have been around five years ago.

She nudged her captive's ear once more. "Tell your buddies to cut out."

"What?" His voice had a squeak in it that hadn't been there before. She was gratified to know he was scared.

"You heard me. Get rid of them. Unless you'd rather they all went to jail with you."

"Go, man!" he yelped. The three scrambled to comply, leaving them alone in the alley a dozen yards from where young Jaime had died.

"Now," Kit said, easing up on him, letting him sit but keeping the knife in his line of sight. "You got a name?"

"They call me Mako."

Charming, Kit thought. "Like the shark, I presume?"

He nodded, a tiny bit of the gang swagger returning.

"Okay, Mako, here's the deal. On the one hand, I can run you in for assault on an officer. Possession of this weapon should add to that, and whatever else I might find on you could make it even more interesting."

His eyes widened slightly, and she wondered what he did have stashed on him. It went against the grain to let it pass, but she had to keep her eye on the bigger goal.

"On the other hand," she continued easily, "I'll make you an offer. You tell me what you know about that night, and you walk away."

He looked at her doubtfully, his distrust obvious. "Just like that? I walk?"

"Yep."

"No cop ever done me no favors before. Hell, they're either hasslin' me or shakin' me down. I hate cops."

Kit sighed. "I'm sure the feeling's mutual. Have we got a deal?"

"I just tell you what I know, and it's over?"

"It's over."

She flipped the knife shut with a handiness that seemed to impress the kid. She thought. Being taken down at all had to have been a blow to his pride. That it was a woman would make it almost irrecoverable. And these kids lived—and too often died—for that pride. If she gave him a chance to recover some of it, he might give her what she needed.

"Tell you what," she said, "you can even tell your buddies that you sweet-talked your way out of it with the lady cop."

She could see that idea appealed to his burgeoning macho aspirations.

"Do I get my blade back?"

"If I like what I hear."

She didn't like what she heard. She hated it. Hated the idea, hated the ramifications, hated the position it put her in.

But she wasn't surprised.

"Ouch," Kit said.

"Tough," Dr. Roxanne Cutler retorted as she swabbed antiseptic into the cut on Kit's forearm. "You Trinity West people keep disrupting my day, you can just be quiet and take your medicine.

"Yes, Roxy," Kit said meekly. "But do you have to administer it so gleefully?"

"Yes. It's one of my few joys."

Kit laughed despite herself. The young black ER doctor

was a favorite among Trinity West personnel, herself included. Kit knew Roxy had had more than one chance to move out of the ER, but she seemed to thrive on the chaos. And she was exactly the distraction Kit needed right now. She was in an ugly place and she didn't know what to do about it.

"You should laugh," Roxy said. "You're darn lucky. Your jacket sleeve saved you. A little bit deeper and you'd be looking at my needlework for the next week."

Kit wrinkled her nose. "Thank goodness for that."

"Don't you be casting aspersions on my seamstress skills," Roxy said as she applied some small adhesive sutures to the cut, then began to bandage it.

Kit heard voices coming from the desk area as a new arrival spoke to the nurse. She caught herself listening intently, then gave an inward groan. Even here, she thought. She could have sworn that sounded like Chief de los Reyes. She couldn't get the man out of her mind even here. She'd been thinking about him far too much lately. She'd been thinking about how different he seemed compared to the laughing, happy man he'd been when Anna had been alive. She'd been thinking how much she'd like to see him like that again.

She'd been thinking how much she liked seeing him, period. And that was worse than dangerous territory—that was idiocy. Even beside the impossibility of it for work reasons, it felt odd, somehow, to begin to think of him that way. Not quite wrong, but not quite right, either, for the simple reason that he'd been Anna's husband, and Anna had been her friend.

Not that it mattered how it felt to her. He would certainly never even think of her that way. He was still in love with Anna, and even if he wasn't, Kit knew she wasn't his type. Anna had been tiny and sweet, all dark eyes and sleek, long, raven dark hair. She was too tall, too fair and far from sweet.

No she wasn't his type at all. He would want someone like

Anna. If he ever wanted anyone again in the first place. And she told herself that was really what this was all about, that she wanted to see him no longer so alone, not that she wanted him herself.

That made perfect sense to her, and she was pleased she had finally figured out her confused thoughts.

"Kit!"

Her head snapped up. She gaped at him as if she wasn't quite sure she hadn't imagined him. But there was no denying it. Miguel de los Reyes was hurrying across the emergency room toward her, looking much more concerned than this minor cut warranted. And looking so familiar and yet so different.

It had been a long time since she had seen him in anything except his uniform or the somber dark suits and button-down white shirts he wore to work. The shirt was the same, but it was open at the throat and the sleeves were rolled up on his forearms. And he had on a pair of snug, faded jeans that made her wonder if there was another forty-four-year-old man out there who could look so darn good in the things. If this was his standard Saturday attire, she was all for it.

He came to a halt in front of her. "Are you all right?" Before Kit could assure him she was fine, he turned to Roxanne. "Is she all right?"

"She's stubborn, overworked and has no social life," Roxy said calmly. "But other than that, she's fine."

Kit could have throttled her attending physician at that moment. "What are you doing here?" she managed to ask him.

He seemed to relax slightly when she spoke. "Dr. Cutler called me when you came in."

Kit shifted her gaze to Roxy accusingly. "Standing orders from the man," the doctor said with an exaggeratedly innocent expression. "If one of his people comes in, he gets called. I do as I'm told."

"Your obedience is exemplary," Kit muttered. She knew darn well Roxy did as she pleased.

Roxy, ever unruffled and clearly not at all intimidated by Kit's glare or the presence of the chief of police—after all, she had once saved his life—merely shooed him into the waiting room, telling him, "You can have her back in a minute."

"Darn it, Roxy," Kit said as soon as he was gone, "that's the chief, for crying out loud. A little discretion, please?"

Roxy taped the last of the gauze with an enthusiasm Kit could have done without. Then the young doctor put her hands on her hips and looked at Kit straight on.

"Honey, if that man would look at me the way he just looked at you, I'd throw discretion to the wind."

Kit gaped at her. "What?"

"I've had the hots for that man since I first laid eyes on him. But he's *never* looked at me like that," Roxy said cheerfully. "And the way he rushed in here in a panic, thinking you were going to be fastened to a bank of machines and IVs? Mmm-mmm, girl. If you don't go for it, you're a fool."

"Roxy," Kit said when she had recovered enough to speak, "I think you've finally cracked."

"Uh-huh. That's why when you saw him come in, you looked like you'd seen the Holy Grail."

Kit blushed furiously, felt it and wondered where all the control she'd worked so hard for had vanished to. She was too old to be blushing like this. She was thirty-six, for crying out loud, how long did it take to outgrow it?

"Lovely color, honey," Roxy said, patting her uninjured arm. "Now let me get you those antibiotics and you can let that gorgeous man take you home. And if you can get him to put you to bed, more power to you."

"Roxy!"

Roxy only laughed.

He hated hospitals.

Of course, he didn't know anyone who particularly liked

them, but he had a special aversion and particularly to this one. And it wasn't solely because of Anna. She'd spent more than her share of time here, but she had died at home in her own bed, the last gift he'd been able to give her. And it wasn't solely because of the time he'd spent here after the shooting that had killed Chief Lipton and nearly killed him.

No, it was because too much Trinity West history was in this place. Too many times that thin blue line had ruptured, and this was the result. A trip to the emergency room for an injured or dying cop.

It had always bothered him, but it had become especially difficult since he had become chief. He felt responsible. He felt an empathetic pain. He worried, felt a need to be involved beyond the inherent obligation to be sure the family was all right.

But when the call had come about Kit, all he'd felt was a sudden jolt of fear.

He barely remembered the call, hadn't been able to believe the reassurances that it was a minor cut. He'd had to see for himself. He'd had all the sick feelings, felt the fear, the worry, chanted the too familiar mantra—"Let it be all right"—everything he always did when somebody from Trinity West was hurt.

But this time it had all been overlaid by a sense of panic he hadn't felt in a very long time. Panic that had had him driving to the hospital even faster than he usually would after one of those calls.

And it hadn't gone away until she'd looked at him and asked what he was doing there. Only then had he realized she really was all right.

"What am I doing here, she asks," he muttered as he paced the waiting room. He was always here when one of his own got hurt. However, he had to admit he wasn't usually in such a state over what was apparently a minor injury.

Before he could dwell on what that might mean, he heard Roxanne Cutler's voice and turned. The doctor had returned to the emergency room, but Kit was walking out, holding her left arm horizontally at her waist. Concern made him wince. He could imagine how it would be throbbing until it settled down, and how letting it fall naturally at her side would worsen the pain.

But she seemed well enough, was walking steadily enough, and he took heart from that.

"At least you didn't have to have stitches," he said as he walked toward her.

She looked up as if startled. "You're still here?"

He frowned. "Of course I am. Why wouldn't I be?"

"Because it's really nothing. I almost didn't come in at all, but I was close by and—"

"Roxanne said it was a nasty cut. That's nothing to mess with, it could get infected."

Kit's mouth quirked. "The knife was clean. I think the guy polished it daily."

He froze. "Knife?"

Kit blinked. "Oops. Didn't Roxy tell you? I figured that was why she called you."

"I've told her to call me anytime anyone from Trinity West came in with an injury, no matter the cause. If one of my people is in the hospital, I want to know about it."

"I'm not *in* the hospital," Kit said. "I could have gone to a walk-in clinic or done it myself, but like I said—"

"You were close by. Now, you want to tell me about this knife? And who cut you with it? Is he in custody? Did you—"

She held up her right hand as if to stave off the flood of questions. That, he thought ruefully, wasn't like him, either. He wasn't reacting with his usual calm. Especially since it was clear Kit was going to be fine. She hadn't needed stitches, he reminded himself.

"It's a long story," she said.

"I have time."

She looked at him. "It's Saturday. Sure you don't want to wait until Monday?"

She seemed oddly reluctant, and he wondered why. "I don't have a thing to do except hear how this happened."

She lowered her gaze and began rummaging in her small purse. She was muttering about keys, but Miguel had the feeling that was only an excuse. Something was bothering her. He knew that intense air. He'd seen it before, when she was deep into a case or when she was particularly outraged by some victim's plight or a miscarriage of justice. He'd worried about it before. That kind of intensity could easily lead to burnout, and he didn't want to see Kit Walker burn out.

And he didn't like seeing her hurting. At all.

"Maybe you shouldn't drive," he said when she pulled out a ring with a couple of keys on it and turned toward the door.

"It's just a cut," she insisted. "I'm fine."

"But you should go home and rest. I'll drive you."

Her gaze shot to his face. "I'm *fine*," she repeated with emphasis. "I don't need to be babied." Then, as if she realized what she sounded like, she added, "Sir."

For some reason, that put his teeth on edge. "Will you drop the sir, please? Let me drive you, and you can save time and tell me what happened on the way."

"But my car is here."

"I'll have somebody pick it up and bring it to your place."

"That's not necessary."

"I think it is. Do you need a key off of there for your house?"

"No, I keep them separate. But—"

He held up a hand to stop her protests. "Don't make me pull rank, Sergeant."

She looked at him, her expression as intense as before, but somehow enigmatic. "Is that what you're doing?"

There was a moment of silence before he let out a long, compressed breath. ''No.'' His mouth twisted. ''Guess I can't have it both ways, can I? Tell you to drop the sir and then pull rank on you?''

She lowered her gaze, but her mouth curved slightly as he acknowledged the contradiction. That mouth…

He slammed the door on that thought. ''Look,'' he said, ''can you forget the rank for a while and just let a friend feel like he's doing something useful and taking you home?''

''All right.''

He hadn't expected the capitulation, and his gaze narrowed. Was she feeling worse than she was letting on, not up to a fight over this?

He nearly laughed at himself. He'd gotten what he wanted, and he still wasn't happy. He took the keys from her, slipped them in his pocket, took her uninjured arm and led her toward his car.

As he drove, Kit leaned her head on the headrest and closed her eyes. Despite his suggestion that they save time by her telling him the story on the way, Miguel hesitated to say anything, not wanting to disturb her if she was truly resting. He knew that no matter how minor the injury, there was a certain amount of shock involved, and if she'd received it in some kind of altercation, there was the post-adrenaline crash to consider.

He slowed as he made the turn onto Marina Avenue. He hadn't been here since Anna had died, since the last time he'd dropped Kit off after she'd gone rushing home with him when Anna had had a particularly bad day. But the small house she'd bought a couple of years after Bobby Allen had been killed looked the same—neat, with a colorful garden in front behind a low fence and a graceful twisted juniper casting welcome shade across the grass. The lawn was a bit long, and he supposed she'd had little time to deal with such things since Gage had left early this year. He had to get her some help, before she ran herself into the ground.

He stopped the car gently in her driveway, not wanting to jar her.

"Kit?"

"Hmm?"

She did sound drowsy. Her lashes lifted halfway, and she turned to look at him, giving a warm, sleepy-eyed smile that rattled him even more than that husky note in her voice.

"We're here," he said, aware his voice was a bit tight but unable to help it.

"Oh." She blinked and sat up. "I'm sorry, I didn't mean to go to sleep."

"Don't worry about it. Let's just get you inside. Have you eaten anything today?"

"I had breakfast."

He grimaced. "It's three in the afternoon. Did lunch ever occur to you?"

"I was busy."

"Apparently." He eyed her bandaged arm. He knew she was fit and strong, he'd seen her in action, but somehow the wrist beneath that bandage seemed delicate, almost fragile. And it amazed him once again that she was able to do her job so well, even though he had always been a firm believer in using wit before brawn. To him, muscle was the last resort, not the first.

"I suppose you want the story now," she said with a sigh.

"If you're up to it."

"Come on in."

He hesitated, questioning the wisdom of this. But he knew he needed to know what had happened, told himself he was here in an official capacity, and followed her into the house.

It was much as he'd remembered, warm, homey, cozy instead of cramped despite the small size. The furnishings were simple and uncluttered, like Kit. The wall of bookshelves told him she still loved to read, and he knew if he checked the titles he'd find a little of everything. A wall of framed photographs, landscapes mostly, interspersed with the occasional whimsical juxtaposition of unlikely subjects, like the lovely butterfly hovering over a rusty can, reminded him of another interest of hers. He wondered if she had time to get out her camera these days.

"Got any food in the house?" he said as she set her purse and keys on the round oak dining table.

She glanced at him, seeming a little startled. "There's some leftover chili, I think, or I can put something together, if you're hungry."

"I meant for you," he said dryly.

"Oh." A faint wash of color tinged her cheeks. Funny, he hadn't noticed her blushing so often in years.

He hustled her into the kitchen, which was also as he remembered, bright and cheerful in blue and white, compact but efficient. The door to the back yard was next to a tiled breakfast bar that divided the room from the small dining nook. The bright blue and white scheme was continued in the tile of the bar, the counters and the wall behind the sink. It suited her, he thought.

She went to the refrigerator and opened it. He saw the detective division days-off schedule held on the door with a magnet in the improbable shape of a trout.

"There's more than enough for two here," she said. "Do you want some?"

"Is it your chili?" he asked.

"Yes. I made a huge pot last week. Should be about ripe by now."

"Then yes," he said. "You always did make the best chili I ever tasted."

"Thank you," she said, looking pleased.

"Can I help?"

She shook her head. "I'm feeling better," she said, giving him a sideways look, "after my nap."

He smiled at her. For a moment she seemed to stare at him, then turned to dump the spicy brown concoction into a pan to be heated. He remembered her telling him that she never microwaved it, swearing it changed the flavor. He'd eaten her chili more than once, in those dark days before Anna had finally lost her valiant battle.

"I don't know if I ever thanked you properly." It was out before he'd realized he was going to say it.

Kit looked over her shoulder at him. "For what?"

"All that you did. When Anna was sick."

Kit went still. "You don't have to thank me for that."

"But I do. All the times you came over—" he gestured toward the pan on the stove "—with food or with some little thing to distract her from the pain or just to sit with her..."

His voice trailed away. He couldn't go on, couldn't tell her how moved he'd been by the way she'd always seemed to worry as much about him as Anna, making sure he took a break from the constant care giving for at least as long as she was there.

"She was my friend," Kit said simply. "And so were you."

And what am I now? The thought formed before he could stop it. He turned to what had, ironically and amazingly, become a safer topic.

"She thought the world of you. She always said so."

"I...thank you. I'm glad."

He swallowed tightly, feeling the lump in his throat that would make the next words hard to get out, but he knew they should be said. And finally, he managed it.

"I'll never forget that day, the year after she died, when you came to me. You'll never know how much that meant to me."

She'd shown up at his door on the first anniversary of

Anna's death, laden with photos she'd taken over the years. He hadn't wanted to look, hadn't wanted to see his wife's smiling face. But Kit had made him look, and with each photograph she'd had a story to tell him, a funny story that reminded him what a happy, cheerful person Anna had been, words that had been unexpected balm to the still-gaping wound of her death.

He knew his healing had begun that day and that even though it had been a long, agonizing process that was probably still going on, if it had not been for Kit and her gentle determination that he remember the good as well as the bad he never would have made the turn at all.

There was still a huge hole in his life, and he knew he'd fallen into the habit of living with it, living around it, but if not for Kit, he wasn't sure he wouldn't have fallen straight into it. He certainly wouldn't have been in any shape to take over Trinity West.

"It just seemed like the right thing to do," Kit said. "You needed to remember that it hadn't all been pain and loss, that you'd had so many good years. I know it was presumptuous—"

"It wasn't presumptuous. It was the act of a good and perceptive friend. You saved my life, Kit. I don't think I would have made it if you hadn't done that when you did."

She stared at him and swallowed hard. "I'm glad," she said in a small voice, and quickly turned away as if overcome with emotion.

He knew the feeling. It was difficult to speak of that time, although the pain was much less immediate now, more of a distant pang. And thanks to Kit's intervention, he'd managed to learn the knack of replacing the sad memories with happier ones until he'd achieved some kind of balance.

It wasn't until the steaming bowls of chili, topped with fresh onions and melting cheese, were in front of them that he brought up the reason he was supposedly here.

"You want to tell me the story now?" He gestured at the chili. "You can take your time. Between bites is fine."

With a sigh, she gave in. He ate and listened as she ate and told him of her meeting with Martin Rivas, of her visit to the scene where Jaime Rivas had died and how she had decided to ask around a bit as long as she was there. And how that had eventually led to the encounter with Mako.

Looking wary, as if she expected a reprisal, she told him of the bargain she'd struck with the young gang member. He shook his head.

"Sometimes you have to let a smaller thing go by to get what you need on a bigger thing," he said. "Go on."

She took a deep breath, dropped her spoon in the empty bowl and took a drink of the ice water she'd poured for them both. He said nothing, just waited. Finally she went on.

"Mako said he'd been in the neighborhood that night, around midnight. He'd seen Jaime."

"He didn't see the beating?"

"No. He just saw Jaime walking toward home."

"He knew him?"

She nodded. "Knew him because they'd been in school together, before Mako dropped out. He seemed to respect him for being smart."

He nodded. "Then what?"

"He said he saw somebody else in the neighborhood at the same time, too, only a block away and headed in the same direction. Said it was a guy all the kids knew to beware of back then. Made everybody on the street call him Boss, and if you didn't, he'd mess you up."

"Is this guy still around?"

"As far as Mako knows, he's still around. But it seems he sticks to the younger ones, the ones he can scare. Mako got too old or too big for him, apparently, and he quit hassling him. Same with his buddies."

"Big man," Miguel muttered. "He got a name?"

"Mako didn't know a name. Just knew him as Boss, like all the other kids the guy intimidated. They didn't ask questions. It only made him mad and he'd come after them."

She didn't go on, and he wondered why. Was he going to have to ask the obvious? This Mako obviously had to know what this guy looked like. And Miguel knew Kit well enough to know she wouldn't have let the kid go before getting a description. So why didn't she just get on with it?

Only one answer came to him, and he didn't much like it. But he knew he had to know, had to ask.

"Was Mrs. Rivas right?"

Kit looked at him across her table. She didn't speak, but the answer was clear to him in the tension of her body, the shadow in her normally clear hazel eyes. She looked like a person caught in a trap, unable to free herself yet unable to resign herself to what had happened. He knew why she was hesitating. She was afraid if she told him and it came to nothing, if she was wrong, she could kiss her career goodbye.

"This is just between us, Kit. And you know if I say that, I mean it. This guy he saw that all the kids were afraid of, it was a cop, wasn't it? And you know who he described."

After a long, silent moment she nodded. And when he pressed, she rattled off the description as if it had been tumbling around in her head repeatedly. Maybe it had. But it left little doubt. Even five years old, the description fit only one person, a person whose appearance hadn't changed in thirty years.

Lieutenant Ken Robards.

Chapter 7

It seemed impossible to believe even of Robards, Miguel thought. But it made a twisted sort of sense. If there had been any legitimate reason for the confrontation, if he'd caught Jamie committing a crime or the boy had assaulted him, Robards, with more bravado than any three men, would have said it was justified and reported it.

It was a method Miguel suspected Robards had used before, when he'd had to "get tough," as he put it, with somebody, somebody who was inevitably smaller and weaker than he was. It had worked for him before, especially when everyone had known he had the personal backing and friendship of Chief Lipton.

But no one had ever died before, Miguel amended silently.

So the fact that Robards hadn't reported it could mean they were way off base with their suppositions, that the man was innocent and the things Kit had discovered merely coincidence.

Or it could mean the alternative—out-and-out unprovoked

homicide. That would have been too much for Robards, even with all his internal support, to try to bluff his way through. But it also seemed too far out there even for this man. Robards was, they agreed, a jerk, a bigot, a racist, a sexist and a dinosaur, but for a cop, even one like Robards, the step to murder was still a long one.

Miguel didn't know whether to be angry, to despair or to rejoice. In the end, he gave free rein to all three. He was angry because being a cop was tough enough without vicious idiots like Robards making it tougher and despairing because, if Kit's information was accurate, taking this particular cop down was going to be a high-wire act he didn't know if he could pull off.

But underlying it all was a feeling of grim satisfaction that could pass for rejoicing. He'd been waiting for this chance for a very long time.

They didn't talk as he helped her clean up, or as they walked into the living room. He paced the length of the room a couple of times, then sat on the comfortable sofa when she took a seat in an overstuffed chair. She waited silently, and he knew the ball was in his court.

For a long moment he looked at her before he said, "If you want to drop this, now's the time. I'll walk out of here, it will end right now, and you'll never hear another thing about it."

She looked startled. "It's not up to me. Is it?"

He held her gaze steadily. "It's got to be, Kit. You're the one who stumbled across this. Robards already knows that. Even if I tried to take it over, keep you out of it, he'd know you started it."

"I know that."

"If we pursue it," he went on, "it's going to be ugly. Uglier than just about any internal investigation I can think of, considering who's involved. And there's no way to keep you out of it once it starts."

"But we can't just let it go. He may have killed that boy!"

"I just want you to be sure." He leaned forward, resting his elbows on his knees. "But be sure of something else, too, Kit. I'll be there. Every step of the way. This is big enough and we're shorthanded enough that I can justify doing the investigation myself. You'll have whatever clout I've got behind you, no matter what happens."

It wasn't much, he thought, when weighed against what she'd be risking. If they were wrong, Robards could bring the whole thing down around their ears. And if they were right, it could cause nearly as much damage in a variety of places and ways. And no matter how much he tried to shield her with his office, Kit would be the center of the storm, the one who initiated the action. Inevitably there would be sides chosen, and she would bear the brunt of it.

She met his gaze unflinchingly, and he saw in her expression that she knew it, that she'd thought of all this before she'd told him. And she'd trusted him enough to tell him despite it all.

"We can't let him get away with it," she said simply, as if there was no other answer possible.

Emotion flooded him, a tangle of the respect and admiration he'd always had for her mixed with something new that he didn't recognize but that made him want to... He wasn't sure what it made him want to do, only that he didn't dare do it. Didn't dare even think about it. He had to wait a moment to steady his voice.

"We go ahead, then?"

She nodded without hesitation. "We do."

"I'm very proud to know you, Kit Walker."

The glow that lit her face seemed out of proportion to the simple words, but it warmed him nonetheless. As did her trust. He knew that trusting her was the least he could do.

"It's only fair that you know something," he said. "I'm

not unbiased here. I've been looking for years for a way to take that man down.''

"I suspected as much," she said. She held his gaze evenly. "You're at the head of a long line, sir. There are a lot of people with reason to despise him. And I confess I'm among them."

"That's why I—*we* have to be very, very careful. This can't be personal or look like a vendetta."

He knew she was aware that Robards had been the loudest voice protesting her promotion to sergeant and her transfer to detectives. Miguel had had to overcome the man's fierce fighting and lobbying every time he'd been up for promotion. They would have to be very careful.

Kit nodded in understanding. "I've known I had to walk carefully since I saw his name on that crime report. And I admit I would dearly love to see him in the wrong. But not enough to embarrass the department without cause."

"And it would do just that," he agreed. "But then, just having a cop like that around is an embarrassment."

"And then some." She looked thoughtful. "It fits," she said.

"What fits?"

"He wasn't always so blatant. It's gotten worse in the past few years. I used to think it was just that he was getting older."

"But maybe he was just getting more arrogant." He didn't say, *Because he thinks he got away with murder,* but he knew they were both thinking it.

"I *hate* this," she said fervently. "But I hate what he's done more."

"I know, Kit. But not everybody who looks at what we do next is going to know what kind of man we're dealing with. They're going to see a thirty-year cop, a lot of experience." He smiled wryly. "Some may agree with his approach. There are a lot of disgusted people out there who think we'd be better off if we went back to his era. Some might even figure we're trying to dump him in some kind of age discrimination thing."

"Then we'll just have to make sure they do see what kind of man he is, won't we? If he beat Jaime Rivas to death, I want him hung out to dry, cop or not."

He nearly smiled at her grimly determined tone. Kit Walker was as tough as she had to be, and then some, he thought. But then, no fragile female would have survived the job, let alone the kind of abuse Robards heaped on her, just as he did anyone else who didn't meet his WASP male standards.

"So do I, Kit," he agreed, "in the worst way. I don't just want him gone, I want him punished. But you realize we may have to settle for…less."

"Less?"

He got to his feet, restless, and began to slowly pace the small room as he answered her.

"After all this time, with the one real witness dead, and this Mako only seeing him in the area, all we have is hearsay. And most of that secondhand."

"And inadmissible," Kit said glumly.

"And the rest is all circumstantial."

"And," she added wearily, leaning back in the big chair, "every circumstance could have an innocent—well, not criminal, anyway—explanation."

He turned to face her and nodded. "That he was seen in the area, that he wrote the reports himself, that he was rousting and intimidating kids on the street, that he didn't call the medics, that he did the bare minimum on the investigation and probably had his buddy Detective Brennan do the same—it all adds up to a mean, sloppy cop, but it doesn't come anywhere near a murderer. Not in court."

"But I'd swear on my badge he remembered that case instantly. He knew what it was before he looked inside that file."

"And I believe you. You're observant, and you have good instincts. But—"

"I know. My instincts would get laughed out of court by any hotshot attorney."

Reluctantly, he nodded. Every cop knew that instinct, that gut-level feeling you couldn't explain, that something was wrong, that that guy walking down the street was on the wrong side of something, was a big part of being a good cop. They also knew there was nothing more vulnerable to the vagaries of the current justice system. You could catch a serial killer with a trail of bodies from coast to coast, but if your only explanation for why you stopped him was, "I just had a feeling about him," you were in for trouble from the defense lawyers. It could end up with the killer walking free. Years of investigating experience to cite as authority softened the blow, but a high-power attorney could take that apart, too.

He didn't say any of this. He knew Kit knew it as well as he did. And it suddenly exhausted him. He sat on the sofa, rubbing tiredly at the back of his neck.

"So what's the bottom line?" she asked.

"You mean after eliminating the option of simply beating him to a pulp?" he asked wryly.

"If we must," she retorted, deadpan.

The corners of his mouth twitched at her tone despite the ugliness of the topic. But then, Kit had always been able to do that, make him laugh with her quick wit. He'd forgotten how much fun they'd all had together, although Anna had had her doubts about Bobby. "I'm afraid he's going to short-change her if it comes to putting her or the job first. Kit needs someone like you," she'd told him one night after they'd all been out for pizza.

Someone like you.

Fire kicked through him, hot, swift and unexpected. One second he'd been remembering Anna, snuggled in bed beside him, and the next he was imagining himself looking at her—but it was Kit's face he saw.

Shock hit him as fast as the fire had and doused the heat with chilling efficiency. More warning signs than he could count were in his mind, and he shook his head sharply at the sudden pressure. Absurdly, a picture of an ancient map popped into his head with the limits of the world as it had been then known and in the far reaches the ominous words, "Here there be dragons." He suddenly knew the feeling.

"Er..."

He swallowed and tried again, afraid to look at her for fear she'd be staring at him as if he'd suddenly lost his mind. As, perhaps, he had. He made himself focus, wondering why what had always been easy suddenly seemed so difficult.

"The real bottom line is getting him off the force." He finally managed to get the words out. "We may not be able to put him in jail, but for Robards, I'm not sure taking away his authority, the badge he uses for intimidation, wouldn't be worse."

Kit's brow furrowed. "But with all his time, wouldn't you have to have just about as much to fire him as you would to charge him?"

He was able to make his voice light. "You want my job? You obviously already understand the most frustrating parts."

"Not just yet," she said in a mockingly formal tone.

He chuckled before going on with the facts he found far less amusing. "I may have to settle for a lot less than I want. We don't have any solid proof, we only have leverage. But maybe, if I play it right, enough leverage to get him to retire early. Like now."

"Retire?"

"I know it's not much. But it may be all we can get, and this may be the only chance we ever get. He's a savvy old goat and he knows how to work the system."

"I'll get more," Kit said, determined. "I'm tracking down

the patrol officer who responded to the scene so I can talk to him, find out why he didn't do a supplemental report, at least. Maybe Robards said something to him. And I want to check out the story on that conveniently dead witness. If there's anything, I'll find it. Just give me some time."

"Kit, you've already been hurt—"

"This?" she said, gesturing with her bandaged arm. "This is nothing. Besides, it comes with the territory. You," she added softly, "should know that better than anyone."

For an instant those quiet words took him back to those endless days of red-hot agony after the shooting, when he'd first been afraid he would die, then afraid he wouldn't. He'd thought in those long days that if they'd just quit trying to save him, he'd be glad enough to go. Maybe Anna really would be waiting for him. He'd seen her often in those wandering dreams, but the pain that even the heavy doses of drugs couldn't hold completely at bay would always make her image shift, then fade.

Kit had been there, too. She'd been at his bedside often during those dark days. She'd talked to him, he remembered that. Exhorting him to live, sometimes, it seemed, even begging him. And sometimes, when he'd groggily opened his eyes, he'd seen her there.

And sometimes he'd seen her even when he closed his eyes. He'd seen her nearly as often as Anna until he'd lost the line between them, wondering in his dazed mind if he was confused, if Anna was still alive or Kit had joined her in death. That last memory made his stomach knot fiercely, and he had to fight it down with an effort.

He'd never realized before what a part of his life she had always been, and what a hole there would be if she left. When the spate of weddings at Trinity West had begun last year— Caitlin and Quisto followed by Ryan and Lacey for the second time, Cruz and Kelsey, then Gage and Laurey—Miguel had wondered if Kit would somehow get caught up in the string. He didn't know that she was seeing anyone. He realized he knew very little about her personal life, but still the thought had come to him, and he hadn't known what to call the odd feeling it had given him.

He wasn't sure what to call it now, either.

"Just a little more time," she said, more urgently. "If I don't find anything else, we're still where we are now. But if I do, maybe we can see that he gets what he deserves. Please, Chief, let me keep going."

Pulled out of his memories, he focused on her. She wanted this badly. As badly as he did, it seemed. And it burned so bright in her, this anger at injustice, while he had to fight to hang onto it every day. He envied her. He wished she could somehow loan him some of that energy, that spirit she never lost. As she had those days when he'd lain in a hospital bed and she'd loaned him her strength through the simple fact of her presence, her bright, caring, understanding presence.

"Under two conditions," he said.

"What?"

"First, we do this together. If it falls apart, I don't want you taking the heat alone."

That had been a trait of his predecessor. The only thing he'd done faster than usurping the credit for the work of others was shifting any blame that came his way to someone else's shoulders. Miguel been the victim of that trait more than once, and that was all it had taken to convince him there was no quicker way to alienate people.

Kit was looking at him rather oddly, nodding, but in a way that seemed less like agreement and more like he'd said something she'd already expected to hear.

"All right," she said. "And condition number two?"

"When we're alone, I'm just Miguel."

She blinked. She looked at him a little warily. Something flickered in her eyes. He wasn't sure what it was, but it drove him to say lightly, "Or Mike, if you must."

She looked startled. "Oh, no. You're not a Mike."

He grinned. "Thank you. Then Miguel it is. No sir, no chief, just Miguel. I won't make it an order, but I will say please."

She laughed, sounding almost relieved. "All right," she said.

He was still wondering about that wary look in her eyes when he left her to get the rest Roxy had ordered.

Do not, Kit ordered herself, *read anything into this.*

She'd lost track of how many times she'd thought it or muttered it out loud since he'd left. In another minute she would be chanting it, she told herself sourly. It didn't mean anything, except that he was more comfortable with a less formal atmosphere since they were partners in solving this crime. If they were going to be in touch a lot, there was nothing unusual in the request.

She lay in the dark, feeling the slice on her arm throb a bit, wondering if maybe she'd been hasty in declining the painkiller Roxy had offered. But then she decided it was better this way. She was glad for the distraction the pain offered. It wasn't that bad, and it gave her something to think about. Something besides a deep, rough-edged voice saying, "When we're alone, I'm just Miguel."

She didn't know why such a simple request was having such an effect on her. Was it because he'd outranked her since she'd known him? He'd been a sergeant when she'd come on the job, and he'd made lieutenant a couple of years later and captain six years after that.

But she called others on the department by their first names, even some of higher rank, ones she'd known for over a decade. True, she'd been careful, especially as a woman, to wait until she was asked to forgo the formality of rank, but once that had happened, she'd had no problem. Except for Robards—whom she called lieutenant, to remind herself to respect the rank if she couldn't respect the man—she called most everyone by their first name, as they did her.

But she had never, she realized, called Miguel de los Reyes by anything other than his rank, or sir. With him, familiarity seemed to run downhill. He called her Kit, she called him chief. Even on social occasions she had done it, or avoided using any title at all, speaking to him without preamble. It puzzled her that she'd done it and never realized it. Why? Why had she treated him differently? Had he realized it even though she hadn't? Had he been wanting to say something about it for a long time?

She nearly laughed at her crazy imaginings. But she couldn't help wondering if she had clung to his rank as some kind of buffer between them, a way to keep a certain distance. But why him and no one else? And why did this whole thing unsettle her so?

Because Miguel de los Reyes unsettles you.

The silent answer came to her so swiftly she knew it had been in her mind for a while although it had never surfaced before.

Or she had never let it surface.

God, could it be? Could it be that she had treated him differently because…because why? Because she not only admired and respected him but felt something more? Had she kept that distance between them because she was afraid something more might show? He'd been Anna's husband, and Anna had been a good friend, and she would never have done anything that would hurt her.

Not that there ever would have been an opportunity. Anna's husband had loved her thoroughly and completely. And unlike many cops, he'd never made any bones about it. He'd never referred to her in the derogatory way so many cops did, as the "old lady." Anna's husband had been as proud of his place in her life as he'd been of his place in the department.

Kit realized something else, too. She had, in her mind, thought of Miguel in only two ways—as Anna's husband or as a superior on the job. She realized it had been an effort to keep him in those categories only. Some part of her had always wanted to see him as a man, and she didn't dare.

She sat up in bed abruptly, shivering, although the night was far from cool.

Kit had always thought she knew herself fairly well and that she was as honest as she could be in her dealings. It was a shock for her to realize she hadn't been very honest with herself. She'd never noticed the care with which she'd kept one man and one man only at more than arm's length. The fact that he doubtless didn't want to be any closer didn't matter. What mattered was that she'd done it, and done it unaware, at least consciously.

Which meant that subconsciously, there was a reason. And the most logical reason she could come up with made her very, very uncomfortable. In fact, it scared her, scared her in a basic way. And not simply because of the impossibility of it all. He was, after all, the chief and her boss in a male-oriented world that, given half a chance or less, would chew her up and spit her out. No, her fear stemmed from a much more basic fear.

She had sworn, after Bobby was killed in the line of duty a month before they were to be married, that she would never fall for a cop again. She'd renewed the pledge fervently when Miguel de los Reyes had lain near death, almost grateful that Anna wasn't here to go through this hell.

Now she could only sit in the darkness and hope she hadn't remembered that vow too late.

Chapter 8

The room hushed for a moment when the door opened, and Kit looked up. The new arrival, looking both curious and a bit uneasy, glanced around. It was a moment before the normal noise and chatter of the Neutral Zone picked up, but no longer than for any other unknown visitor.

Which, Kit told herself, was a good sign. It meant the kids probably didn't realize the chief of the Marina Heights police had just walked into their sanctuary. Lord knows what would happen if they did.

She finished with the glass of soda she'd been filling and handed it with a smile to the young girl across the bar. Gloria, a pretty fifteen-year-old who dressed like she was thirty and tried to talk like she was forty, turned and saw the tall, lean man approaching. She let out a low, earthy comment of appreciation.

Kit only knew a couple of the Spanish words, but it was enough to get the gist. Despite his advanced age, from Gloria's point of view, Miguel de los Reyes was one fine piece of male. And as she looked at him, dressed in jeans—black ones this time—a gray knit shirt and a black belt with a silver buckle and tip that emphasized his lean waist, she couldn't help agreeing.

"You said it, sister," she muttered, winning a grin and a wink from Gloria before the girl went to join her friends, taking time to eye the approaching man once more as they passed each other.

"Sorry I'm late," the chief—Miguel, she corrected herself, still not used to the familiarity—said as he reached the bar. "That budget meeting with the city finance director ran long. And I wanted to change clothes. This doesn't seem the place for a suit."

"Hardly," she agreed with a grin. "No problem. I'm here for the duration, anyway."

It was her night to run the club while Caitlin stayed at home with little Celeste, so they had agreed to meet here. All of Caitlin's friends, from Trinity West and elsewhere, were pitching in, knowing that while her dedication to the Neutral Zone hadn't changed, her available time had. The little girl who had been named for Quisto's mother was keeping her more than busy. So they were all taking turns donating an evening, keeping the place going as it always had.

"How's your arm?" he asked.

"Fine," she assured him.

He'd called yesterday afternoon to be sure she was all right, and she hadn't known whether to be gratified or nervous. She hadn't seen him at the station today, although a brief chat with Rosa had yielded the information that he was tied up at city hall and probably would be all day. But he'd called that evening just before she'd left Trinity West, and when she'd told him records had tracked down the case number on the drive-by shooting involving the supposed witness to the murder and she was going to stop by the storage room on her way out and dig out the file, he'd wanted to meet to go over it.

"Coffee, soda?" she offered. "Or maybe one of Quisto's favorite root beer floats?"

He laughed. "Just coffee, thanks."

"Grab a bar stool."

"It looks different," Miguel said as he looked around. "I was in here right after she opened, when we were still trying to convince her she'd be safer closer to Trinity West, but I haven't been back." He grimaced. "I thought it might make the kids nervous if they recognized me."

Kit paused, coffeepot in hand. "I never realized how much your job affected your whole life."

He shrugged. "It has its moments."

He took the mug she offered him and looked over the rim to the wall behind her. Kit knew what he was seeing, the cheerful, bright yellow expanse Caitlin had added as counterpoint to the dark, grim wall on the other side of the big room. Over there, photos of young people, some still children, some mere babies, hung in stark profusion, with only one thing in common—they were all, every one of them, dead. Murdered with intent, or by the accident of being in the wrong place at the wrong time, they were mute testimony to the ugliness of the streets, and to Caitlin Romero's determination that they not be forgotten. It was that wall as much as anything that brought the kids here. It had become a shrine to lost brothers, sisters, uncles, aunts, parents and even the children of these children.

But the yellow wall was the antithesis of the brutality of the dark wall. It was the home of hope, of photos of new babies born, of graduations and weddings and gamboling puppies. And it gave these kids something to think about when too much of their time was spent wondering if they would live to adulthood.

Kit got a towel to wipe off the top of the highly polished

bar. It wasn't fancy, but Caitlin saw to it that it, like everything here, was taken care of. It was all part of her campaign to make the kids see things didn't have to be expensive to work and look nice.

Kit saw Miguel smile as his gaze reached the spot over the root beer tap. She knew why, knew that he was looking at Caitlin and Quisto's wedding picture, hung in that place of significance for them both.

"I've noticed," Kit said thoughtfully, "that whenever Quisto or Cruz or Ryan do a shift here, the female population seems to get a bit silly. Why is that, do you suppose?"

Miguel laughed, and Kit thought the genuine, lighthearted sound the sweetest thing she'd heard in a long time.

"I can't imagine."

Kit glanced at the pinball machine, where Gloria was clustered with three other girls, giggling and looking this way. "Hmm," she said. "I was just wondering if you knew, since you seem to be having the same effect."

He looked startled and glanced over his shoulder. Caught, the girls shrieked and turned away, then started giggling again.

When he turned to her, still looking puzzled, Kit laughed. "It's really nice to see them acting so...normal. Most of them are pretty tough cookies when they start coming here, but given the chance Caitlin gives them, they revert to young girls pretty quickly. Especially with a good-looking guy around."

His expression shifted to a smile she would have called, had it been anyone other than him, shy. "Was there a compliment in there?"

Kit stopped dead in her rhythmic wiping motion, surprised at his almost hopeful tone. He had to know. The man had mirrors in his house, after all. And she'd teased him often enough about his aristocratic good looks in those old, comfortable days when he'd been safely off-limits, marked by the biggest stop sign in the world to her, the wedding band on his left hand.

But she hadn't said anything like that since Anna had died nearly six years ago. It had seemed wrong, somehow, even after he'd taken off the ring, two years after her funeral. And she hadn't been comfortable about saying such things without that buffer.

And it had never occurred to her that he might need to hear it.

"I guess I didn't think you needed to hear the obvious," she said. "But what I used to tell you still goes. More so. You..." She trailed off, unable to summon up one of the teasing compliments she used to throw at him about looking like an Aztec god.

He looked at her steadily, an oddly intent expression on his face. "Sometimes," he said, "it's not so much the compliment as it is the source."

She was very much afraid that she was gaping at him. She had no idea how to take that remark. The most obvious insinuation seemed impossible.

"Shall we get started?" he said briskly, as if he hadn't just rattled her to the core. Or as if it had meant nothing to him at all.

"Sure," she said, glad for the excuse to turn from him and hang the towel on its hook behind the bar. They retreated to Caitlin's office through a doorway at one end of the long, yellow wall.

He seemed to make the oblong room, which wasn't that small at seven by twelve feet, shrink somehow. She walked to the desk beneath an old, schoolroom style clock, where she had put the file she had taken to carting around with her. The small desk was rather cluttered, with a single-line telephone sitting atop an old but still functional answering machine, a well-used-looking rotary card file, a new photo of a happy-looking, dark-haired baby and a small stack of notes and papers in a plastic tray.

Dodging the file cabinet that sat beside the desk at a right angle, she walked past the long, narrow table against the side wall. It held a coffeemaker, a small radio and odds and ends of whatever projects Caitlin was involved in at the moment, from helping kids with homework to helping them find jobs. Her goal was to keep these kids out of someplace like Kelsey's place next door, the halfway house for runaways. Kelsey had often said that if there were more people like Caitlin, and more places like the Neutral Zone, she'd be happily out of business.

At the other end of the office, opposite the desk, was a sofa and a small lamp table that barely fit along the narrower wall. Kit gestured Miguel to sit down. When he did, she took a seat at the other end of the sofa and set the folders she'd picked up safely between them. If he noticed her purposeful action or saw any significance in where she chose to sit, he didn't comment.

"I haven't had a chance to even look at this yet," she said as she pulled the file out of the large manila envelope she had stuffed everything in when she'd decided she didn't want to risk leaving it in her office. "I was running late, so I just signed it out and ran. I'll make copies later and put it back."

His dark, arched brows lowered. "I meant to tell you to sign anything you pull on this out to me. Just in case. I don't want Robards on your back any more than he already is."

"Thanks," she said, genuinely appreciating the thought. "But I don't think he has any idea I haven't dropped it yet." She tapped the folder with a finger. "It took a while to find the thing. It was misfiled by a year."

He frowned. "Conveniently inconvenient."

"That's what I thought," she said. "It was right where it should have been, only a year off."

"And easily explainable as a simple filing mistake."

She nodded. "I'm not even sure why I looked there."

"Those good instincts of yours." His mouth twisted. "And yet another irregularity that could go either way."

"They just keep piling up, don't they?"

"Smoke," he said.

She lifted the file folder. "Maybe this will tell us if there's a fire."

She offered it to him, but he shook his head, indicating she should go ahead. A small thing, she thought, but typical of the man. She opened the file, which was considerably thicker than the Rivas file. She scanned quickly, and it was clear this was a much more thorough investigation. Of course, there had been several witnesses and the evidence of spent shell casings from an automatic weapon.

"Looks like a typical gang drive-by. Downtown Boys versus the Charros. No plates on the suspect vehicle, and the driver, at least, wore a ski mask. Victim was a long time Charro and had several homies with him. With the mask, nobody could ID the driver, and they couldn't tell if anybody else was in the car, so the driver may or may not be the shooter. But they all recognized the car as belonging to one of the Downtowners."

"Robards didn't do the reports on this one, did he?"

Kit had looked at that first, not that she'd needed to. The printing on the pages was neat and firm, not Robards's crabbed scrawl. She glanced down to see who had done the report, and something else caught her eye. She looked at him.

"No," she said, "Carpenter wrote the initial report. But you approved it."

He blinked. "I did?" She nodded. "Odd. I was a captain by then. Why would I be approving a report instead of the watch commander?"

"I don't know." She pulled the crime report free of the metal fastener and handed it to him. "See if you remember."

She noticed the detective follow-up on the murder of the

young man known as El Tigre had been done by then detective Cruz Gregerson. It had happened just before he'd been promoted to sergeant and had taken over the felony unit. She read his report, expecting and finding Cruz's usual thorough job.

"I do remember this," Miguel said suddenly. Kit looked up. "I remember it pretty clearly. We almost had a riot on our hands that night."

"A gang riot?"

He nodded. "The Charros insisted El Tigre hadn't done anything, hadn't trespassed on Downtowner turf, hadn't dissed anybody connected to them. They were ready to go to war."

She'd dealt with enough gang members and their families to be able to guess exactly how volatile the situation must have been that night.

"How did you end up involved in it?"

"I was acting watch commander that night. I was covering for Lieutenant Lerner. He had some family thing going on."

Kit nodded. It was unusual—no, practically unheard of—in the past for the Trinity West captain to do such a thing, but Miguel de los Reyes had been different from the beginning. He didn't feel he was above any job his people had to do. And if he was the only one available to help out, then he helped out.

"In fact," he said, gesturing with the report, "this was the case that got Cruz promoted. He'd been up for it before, but Robards slammed him down because...well, he had a dozen excuses, but you know what the main one was."

"Yes," Kit said, anger welling up on behalf of her friend. "Half-breed was the nicest of what he called him."

"But this made it impossible for Robards to stop the promotion. Cruz did an amazing dance that night, keeping those two gangs from going to war right there in the street. It was as much a time bomb as the one they gave him the Medal of Valor for disarming.''

"He says here you had a lot to do with it.''

Miguel looked surprised. "What?''

She indicated the follow-up report. "He says you offered yourself as a hostage if the two sides would talk instead of shoot. That it was the weight of having the chief of police do such a thing that got them thinking more about how powerful that made them feel than about retaliation.''

"I didn't approve *that* report,'' he said dryly, seeming embarrassed by Gregerson's praise.

"No,'' Kit said, "Mallery did. But now that I read it, I remember hearing about it from Cruz. I think that was the day he told me we were all going to be working for you someday. And that he'd be happy to see that day come.''

He didn't say anything, but he looked pleased. And that pleased Kit.

"Didn't they track down the car?'' he asked. "I seem to remember something like that.''

Kit went back to the report, then nodded. "Cruz found the car's owner, one Lorenzo Morales, known to his intimates as Choker.''

"Choker? Cute. Go on.''

As she read on, she nearly laughed at the familiar ruse, seen so often when a vehicle was used in a crime. "My, what a surprise. Choker told Cruz his car had been stolen that very day, in fact merely hours before the shooting.''

"How convenient,'' Miguel said dryly. "Again.''

"Yeah.'' She grimaced. "You'd think they'd come up with a new story. But Cruz says here there were several witnesses to back up his story. All his homies, of course, since they were at the residence of one of them.''

"Of course.''

"But you're right, they did find the car abandoned the next day, down in Marina del Mar, near the beach. And there was nothing in it to connect Morales to the shooting. We had to buy his story for lack of evidence to the contrary."

"Wonderful," Miguel muttered.

He scanned the crime report again. Kit stole a moment to look at him, to wonder how his age of forty-four showed only in and around his eyes. And that, she knew, could be as much the job as anything else. It aged them all eventually. Otherwise he looked a decade younger, not much older than she did. Of course, there were days when she felt a decade older than she was. She knew that was the job.

She found herself staring at the twin sweeps of his dark lashes, which looked impossibly long and thick from this angle. They, along with the fine arch of his brows, were a distinct contrast to the sharp, masculine elegance of his face. Even his mouth seemed masculine, or perhaps it was simply that when she looked at the shape of it, she kept wondering what it would be like to kiss. And wondering even more what it would be like to be kissed by it.

He reacted to something he read, and Kit jerked her mind out of the rut it seemed to fall into every time she was with this man. And just in time, because he looked up.

"Funny description of the driver from that one witness," he said.

"What?" She'd only skimmed the witness statements before handing the report to him.

"He said the only thing he could tell, with the ski mask, was that the guy had a fat head."

She let out a short laugh. "In more ways than one," she said. "So, we have a fatheaded Downtowner shooting a Charro called El Tigre, in typical fashion. Witnesses abound, but still nobody in jail for it."

"I'm surprised the wits were even that helpful," he said. "Usually they won't talk at all."

"I know," she said. "Usually they're in too big a hurry

to retaliate. But Cruz can talk their talk. I'll bet he took that part over from Carpenter when he got there.''

"Probably. It's just like him to do it and not take credit.''

"Like somebody else I know,'' she said pointedly. And had the pleasure of seeing that little smile again.

"What I don't see,'' he said after a moment, "is any clear connection between the two murders. Other than one we can't prove.''

"I don't, either. Even the lack of a motive for the Downtown Boys to go after El Tigre doesn't mean much.''

He expelled a frustrated breath. "No. They'll do it for no reason at all often enough, shoot somebody for just not being one of them.''

Kit sighed. "It's such a waste.''

"I know. But those kids, they don't see any other choice. Sometimes it comes down to something very basic—join up or die.''

Kit had no answer to that. It was true, and she knew it. They went through the reports once more and found nothing that seemed to have any significance. Kit gathered the papers and stuffed them into the envelope. Miguel watched her close the envelope and fasten it with the metal clasp.

"I think perhaps we should keep these files in my office, rather than yours.''

Kit's gaze shot to his face. "You do?''

"I'd rather they be in my possession than yours. No one can really question why I have them, and there's less that he can do.''

He didn't define the "he'' and Kit didn't have to ask. "All right,'' she said carefully. "That's probably a good idea.''

He gave her a sideways look. "I've worked for the man, too, Kit. He was my sergeant when I first came on.''

"And you survived?'' she quipped.

"Barely,'' he said, his tone dry. "But I'm quite aware of his management style.''

And he obviously knew quite well Robards's unpleasant style included snooping and spying on his people whenever he got the chance, Kit thought. He probably even knew the running joke as Trinity West slowly joined the computer age was that Robards was torn between hating the new technology and liking the fact that he would be able to conveniently spy on all his subordinates from one place.

She wondered if there was anything that went on in Trinity West this man didn't know about. Wondered how he'd managed to reach the top of the heap and still hang onto his understanding of what it was like to be a street cop, to be part of that thin blue line, part of a world no one who hadn't been in it could ever really understand. Wondered how he'd kept his sense of fairness, his courteous manner through the various public, media-hyped incidents that had put some tarnish on the shields of all police, and through his own personal tragedies.

But he'd done it all. In a time when Trinity West—and the city of Marina Heights—had threatened to implode, he had taken over and turned it around. He'd begun by running things with what bordered on a siege mentality, rebuilding the bond between the men and women of Trinity West until they were once more a cohesive unit.

Once he had a functional force again, he had turned his attention to a city on the edge of disintegration. He had adapted techniques some detractors had called nothing less than guerrilla warfare, but no one had been able to argue with the spectacular results. The detractors had been largely ignored as troublemaking outsiders. The law-abiding residents of Marina Heights called their new police chief a miracle worker.

It was an honor to work for him. It was an honor to have his trust.

Kit just hoped she didn't destroy that trust by doing something stupid. Like letting him know she was having a lot of trouble looking at him as the chief. Like telling him that Miguel the man was overtaking Chief de los Reyes. Like letting it slip that the buffer first Anna, then his rank had always been, weren't working too well anymore. Like asking him what he meant when he said sometimes it was the source more than the compliment.

She wondered if the most dangerous part of this entire situation for her wasn't going to turn out to be, not Robards, but the simple fact that she was going to be spending time with a man who could all too easily turn her life upside down.

Chapter 9

"You're sure you can't stay for lunch, Kit?"

Kit smiled at Kelsey Gregerson and regretfully shook her head. "As much as I hate to miss out, I'm playing hooky as it is."

She meant it. One of Kelsey's meals wasn't something she refused lightly. Between Kelsey and her friend Dolores Lamana, the Oak Tree Inn was gaining quite a reputation for fine food. And for ambiance, as well, and well deserved, Kit thought as she looked around. The large room that served as a lobby and gathering place was a charming haven of soft tans spiked by touches of rich, deep green and jewel red. Two comfortable sofas and a couple of temptingly cushioned chairs were arranged invitingly near a stone fireplace, and before them was a low table that held the cups of fragrant, perfectly brewed coffee Kelsey had fixed when her unexpected guest had dropped in. With the knack of a true innkeeper, Kelsey had never turned a hair, but welcomed Kit with every evidence of delight.

Kit took a sip of the rich, savory liquid. She'd also meant it about playing hooky. She was taking a risk being gone this long when Robards was riding her back, but she'd finally located the cop who'd been there the night of Jaime Rivas's murder, and since Welton had been going out of town on three weeks vacation, she'd had little choice but to catch him before he left. The side benefit had been his proximity to Kelsey's place.

"I don't know how you do it," Kit said. "Keeping this place going, plus your shelter in town."

The inn was a good hour outside Marina Heights. Kelsey's shelter for runaways was in the heart of the worst part of the city. A lifelong runaway, Kelsey had been running a sort of halfway house out of the inn before she'd met and fallen for Cruz, which had brought her well-intentioned but unsanctioned activities to a halt.

Her shelter in town, which she had dubbed Oak Tree East, was beginning to reap the benefits of the reputation she'd built. The runaway grapevine was as effective as the old hobo grapevine had been, and kids knew they could come to her for food and shelter and that she would give it to them before making them face any questions. Her rules were simple but strictly enforced—no drugs, no booze, you agree to get some kind of help to resolve the problem you're running from, and you tell her the truth.

She'd been where they were, Kit thought, and that's why it worked, why they trusted her. But whatever the reason, Kit admired the green-eyed woman tremendously and did whatever she could to help out, as she did with Caitlin Romero and her Neutral Zone. Kit was convinced the answer to handling runaways lay with people like them more than with the police.

"It's not easy," Kelsey admitted. "But Sam does a lot around here, and Cruz helps when he can. He's learned the basics of being a good innkeeper, so I can spend time at the shelter."

Kit smiled. "He's got the personality for it."

Kelsey smiled at her. "Yes. Rock solid, kind, thoughtful, good-natured…"

"Don't forget drop-dead gorgeous," Kit teased.

"That, too," Kelsey agreed with an easy laugh. She knew Cruz and Kit had once dated, but Kit had made sure Kelsey knew she was more delighted than anyone about the love they'd found.

"Speaking of drop-dead gorgeous, I understand you had company last night at the Neutral Zone."

Kit instantly felt her cheeks heat and tried to cover it with a laugh. "Nothing wrong with your grapevines, runaway or otherwise."

"Someone mentioned it to Caitlin, who mentioned it to me. After all, the chief of Marina Heights PD doesn't pay many visits to the Neutral Zone."

"He's afraid he'll scare the kids away if they find out who he is."

Kelsey studied her. "Considerate of him. But then, from what I've seen, Chief de los Reyes is every inch a gentleman."

And every inch drop-dead gorgeous, Kit thought. Every inch she'd seen, anyway. And she didn't doubt the rest of him matched. Not that she'd be averse to finding out first-hand—

She made herself stop. She'd been spending far too much time in that particular rut of late. It seemed every time she wasn't completely focused on something else, the images would slip into her mind. Vivid, heated images of what it would be like to kiss him, what it would be like to hold him, to touch that long, lean body, to have him touch her in turn, to see the gentlemanly calm leave him, replaced by the rising heat of desire. The desire she had, in her wilder moments, fancied she'd seen in his eyes, brief, fleeting glimpses of a need she'd never expected, never dared to hope for, not for her, not from him.

"Kit?"

Kelsey's gentle, curious prompt made Kit realize she'd been sitting there lusting after the man for far too long. She spoke quickly.

"He did cause quite a stir with the kids. The girls, anyway."

"All of them?" Kelsey asked with an arched brow.

Instantly on guard, afraid Kelsey had somehow read her mind, Kit asked, "Meaning?"

"Oh, nothing. Just that he's a very attractive man, you've always liked him, and Cruz says he thinks the world of you."

Kit blinked. "He said that to Cruz?" Miguel had told her in other words that he respected and admired her, but the fact that he'd said it to Cruz startled her.

Kelsey nodded. "Cruz told me the chief told him once that when he was shot, sometimes the only thing that kept him going through the pain was knowing you'd show up sometime that day with some silly joke or something. He said he used to tell himself he could hang on at least that long, until you got there, and when he made it that far, he knew he'd make it through the rest of the day."

"My God," Kit breathed. He'd told her her visits had meant a lot to him, but she'd had no idea...

"So, come on, girlfriend, spill it. What's going on? What brought the elusive and ever so eligible Miguel de los Reyes to the Neutral Zone? I figure it must have been you."

"Hardly," Kit said wryly. "He—" Kit broke off, realizing she shouldn't be mentioning the case, even to Kelsey. In fact, especially to Kelsey. Her marriage to another of Robards's beleaguered detectives could put her in a very awkward place, should all of this blow up in their faces.

"Don't underestimate yourself, Ms. Walker. The guys all

think he'll never get married again, but we girls think you just might be the one to change his mind.''

"Change his— Married?"

Kit nearly squeaked in shock that this had been a topic of discussion among Kelsey and Caitlin, probably Lacey Buckhart, too. Hell, probably little Sam had even gotten in on the act, and maybe Laurey, by phone from Seattle, she thought ruefully.

Kelsey laughed at her tone and the expression Kit was sure was on her face. "Don't be so shocked. It happens to the best of us. And all of us agree, the two of you are definitely among the best of us."

Kit took a deep breath and tried for equilibrium. After a moment she thought she could risk speech. "So that's it. Since all of you are so annoyingly happy, you want to spread it around, and you picked us two poor singles to target."

"Of course," Kelsey said brightly. "There aren't many more we care that much about, and you two are obviously perfect for each other. And it's not like there's any rule against it at Trinity West, after all, not like there is in some places."

Kit shook her head. "Forget it, Kelsey. There are more reasons this is a crazy idea than I can count."

"Such as?"

"Such as I work for him, which could put us both in hot water. Such as he's been a friend for years, and I don't want to mess that up. Such as I was a good friend of Anna's. Such as he still loves her. Such as the guys are probably right."

Kelsey gave her a look of satisfaction that stopped just short of being smug. "I see you've been seriously thinking about it, to come up with all those so quickly."

Kit didn't even try to hide her blush. She knew it was useless. "You," she said, "are a dangerous woman."

"So my husband tells me." Then, seriously, Kelsey added, "We've all faced problems that seemed insurmountable at the time, Kit. You know what Cruz and I went through, and Caitlin and Quisto after that boy was murdered. Gage and Laurey had to get past the fact that he arrested her, for heaven's sake. And look at Lacey and Ryan. They had to overcome the death of their baby, to forgive each other so much..."

Kit felt a sudden moisture in her eyes as she remembered Ryan in those days after Lacey had divorced him. He was the biggest, strongest man she knew, and Lacey had brought him to his knees. But he'd never stopped loving her, nor she him, and now they stood together in a united front like none she'd seen.

God, she had to stop this, or Kelsey was going to have her believing it was possible, and she knew it wasn't.

"I've got to go," she said abruptly. "I have an appointment at eleven." She got to her feet, then realized how short she had sounded. "Kelsey, I—"

"Never mind." Kelsey waved off the apology she'd begun with a smile. "Believe me, I understand. I've been there. And I shouldn't have teased you about it. It's between you two and nobody else's business."

"Thank you," Kit said.

"But we'll still hope," Kelsey warned with a grin, ending the conversation on a cheerful note.

Kit took her leave with a smile, but her mind was seizing on just how long it had been since she'd been any part of a joint "you." Very long. That was probably why she was all messed up—she'd been alone too long. She'd tried, a couple of years after Bobby's death, to get out, to meet people, but it had always seemed more trouble than it was worth, and except for the brief time with Cruz she'd either been bored or annoyed, and the time spent had seemed a waste.

But it had been eleven years since she'd buried the man she'd loved, and it was time to get on with her personal life— if she ever wanted to have one again.

She wished that when she thought about it, her mind didn't

always plunk Miguel de los Reyes right in the middle of that imagined life.

She was halfway to Trinity West when her pager went off. She glanced at it and saw that it was a message from Betty. The detective secretary didn't normally page for routine calls, so this had to be something out of the ordinary.

Robards, Kit thought grimly as she reached for her cell phone.

Maybe he was asking Betty about where Kit was. She'd made sure she had a legitimate reason for being out of the city—she needed to talk to a rape victim who lived near the Oak Tree Inn. The visit to see Kelsey had been an extra she'd write off as her lunch period if she had to, no problem there. It was her appointment with the former Trinity West cop she had to be careful about. She didn't want to have to explain that.

"Betty?" she said when the woman answered. "It's Kit."

"Oh, good," she said, not sounding particularly ruffled, as Kit imagined she would if Robards had been riding her. Kit relaxed slightly. "You got the page?" Betty asked, rather unnecessarily; she always seemed a bit amazed that such pieces of technology actually worked.

"Yes," Kit said. "What's up?"

"Well, usually I won't page you for just a phone message to return the call, but since it was the chief…"

Kit's relaxation vanished. "The chief called? For me?" She'd told him where she was going this morning, and she wondered if he'd found out something she needed to know.

"Oh, don't worry," Betty said soothingly, "he didn't sound angry or anything. Not that he ever gets angry, but you know what I mean."

"Yes," Kit said again. "What did he want?"

"Why, didn't I say? To call him back."

With a sigh Kit pressed on. "That's all he said?"

"Yes."

"All right." Then, as something else occurred to her, she asked, "Why didn't you just page me to his number?"

"Oh, because he's not here. He's at city hall."

Kit sighed again. She adored Betty, but she'd been beyond distracted of late. Her young granddaughter was getting married—to the relief of all the single men of Trinity West, who had raised dodging Betty's efforts to set them up with the rather bubble-headed young lady down to a fine science—and her concentration seemed shot.

But her distraction of late gave Kit a patience she might not have otherwise had. "Did he leave the number there?"

She heard the embarrassed laugh. "Oh, dear, of course. I don't know where my mind is," said the usually efficient woman.

I know just how you feel, Kit thought. Except she pretty much knew where her mind was. She just wished it would quit going there.

"Here it is," Betty said, rattling off the number. Kit keyed it into the number pad of the cell phone, thankful for the feature that let her do that while still on one call, then hang up and dial the next. Which she did as soon as Betty had apologized once more and hung up.

She used the time as it was ringing to steady herself, to be sure she was braced to hear his voice and not let her mind shoot to her conversation with Kelsey. She was concentrating so hard that when a strange, female voice answered she was taken aback.

"City manager's office."

Poor Miguel, Kit thought. *Two days in a row fighting city hall.*

She identified herself and asked for him, saying she was returning his call. She was subjected to several moments of annoyingly bland canned music and wondered if the stuff was piped into city hall. She thought they'd get a lot more done if they had a little country or rock or even some Vivaldi to listen to.

Funny, she didn't know what Miguel liked in the way of music anymore. And that was usually something she found out early about a person. Music was important in her life, and she believed taste in music and reading told you more about a person than just about anything else. Years ago he'd played a lot of rock, but that had been Anna's choice.

Classical would seem to fit him now, she thought. She could picture him with Mozart booming. Which means, she thought with a grin, he probably adored heavy metal. Or maybe—

"Kit?"

She was startled by his voice. She'd been so lost in her speculations that when she heard him it seemed as if she'd somehow conjured him up, and it was an instant before it all came back to her.

"Hi," she managed to say. "I got your page."

"Page?"

"You wanted me to call?"

"I called your office, but I told Betty I'd get you later."

"But she said—" Kit sighed. "Never mind. I'll just be glad when that wedding's over."

She heard him chuckle, a low, husky sound she thought far too sensual to be used in a city manager's office. "I gather she's a bit distracted."

"And then some. But she'll get over it and get back to being Betty of the iron hand soon. Did you need me?"

There was a pause that made her wonder what he was thinking. And gave her time to wish she hadn't said it like that. God, her mind was charting its own reckless course these days. She had no room to talk about Betty.

"I wanted to know how it went today," he finally said.

"It was interesting," she said carefully, not sure she wanted to talk about it on a too easily monitored cell phone.

And he picked up on her hesitation as easily as if he could read her mind.

"Perhaps we should discuss it in person. Can you meet me in, say, a half hour?"

She had no good reason to say no, although with all the thoughts Kelsey had stirred up she would have preferred some time to quash them.

"Of course," she said. "Where?"

"Someplace close to here," he said, sounding a bit rueful. "I'll be coming back."

"My sympathies," she said. "A day at city hall is certainly not my idea of a good time."

"So rescue me."

But who's going to rescue me? she wondered.

"Have you had lunch?" he asked.

"No, not yet."

"Neither have I. Let's eat, then."

To her surprise he suggested a fast food outlet across the street from city hall, apologetically saying that was about all he had time for.

When she pulled into the lot she didn't see his car but figured he'd probably walked over. After she parked, she saw him by the front door. For an instant it hit her again. He seemed so alone. Even with locals and tourists milling around, he seemed to stand apart, isolated. It tugged at some place deep inside her, made her want to hold him and let him know he wasn't really alone.

Even his expression seemed distant, she thought as she got out of her car and headed toward him. As if he was watching the world but didn't feel part of it. As if he noticed everything going on around him, but it didn't affect him.

Then he seemed to sense her coming, because his head came around and he looked her way. She saw him focus on her. And then she nearly missed a step. His eyes lost that distant look in an instant, and a wide, unrestrained smile curved his mouth. The sudden change and the undeniable fact that it was the sight of her that caused it brought back every image she'd been fighting off, every idea Kelsey's words had given rise to.

Rather recklessly she smiled back, for a moment putting all the obstacles aside and letting herself enjoy the simple fact that a very attractive and usually reserved man had lit up at the sight of her.

When she got closer she thought she saw his arms start to come up and thought of that moment when she'd wanted to hug him. But then his right arm went to his side, and his left arm reached for the door as if that had been his intent all along.

And I, she told herself firmly, *would be much better off believing that.*

It felt decidedly odd, being in such a familiar, ordinary place as this with him, standing in line, reading the backlit menu as both of them had undoubtedly done countless times, but never together. She smiled when he ordered a chocolate shake, but it faded when he muttered something about it settling his stomach.

"Maybe you'd better rethink that running for office idea if that's what city hall does to you," she said as they sat in a corner booth, as far away from the crowd and the windowed front of the building as they could get.

"The point is to change things so it doesn't give *anybody* an ulcer."

"You're not serious?" she said, concern creasing her brow. "About an ulcer?"

He looked at her steadily for a moment before he said quietly, "I'm fine. But be careful, I could get used to you worrying about me."

"I've always worried about you."

"That's not what I— Never mind," he said. "Did you talk to Welton?"

It took her a moment to tear her mind away from wondering what he'd almost said and focusing on what he'd asked. "I...yes."

"And?"

"He remembered the night pretty well. Said it stuck in his mind because he'd never seen Robards offer to tie his own shoes before, let alone take a felony report."

Miguel's mouth quirked, but he only nodded.

"But what's really interesting," she continued, "is that he says he filled out a supplemental report. A short one, since Robards made him leave the scene almost immediately, but he did one."

"But it wasn't in the file," Miguel said.

She shook her head. "I asked him who he turned it in to. You won't need three guesses."

He lifted a brow. "Would Welton be willing to swear to that?"

"He would," she confirmed. "He's very happily not a cop anymore, so he's got nothing to lose. And he doesn't harbor many fond memories of the man."

"I'm not surprised." He nodded at her to go on.

"Welton said he took offense at first, when he was ordered off, thinking Robards was implying he couldn't handle it. He was ticked enough to say so to him."

"Don't blame him. Didn't you say he'd had seven years on?"

She nodded. "Anyway, he said that just made it more memorable, because Robards was almost nice about explaining that that wasn't the case."

Miguel's brows shot up. "He actually used *nice* in the same sentence as *Robards?*"

She gave him a rueful smile. "He was as amazed as you sound, but he said it was true. Of course, he also said he knew very well he wasn't on Robards's list. 'I'm WASP enough he stayed off me pretty much,' I think was how he put it.''

Miguel looked thoughtful. "I didn't realize everybody was so aware of his predilections.''

She lifted her hamburger for a bite, then looked at him over it. "Did you think only his victims noticed?''

He stirred his shake, took a sip, then said honestly, "Maybe I just thought only his victims cared.''

"Do you think Gage didn't care? He was as close as Robards got to a fair-haired boy, and Gage hated it. He went out of his way to aggravate the man just because he hated not being hated by him.''

He half-smiled at the words, then apologized. "I know he did. And others. It's just that sometimes all I see are walls.''

"There are doors. And windows. They're just not as obvious as the walls.''

"And you would know as well as anyone, wouldn't you?'' he asked softly.

Something about the way he said it made her shiver, but not from cold. He lowered his eyes to his tray, and she stole the moment to watch him, to see the thick sweep of his lashes and the softness of his mouth, features that kept his countenance from being forbidding.

He stirred the shake again, and she managed to shift her gaze to her meal before he looked up and asked, "Anything else from Welton?''

"Just that Robards was pretty adamant that he not only leave him to do the report, but that he leave, period.''

The dark, arched brow rose again. "Odd. Felony crime scene like that, you're looking for help, not sending it away.''

"I asked Welton about that. He said he just wrote it off to the fact that it was a busy night and they had calls backed up all over town. Said Robards told him since he'd caught it, he'd clean it, and to get back to work. And to keep quiet about it, so neither of them got in trouble over it.''

"Uncharacteristically noble of him," Miguel observed dryly.

"Very."

"And something we'd have a hard time proving wasn't true."

"I know. I'd hate to have to get up in front of a termination board and explain that something wasn't right because I just know Robards would never be so concerned. I can hear his self-righteous defense now."

"You'll never get a thirty-year cop fired on the basis of that," he agreed, sounding rather glum.

"But we already knew we probably wouldn't be able to get him fired, let alone arrested. He covered his tracks too well."

"And made sure there's an innocent explanation for everything."

She sighed. "If it was any cop but him, I'd believe those innocent explanations."

"Second thoughts?" he asked.

"No," she said. "I know he's dirty. I—"

"Sergeant Walker, hi!" Kit looked up, startled, then relaxed when she recognized the young parking control officer from... Lord, had it only been last week? "I just saw you here and wanted to thank you again for the other day. You really saved the situation out there."

"No problem," she said.

"You handled that lady so slick—"

The young man stopped abruptly as he noticed, belatedly, who Kit was sitting with. He alternately paled and blushed, his mouth flopping in a way that reminded her of a beached grunion.

"I...oh, wow, I'm sorry, I didn't see you, Chief, I didn't mean to interrupt or anything, sir, I just wanted to thank the sarge for helping me out, and I—"

Miguel held up a hand to stop the gush of words. "It's okay, son."

Kit stifled a giggle at the young man's expression, managing to turn it into a smile. "Go eat your lunch, Larry. You're dripping."

The man flushed all over again, nodded sharply and fled. Miguel watched him go with an amused expression. "What was all that about?"

"That," she said wryly, "is what started this whole thing."

He blinked. "Oh?"

Quickly, she told him the story. "I didn't really do anything except defuse Mrs. Rivas's anger. She's not a mean or nasty person, so it wasn't hard."

"But not everyone would bother," he said.

She shrugged. "There was crowd potential, and I didn't want the kid in over his head."

One corner of his mouth lifted. "I always said you were the best backup around."

He *had* said that, Kit remembered. And she was enough of a cop to recognize the highest of praise in that simple statement. Cops were very particular about who they liked backing them up, often doing without if they didn't like the only officer available.

"Thank you," she said, more than pleased.

"You're damn good, Kit. Don't ever forget that."

"I'm glad you think so," she said, aware even as she said it there might be a tad too much emphasis on that *you*.

"If I didn't, I wouldn't be pushing you to take the next lieutenant's test." He had suggested it, to her surprise. She hadn't thought herself ready. "Which," he added grimly, "will need to be sooner than the city had planned."

"Here, here." Kit lifted her soda cup in a mock toast. "Here's to opening up a lieutenant's spot."

Miguel lifted his shake. They tipped the rims together, and Kit was very proud that she managed not to jump when their fingers touched. She tried not to notice the heat that sparked through her. Tried not to notice that Miguel, too, went very still.

Above all, she tried not to notice the urge to do it again.

Chapter 10

There was absolutely no point in going home, Miguel thought. He was so wound up he wouldn't get to sleep for hours. So he might as well put it to good use. He'd work the frustration and disgust off on that pile of paperwork he'd let stack up while putting together the preliminary budget the city council had just shot to hell.

He had the oddest feeling, as he pulled into his reserved parking place next to the back door of Trinity West, that if it hadn't been for this, he would have thought of something else to keep from going home—if you could call it that. If home meant the place where you spent most of your time, then this plain, square building in front of him had become more his home than the small, stark apartment he lived in.

But the saddest part, he thought as he went up the outside stairs to the private door to his office, was that this place, with its outdated furniture and equipment and all the wear and tear of the years, was probably homier than the small, one-bedroom place he rented. He'd been there for two years, and there were still boxes he hadn't unpacked. True, for a while after he'd been shot he hadn't had the energy. Simply getting up and functioning for a day took every bit he had, and he had come home only to fall into bed and try and recoup enough to get up and do it again the next day.

But even when he had most of his stamina back, when the ugly red wounds had faded to ugly scars, even when he no longer woke in the night fighting off waves of pain—sometimes real, sometimes remembered—he still made no effort to personalize the small space that housed him. It was a place to sleep, fix quick meals and do the work he brought home with him, no more. It was all he wanted.

And after a while, he thought as he put his key in the lock on the door marked Private, it had seemed silly to lug all his work home to do in that place that was just another reminder of all he had lost. He'd put the house he and Anna had lived in on the market on the second anniversary of her funeral, the same day he'd finally taken off the ring she'd slipped on his finger all those years ago. He hadn't wanted to, but he'd known it was time.

And he had grown weary of people commenting on it. They'd thought he didn't hear the whispers, the speculations on whether he'd ever get over it. The ring really hadn't mattered. He'd seen the pale mark it left, then felt the weight of it long after he was no longer wearing it.

Crazy, he thought as he shoved the heavy door open, all these memories stirring. That had been happening a lot lately. Ever since Kit Walker had walked into his office that night—

She was in his office now.

For a moment they both stood, frozen, he with his hand on the doorknob, she with a file folder in her hand. She had on a trim, pale yellow skirt and a brighter yellow sweater. The skirt was not excessively short, but bared enough of her long legs to bring back—once more—that image of her in shorts. The sweater was long and loose, but the way it clung for brief moments when she moved made him imagine the body beneath it far more vividly than any tight, clinging garment would.

Or maybe it didn't matter what she wore, he'd be thinking about it anyway.

"You're here late again," he said rather quickly, and more to stop his wayward thoughts than anything else.

"I was…putting away the copies I made of the drive-by case," she said, and he realized then she had open the desk drawer he'd told her to use for anything relating to their inquiries.

He nodded, but frowned as he let the door close behind him. "You're putting in a lot of extra hours."

"Afraid I'll break the overtime budget?" she teased.

"No," he said, knowing perfectly well she didn't turn in for half of it. "I'm worried *you'll* break."

She looked startled, then a slow smile curved her mouth. "Don't worry about me."

I don't seem to have any choice, he thought. Funny how, when Anna had been alive, he'd thought of her mainly as a colleague and Anna's friend, albeit a friend he liked. And if he'd been vaguely aware of having to put more effort into keeping her in those slots than he should have, he'd managed to ignore it.

As he stood in his office looking at her, he couldn't deny he knew exactly why that task had been harder than it should have been—he'd always known he found her attractive. It hadn't mattered then. He'd loved Anna fully and completely. But as Anna had teasingly said on occasion, being married didn't mean you were dead.

And Kit had made it easier then, because he'd known she had more respect for marriage vows than some of the people bound by them did. She would no more breach them than he would, even if Anna wasn't her friend. The fact that Anna was her friend had meant, to Kit, that those vows were even more inviolable.

But now that wasn't a factor.

And for the first time since Anna's death, it mattered.

Not that he hadn't thought about it before. It had been five years, after all, and there had been occasions when he'd met someone and had realized there was nothing stopping him. But it had never gone beyond that, because no one had stirred him beyond the realization.

Until now.

"Is something wrong?" she asked, startling him into wondering if his thoughts had been showing on his face.

"Wrong?" Dropping his small briefcase in one of the chairs in front of his desk, he hastily grabbed at the only thing he could think of, what had sent him here in the first place. "No. No more than usual, anyway." He grimaced. "City council meeting."

She grimaced in turn. "Ouch. It didn't go well?"

"The subject of money never seems to go well when you're dealing with a bureaucracy."

"The budget?"

He nodded. "At least they make it simple. None of this going in asking for a lot and figuring you might get part of it. They just say keep doing the impossible with nothing."

"Did you tell them it couldn't be done?"

"Yes. They weren't buying."

She shut the drawer she'd put the files in, then gave him a look he couldn't interpret.

"It's your own fault, you know," she said.

He blinked. "What?"

"You've been doing the impossible with nothing for two years. You've spoiled them."

He had heard similar sentiments before and been happy about his accomplishments at Trinity West. But somehow, coming from her, the assessment made him feel a pride he'd not felt before. But he didn't quite know how to say so, wasn't sure he dared, so he covered his uncertainty with a gruff expression of his disgust at the whole process.

"Sometimes I want to go in and bang some heads together just to see if there's a functioning brain cell or two among those people."

She studied him. "I know there have been rumbles about you doing just that someday. Really running for city office someday, I mean."

It had, in fact, been suggested to him more than once by various people. Several citizens and civic groups had broached the possibility repeatedly.

"On nights like this," he said wearily, "I just about feel like doing it."

"If anybody could pound some common sense into them, you could."

"That's a pretty big if," he said dryly, "but I'm flattered by your confidence."

"Don't be. It's true. You'd be good at it." She smiled at him. "And Mayor de los Reyes has a nice ring to it."

"You after my job, Sergeant?" he asked teasingly.

"Me?" She looked astonished.

"And why not?" he asked, grinning at how the very idea seemed to fluster her.

She laughed, shaking her head. "It would never happen."

"Why not?" he repeated seriously. "You've got the brains, you've got the qualifications in education and police background, you're great with people and you can learn the administrative end." He nodded as the idea grew on him. "I think I'd like to see you in this office."

"Now *I'm* flattered," she said, twin spots of color tingeing her cheeks. "But even if you roll straight into the mayor's office, please don't hold your breath waiting for them to choose a woman as your replacement."

"Don't underestimate the respect you've got at Trinity

West," he said. "But you should probably have some time as a lieutenant and captain first."

She laughed. "A long time," she drawled, clearly thinking he'd been joking all along.

But he hadn't been, not really. He could easily see her sitting in this chair in a few years. She had the smarts, the guts, the tenacity and enough of each to overcome the unfortunate fact that in this world, being female put you a length behind before the gate even opened. He wasn't sure he'd wish it on her, though.

"Have you had dinner?" he asked. Only after the words were out did he wonder what had possessed him to say them.

She looked startled, as if she was still a little off balance from his teasing. "I...no. I was going to grab something on the way home."

"Me, too. Shall we do it together?"

Now that didn't come out very well, he thought. He was out of practice—long out of practice—in asking anybody out. Not that that's what this was, of course, but still, he could have done better than that clumsy, faintly suggestive effort.

And she was looking at him as if she was trying to decide just what he'd meant, if that stupid phrase was some kind of double entendre. Disbelief tinged her expression, and he wondered if it was over him saying it at all, or saying it to her. Was it so astonishing to her that he'd want to have dinner with her?

Or, he thought with a sudden qualm, was she thinking she didn't dare say no because of who he was? Had he inadvertently crossed over into the sexual harassment ring?

"We can talk about the Rivas case," he said quickly, "and where we go from here." *That's it, make it safe, make it business,* he told himself. "I can postpone what I came in here for."

And when, after he'd made it safe, she agreed, he told

himself there was no way that could be a hint of disappointment he was seeing in her eyes.

"How's the arm?"

Kit smiled across the table they'd just been seated at. "It's fine. Really. I barely feel it."

"Roxy's good."

"Yes, she is," Kit agreed. He said nothing more, but she imagined they were both remembering that bloody night two years ago when Roxy's quick actions and determination had saved his life. He'd been essentially dead when they wheeled him into her ER, but Roxy never gave up without a fight.

"So, anything new?" he asked after the business of ordering meals had been taken care of. "I've been tied up all day and barely had a chance to check for messages."

"Not really," Kit said. "But I did notice the other case, the original of the Rivas file, hasn't been replaced yet."

"Maybe it's misfiled by a year," he said dryly.

She laughed and took a sip of water. She'd been surprised he'd selected this place, even wondered if he'd done it because she'd mentioned the time she'd come here with Cruz, what seemed like ages ago. If this was a real date, she might wonder if he was testing for some kind of reaction, to see if she'd really meant what she'd said about having no regrets.

But it wasn't a real date, and she didn't think Miguel de los Reyes was the kind of man who would do that, anyway. He'd no doubt picked the Sunset Grill in Marina del Mar because it had recently been brought to mind. And because it still had the reputation Kelsey Gregerson had built on intriguing variety, excellent food and atmosphere. It was now one of the in places in the wealthy resort town with a menu that was never the same twice. It had an airy, open feel with skylights to let in the sun and a unique design that made every table seem secluded and private.

And that thought made her remind herself he had not chosen the place because it also had the reputation of being a great romantic location that took advantage of spectacular sunsets over the Pacific.

She felt silly even having to assure herself of that. She wouldn't have thought it had it been anyone else asking her to discuss business over dinner. It was her own fault she was thinking it now. This man was too big a threat to her peace of mind.

"I was here once before it was the Sunset Grill," he said when their food had come, breaking the long silence.

"When it was just that little hole in the wall? I remember. Bobby and I used to come here then."

He looked at her for a long, silent moment, until she wondered if she'd made a mistake in mentioning it. Then he spoke quietly.

"You were so strong when he was killed. You just kept going, you never let it cripple you."

She nearly laughed but held it back because she knew it would come out as a bitter little sound, and she didn't want it to. She really wasn't bitter anymore. She'd gotten over that years ago. She and Bobby had both known there was always a chance one of them might not come home some night. But when it came to the crunch, that knowledge hadn't helped very much. At the time, she had felt worse than crippled. She had felt broken beyond repair.

"You didn't see me when I holed up in my apartment on my days off, crying around the clock," she said.

"You never let it affect your work," he said. "We all knew you were hurting, we could see it, but we didn't know how to help."

"You did. Everybody did, but you and Anna helped the most by just being there. All those times she called late at night to check on me, all those shifts when you'd show up in the field even though you were a lieutenant and didn't have to be out there, claiming you needed company and a cup of coffee…that kept me going.''

He lowered his gaze to his plate. A man walked by, a woman who appeared to be his wife trailing behind. He paused, and for a moment Kit thought he was looking at them, but as soon as the woman caught up he strode off again, and she realized he must have been waiting for her, although he was soon several steps ahead of her again. One of those impatient types, Kit thought. Or one who wanted to be sure the woman stayed in her place ten steps behind, she amended wryly.

They ate in silence for a while before he spoke as if the conversation was merely continuing.

''Do you still…think about him?''

There was something in his tone and the way he didn't look at her that told her he was after something more than a simple answer. But she didn't know what he wanted to hear. She toyed with her steamed broccoli for a moment before she answered.

''Yes, but it's not a constant thing. Not even frequent, anymore,'' she said carefully. ''I don't think I'll ever forget Bobby completely. I loved him very much. But it's been eleven years.'' A sudden reason for the intensity of his question hit her. She looked at him as she added softly, ''It does get easier. Eventually.''

He didn't speak, looked as though he couldn't. But he reached across the table and covered her hand with his own. His warmth, an almost incredible heat, gave her the strangest feeling, and before she realized what she was doing, she had turned her hand beneath his palm and curled her fingers around his.

As if reflexively, his fingers returned the squeeze. If she hadn't been looking right at him, she might have missed the faint flare of his nostrils. There was no other sign that her action had moved him. Except that he lowered his gaze, this

man who never, ever took the easy way. And after a moment he released her hand.

Several silent minutes passed, both of them picking at half-eaten meals, before he put down his fork and looked at her. "I used to think about how you were, after Bobby was killed. After Anna died, when I used to wonder how I was going to survive, I thought about how brave you'd been and told myself I couldn't do any less."

"Brave?" She stared at him. "I was anything but. I was a basket case. Just not in public, if I could help it."

He lifted a dark brow at her. "And you think that's not bravery?"

She shook her head. "Bravery is coming back, after what happened to you, after the shooting, knowing it could happen again."

"That kind of pain, pure physical pain, is easy," he said.

He didn't go on, but she knew what he meant—that any kind of physical pain was easier to bear than the emotional agony of loss. And she couldn't argue with that, not when she knew it as well as he did. The night Bobby had been killed was etched in her mind so deeply it would never fade. She'd known, the minute she'd opened her door to find Miguel and Anna standing there, Miguel still in uniform, Anna looking at her with such gentle sorrow in her eyes. She'd known instantly the worst had happened, hadn't even asked if Bobby was dead or simply badly hurt because she already knew. There had been nothing of hope in their faces.

And she didn't ever, ever want to go through that again.

She felt herself freezing up and knew that her conversation had turned cool, impersonal. Although the food was delicious, her fish grilled perfectly, she couldn't finish it. And she noticed he seemed to have lost his appetite, as well.

He didn't ask her what was wrong. He was too perceptive not to notice the change, so she had to assume he didn't want to know or perhaps was grateful that they had retreated from dangerous ground.

She lectured herself in a way she hadn't had to in a long time, because no man had ever come close to making her even think about changing her life. She dated occasionally, but never seriously. She had her work, she had her friends, and they provided the kids if she was feeling motherly, and they welcomed her offers to baby-sit. Sam's zoo let her expend her fondness for animals, although it wasn't quite as easy now that they were living at Kelsey's inn. But it was all she needed.

And if she wanted more now and then, well, she got over it. Funny how never before had the desire for more coincided with meeting a man she could think about seeing seriously. That it did now was a measure of how confused she was, she supposed. Because amid the confusion there was only one thing she was positive of.

It didn't matter that there was no formal rule at Trinity West about such things. A relationship with Miguel de los Reyes was impossible. A relationship between the Marina Heights chief of police and one of his line officers was beyond impossible.

Not only was there all the personal baggage, there was the rest. She knew it was hard enough for any cop to have a normal, stable relationship. For a female cop it was more complicated. The only people who truly understood the crazy schedules and the nature of the work were other cops. And even if she hadn't sworn that off, just the idea of the complications of a personal relationship of any depth between a sergeant and her chief gave her chills. The potential for disaster on both sides was tremendous. Her being accused of sleeping her way up the ranks and him of favoritism or sexual harassment were probably just the tip of the iceberg.

With a minimum of discussion they agreed they were finished with dinner. And with no discussion at all they walked to the parking lot. They had both driven, to avoid having to go back for one car. They stopped between the low, red, racy coupe that was her one extravagance and Miguel's plain, gray city car, the car that traditionally would have been traded in for a new one last year, but that he'd kept so the money could go toward a new patrol unit instead.

For a moment they stood, close yet apart. And Kit felt the craziest wish that he would reach for her, that he would end this evening as if it had been the social, personal occasion he'd denied it would be. But they'd very nearly turned it into that, she thought, with all that talk about things so long buried, things so deeply personal. And she wondered what would happen if they ever went over the edge of this precipice they seemed to be skating along.

Then he moved, his hand coming up slowly. She went very still, waiting, wondering what he was going to do. His fingers curved, and he brushed the backs of them over her cheek with a feather-light touch that nevertheless sent her into a crazy upheaval, shivering as if at the touch of ice yet feeling weak in the knees at a sudden burst of heat.

She saw him tense, and for an instant his hand hovered near her face, as if he wanted to repeat the motion. She wished he would. She'd never quite felt anything like that before. But he pulled his hand from her in a jerky little motion that was unlike his usual grace. Then, as if he was resisting some kind of magnetic pull, he slowly lowered his hand to her shoulder. He clasped her, his fingers tightening as if what he really wanted to do was hug her.

She told herself it was wishful thinking. She told herself it meant nothing. She told herself he was an old, dear friend and this was an expression of friendship, as he'd give to anyone. She told herself she was a fool to read anything into the fact that he had brushed her cheek. That the brief, exquisite touch had felt like that of a lover, not a friend, was her fault, the result of too many lonely nights, too long spent thinking of this man in ways she had no right to be thinking.

He drew back suddenly, releasing her. For a long moment he stood staring at her. She saw the turmoil of emotion in his eyes, those light gray eyes that had always made her feel it was pointless to try to hide anything from this man, because those eyes could see clear through her, all the way to her soul.

She supposed he was regretting what he'd done and probably worried that she would misinterpret it. And if she judged by her unruly body's response to that slightest of touches, he was right to be worried. She barely managed not to grimace visibly. She hid the reaction by digging out her keys.

"I was thinking about…that car. The one that was supposedly stolen and used in the drive-by," he said suddenly.

The abrupt statement proved to Kit that her thoughts had been accurate. This rapid change of subject seemed to indicate he was as off-balance as she.

"Me, too," she said, accepting the safe topic appreciatively. "I still want to talk to Lorenzo, aka Choker. They didn't take him very seriously at the time, but…"

"If it really was stolen, he might know something that didn't make the report."

She nodded. "And I suppose even gangsters get their cars stolen now and then. Besides, there might be something that didn't mean anything then that might now. I'll see what I can find out about it tomorrow."

He nodded. "Let me know."

She nodded again and felt silly at how awkward things had suddenly become. All he had done was touch her cheek. And he had quickly altered his approach and grasped her shoulder, making it clear it was merely camaraderie he felt.

It didn't mean anything, it didn't mean anything….

The words marched through her mind as if on a continuous

loop recording, a background mantra she knew she didn't dare ignore.

Uncertain what to do, she mumbled a rather inane comment about it being late. He nodded yet again, as if he was having as much trouble as she was finding coherent words to put together. At last she said good-night and got into her car.

As she reached the driveway, she took a last glance in her rearview mirror.

Miguel de los Reyes stood next to his car. Alone. As always. The confused emotions she'd felt were nothing compared to the tangle she found herself in now, her heart nearly breaking as she looked at that solitary figure.

Miguel watched her drive away until the little red car was out of sight. Then, with a sigh, he leaned against the fender of his car.

This was insane.

He'd meant this to be just what he'd said, a quiet, safe discussion about the Rivas case. Instead, he'd lost control and touched her in the way he'd been aching to for far too long. True, he'd managed to hold it to the merest brush of his fingers against her cheek, but only by sheer force of will, and it had taken every bit of discipline he had to convert the touch to a safe, affable grasp of her shoulder. As if she was nothing more than a friend. As if she was one of the guys. As if he wasn't hurting to touch her in much more intimate ways.

Even the dinner had gotten out of control. They had spent little time talking about the case and far too much time in the kind of talk that stirred up deeply hidden emotions, that brought to the surface memories and longings and wonderings that could be hazardous to them both.

The things they'd talked about reminded him of how much he'd always liked Kit, and only near the end had he realized that the fact they'd talked so easily about things so painful to both of them was a dangerous sign.

And even that brief, sweet contact of their hands had been too much, too dangerous. Had set him to thinking of things that could never be, things he hadn't wanted for so long he'd thought he'd forgotten how to want them. He wondered again why he'd done it—touched her—when he knew what it would do to him. He wondered if he'd developed some kind of penchant for self-torture or if he'd had to see if another simple touch would have the same devastating effect.

But it wasn't simply the touching. Kit read him so easily, always seemed to know exactly what to say. Just as she had in those dark days after Anna's death. She'd been there, with the right word at the right moment, to keep him from going over the precipice into the abyss.

But he couldn't deny she stirred other feelings in him, as well, feelings he'd wondered if he would ever have again, a longing for someone to be there, to not be so very alone, to have somebody to give a damn about him, somebody who understood the difficulties of the job he was trying to do, somebody who could distract him from it, make him think about something else, someone else, somebody who could make him feel alive again somewhere outside his office.

That Kit met all those qualifications and added a few unique ones of her own didn't escape him. And then there was the rather startling fact that he felt a distinct, more than casual sexual interest. It had been so long he almost hadn't recognized it when he'd found himself studying the soft fullness of her mouth or the delicate nape of her neck beneath the short cap of blond hair, or remembering those legs that just went on and on.

He moved suddenly, opening the door to his car. His mind moved even more quickly, backing off the dangerous thoughts. He hadn't forgotten the hellish price he'd once paid for loving a woman. He never would. And he'd meant what he said—the ordeal of Anna's long death had been more painful to him than any physical pain, even the agony he'd gone through when those two bullets had ripped into his body.

And then a memory of two people who had been hurt as badly as he had been by Anna's death came to him. Her parents, their eyes still shadowed by sorrow, photographs of Anna and of Anna and Miguel still adorning their walls. Those two people who were as close to family as he had left telling him with sad certainty that they loved him for himself, as well as for his love for their daughter, and it was that that made them say he had been alone too long, that it was time for him to move on. Anna's mother saying there must be someone in his life, someone he could care for, who would care for him.

Someone he could love.

At the time, he had given them the best smile he could manage and lied, "Maybe someday."

Now, all he could think of was Kit.

That scared him. Deeply. He wasn't ready to try caring again. He didn't know if he ever would be. But even if he was, Kit was off-limits. Never mind that she was a friend, that she'd been one of Anna's best friends. She worked for him, and that was a nest of hornets he didn't dare stir up.

That the realization might have come a bit too late was something he didn't want to think about.

Nor did he want to think about the fact that he was experiencing a profound regret that he hadn't kissed her good-night.

Chapter 11

It was a sad state of affairs, Kit thought, when the only time she felt she could breathe without being watched was in the ladies' room. And she wasn't even certain about that. If there was a way to spy in here, she was sure Robards would have found it. It was with half-seriousness that the women in the department checked the walls of the bathrooms and their locker room for any changes, such as new holes in the walls or ceilings or new pieces of equipment.

Once they found a bug in the alarm clock in the small dressing area adjacent to the showers, but since the clock had been requisitioned out of the department's unclaimed property, they couldn't prove a thing about the origin of the tiny microphone. After that, Kit had occasionally used the department's equipment to sweep those areas for any electronic devices. Although none of the women would speak of it, they all knew what she suspected and were relieved when she passed along an all clear.

And right now she needed that all clear. She needed some

place to think. She'd barely made it in on time today, had woken up so late she'd been running since the instant her bleary eyes had focused on the clock. She hadn't had time to think.

Maybe that was just as well, she thought, her mouth curving into a wry smile as she sat on the bench in front of her open locker. Because what was there to think about except the reason she was running late and had been scrambling to catch up all morning? What was there to think about except the reason she'd slept so late, the simple fact that she'd lain awake long into the night thinking about Miguel.

She still found it difficult to let go of the protection of referring to him by his rank, or even by his full name, especially here. But even more difficult was believing his simple and clearly heartfelt words.

I thought about how brave you'd been and told myself I couldn't do any less.

That she'd been an example, even an inspiration, to anyone during that time was hard enough to accept. That she'd been that to Miguel was almost impossible. She'd been so shattered she'd barely been able to function in those days after Bobby had died. He'd never regained consciousness after being shot, and she carried with her ever since a feeling of incompleteness. She'd said goodbye when they told her it was inevitable, but she couldn't be sure he heard her send him on his way with all the love she had in her. She wanted to believe he heard, that he had known, but...

She had indeed been a basket case, she thought. And when she'd first gone to the hospital after Miguel had been shot, it had taken every scrap of nerve she had to make herself walk into what she was sure would be the same dying situation all over again. The report had been that he'd taken a round to the left thigh that had nicked the femoral artery and a second round through his left side just below the rib cage. The blood loss had been massive, but they'd had a steady replacement supply—nearly every person at Trinity West had donated for him—and Roxy had fought like a demon to keep him alive long enough to get him out of the ER and into surgery. They'd all known it was no small miracle that he'd survived.

After a battle with herself, she had finally walked into his small cubicle in ICU. She had taken one look at him, hooked up to machines and bags with wires and tubes, had seen the ashen cast of skin that should have been beautifully bronze, had seen his tall, strong body laid low, helpless, like Bobby had been, and she'd panicked. She'd darted out of the room blindly, knowing she couldn't go through this again.

Roxy had found her huddled in a small supply room, the first place she'd been able to find to hide from the small crowd in the waiting area and the steady stream of Trinity West people coming in and out. Roxy had begun with her usual teasing, but when Kit had glanced at her, one look at her eyes had been all it had taken for the young doctor to shift gears.

In some vague part of her mind, Kit had known Roxy was using the manner she used with frightened children, soft, warm, coaxing and exquisitely gentle. She'd seen her do it before, in the year since she'd come to work at Marina Heights Hospital. She didn't mind. She felt like a frightened child. With a cup of strong coffee poured into her system, she'd been able to steady herself. She found herself telling Roxy about Bobby, something she rarely spoke of. And Roxy had empathized, sympathized and said all the right things, and then she had returned to her normal, sassy self.

"Now that you've had your catharsis, you listen up. There's one big thing you're not taking into account here."

Kit had looked at her, startled by the sudden change in tone. "What?"

"Me," Dr. Roxanne Cutler said determinedly. "And that man is not going to die, not if I have anything to say about it."

Roxy had been as good as her word. It wasn't really her case, once he'd been passed along, but she haunted ICU, double and triple checked everything that was being done and made some suggestions. The case doctor had at first rebelled, then listened, then acted, and Miguel had recovered.

And Roxy Cutler, Kit thought with a smile, had become a savior at Trinity West.

She heard the door swing open, heard the familiar sound of a cop walking—the steady stride, the slight jangle of metallic bits of equipment on a Sam Brown, the creak of leather. She stood, smiling at the young woman in the dark blue uniform of the Marina Heights police, the name badge precisely aligned over her left pocket proclaiming her L. Wiggens. Lisa, Kit thought as she placed her. She was out of last year's first academy class and out on her own on the street in the past month or so. They chatted briefly, Kit giving what encouragement she could to the young rookie. It was hard, sometimes, she thought as Lisa's excitement bubbled over, to remember ever being that young or that enthusiastic. She had probably less than fifteen years on the young officer, but fourteen of them had been spent here, and it felt more like fifty. She felt a little pang of regret but didn't know if it was because of what she had lost or what this young woman would inevitably lose if she stayed on the job.

The privacy of the empty room lost, Kit decided she'd had enough of a respite. All she seemed to do was get lost in memories these days, anyway. She picked up her purse, slung it over her shoulder and closed and locked her locker. She told herself as she headed for the stairway to the detective division that it was because they were newer that the memories of the past few days were so vivid. But somehow she wasn't quite convinced. She had a feeling any memories of Miguel were going to be vivid, no matter how old they were.

She was dwelling on one, the way he'd looked at her when he'd thanked her for being there after Anna's death, when she opened her office door. The odor warned her before she saw him. That cigar stench was unmistakable. She prayed it was residue, that he wasn't smoking in her office. She wasn't up for that kind of confrontation. They'd had a few of them before, and she always won, because she had the no-smoking policy on her side, but they were never pleasant. She knew Robards forced rather meaningless confrontations like that on occasion, just to keep his people off-guard and to give him a stage to vent his displeasure when he couldn't find any other excuse.

There was, thankfully, no cigar between the smoke-yellowed teeth. However, there was a smile on the heavily jowled face, and that made her nervous. Anything that made Ken Robards smile did not bode well for somebody else in the world. She hoped it wasn't her but didn't really want to wish him on anybody else, either.

"Something I can do for you...sir?" As always, it took determination and a reminder to respect the rank if not the man to get the last word out.

"No, Sergeant, it's what I can do for you."

His smile widened as he said it, and Kit's stomach twisted. This was worse than she'd feared. Robards never, ever did anything good for anybody. Which left only one conclusion.

"What's that?" She couldn't get the *sir* out this time, and as his smile became almost a leer, she didn't regret the lack.

"I can tell you I'll support you if you choose to take action."

Kit blinked. It wasn't often she felt so completely confused, she had to give him that. He didn't usually surprise her. "Action?"

"I know it would be difficult, him being the chief and all, but I'll back your play."

He was still smiling. Beneath that short brush of blond hair he looked like a voracious walrus that had just stumbled across a pile of his favorite food. He reminded her of one of the wood carvings Ryan Buckhart turned out, small, detailed little bits of art that couldn't, it seemed, really have come from that huge knife of his. He'd never labeled the walrus he'd done last year, but anyone from Trinity West who looked at it, who saw its smug, pompous expression, knew who it was. And the fact that Ryan kept it on his desk and got away with it spoke volumes about the miracle Lacey Buckhart had achieved in keeping Robards off her husband's back. Kit had never been able to wiggle out of Lacey what had happened, but it had obviously been effective.

Robards's expression made her nervous. Especially since she had no idea where he was going with whatever this was.

"And what play would that be?"

"Filing a sexual harassment complaint."

Kit's breath stopped. With an effort she stopped her eyes from widening in shock, kept from showing any sign of her stunned surprise. What on earth was he up to, inviting her to file a complaint against him? Not that the women of the department hadn't considered it more than once, but none of them had wanted to go through the emotional turmoil and the hours of deposition, testifying and other chaos it would cause. Not to mention if they lost, their lives would become hell. Right now it was only Robards who gave them grief. This was, for all its advances, still heavily a man's world and a man's business, and they were afraid they'd lose what support they had. A sad thing, she thought, when, with some exceptions like her close friends, you're afraid the men you work with would side with a man like Robards simply because he was a man.

And it struck her that they hadn't brought up the subject of a complaint since Miguel had become chief. That had been another reason they'd never taken action. Chief Lipton had been a contemporary of Robards, and some thought he was, although not as openly, of the same mind-set. Betty, the detective secretary who took nearly as much from Robards as the rest of them, had said that filing a complaint with him would be like the chickens going to the coyote to complain about the fox.

But Miguel, Kit thought, was an entirely different kind of man.

"An all-American girl like you would never see a man like him on a social basis unless she was forced to."

Kit blinked, suddenly drawn to the present. A man like who? Lord, she was truly far gone if her mind could wander when she was face-to-face with Robards. Not only that, it could be dangerous. When dealing with a scorpion, you had to pay attention. Only a fool believed it wouldn't sting if given the opportunity.

And then his words registered. "I'm not sure exactly what you mean," she said cautiously.

And just as cautiously, wishing she'd thought of it sooner, she reached into her purse and clicked on the small tape recorder. She pulled out her notebook to cover the action, then set her purse on the desk in front of him, trusting his aversion to things female in his precious workplace to keep him from looking too closely.

"Don't try to hide it, girl. A friend of mine saw you with him down at that fancy yuppie place in Marina del Mar."

Miguel? Kit thought with a shock. He was talking about Miguel?

"Now, I don't blame you, you had to go, him being the chief and all. But nobody who looks at you is going to believe you went out with him voluntarily. They'll know he must have used his rank to get you to go with him."

It suddenly struck her what he was getting at. Then she told herself she had to be wrong. Even Robards wouldn't sink so low. Besides, he hated her. Why should he suddenly change?

"Nobody who looks at me?"

"Sure. Blonde, fair, you know."

Yes, she knew. *White.* She said it in her mind, her shocked fury rising fast. It was all she could do to keep her voice even, but she wanted him to keep talking, had to be sure.

"I do?" she asked.

"I mean, it doesn't even look right, you together, him being...what he is. Anybody could figure it out, that he wanted to show the world he could do better than another greaser."

An image of Anna, with her laughing dark eyes, her beautiful dusky skin, her melodious voice and slight, aristocratic accent, before the awful regimen of chemotherapy had taken her lustrous dark hair, came to Kit in a rush, and it was all she could do not to hook her foot under the base of the chair and dump Robards on his backside.

Instead, she set herself the task of getting him to hang himself. She'd have to use his name, to make it clear who she was talking to. She hoped she could carry it off without arousing his suspicions.

"So, Lieutenant Robards," she said carefully, loudly enough for the recorder to pick it up clearly, "what you're saying is that you would back me if I filed a sexual harassment complaint against Chief de los Reyes because it's obvious to you that I wouldn't have voluntarily been with him last night because I'm white and he's Hispanic. Have I got that right?"

"I always said you were a smart girl."

Right. When you weren't saying I was an uppity bitch who didn't know her place and a few other choice things.

"I see," she said slowly, wondering if she could get him to go further, hang himself a little more. "Do you think I'd really have a chance, him being the chief and all?"

"With the right people on your side," Robards said confidently. "And there are a lot of men left who aren't blind, who see that a man like that isn't fit to lead."

She injected a note of awed wonder into her voice. "And

they'd even go so far as to support a female officer if it would take him down?''

She wondered, as his eyes narrowed, if she'd overdone it. But after a moment, he nodded. ''Some things,'' he said, ''are more important than others.''

And Robards had apparently decided that getting rid of Miguel de los Reyes was worth the humiliation of supporting a female in reporting something he didn't even believe was a crime.

How comforting, she thought, *to find out his racism has a higher priority than his sexism.*

''You think about it,'' he said, standing up. He walked out of her office with that characteristic gait of his that was half swagger, half waddle. The cigar smell, unfortunately, didn't leave with him. It lingered in the air like the permeating stench of a rotting corpse.

Kit sat down, not in her chair, where he'd been, but in the small upright chair opposite the desk. She didn't want to touch it while it was still warm from his copious body heat and quite possibly damp from his sweat.

She took a long, deep breath to steady herself. The man's evil viciousness made her sick, masked as it had been as concern and support. And the ramifications of being seen with the chief in a clearly social setting didn't escape her, either. The fact that it had been strictly—well, almost—business didn't stop her from realizing once again what an utter mess it would be to try to pursue anything else. And she didn't like the reminder, even though she hardly needed it.

After a moment, she reached in and turned off the recorder. And thought. Maybe, just maybe, there was a bright side. Maybe this could be turned to advantage. If Robards was zeroed in on this, it would keep his mind off the Rivas case. He wasn't capable of handling both at once—he didn't have the brain power.

She waited, worked on other cases, made calls, very aware

of Robards hovering. Apparently he had decided she would be more inclined do what he wanted if he kept an eye on her, if he pressured her with his presence. Every time she turned around he was there, watching, waiting. She tried to ignore him, but it was difficult, and she breathed a sigh of relief when she saw him depart for his usual early lunch.

Quickly she made preparations. She left her desk cluttered with a pen and some papers and, since this area was secure, her duty weapon. After she put the lightweight Glock in plain but not obvious sight, she slipped her smaller plainclothes weapon, a classic two-inch, five-shot Smith and Wesson, into her purse. She left the jacket she used to hide it when wearing it over the back of her chair. It wasn't cool enough to need it, since she had a sweater on, a long-sleeved one that would cover her forearm, although she'd changed from Roxy's carefully wrapped gauze to a couple of adhesive bandages yesterday.

She hoped all this would stall any inquiries by giving the impression she was in the building. She didn't sign out officially, but told Betty she was leaving and that she'd be on her beeper. She didn't want the woman to get in trouble. Betty could find her, and Kit could take the heat for not signing out.

Her first goal was thwarted. The chief—she caught herself again thinking of him that way within the walls of Trinity West—wasn't in his office. Rosa told her he'd come in briefly this morning, made a few calls, then left.

So Kit adjusted her focus to her second goal, the next step in the plan to take Robards down.

It was the sudden awareness that sparked through his genial companions that first alerted him. The lewd comments and the wolf whistles that followed told him what, and some inner sense he was barely aware of told him who. So he wasn't surprised when he looked over his shoulder and saw Kit approaching.

Miguel knew she understood some Spanish, but not how much. If she understood any of the more descriptively lewd terms or the suggestions they had for her, it didn't show. She moved confidently, easily. She was wearing a soft, white sweater over blue jeans this morning, jeans that made her legs look even longer by the time they ended at a pair of scuffed white running shoes.

She hadn't seen him yet, he guessed. He was pretty well hidden from her where he sat on the low wall beside the dingy stairway, especially with the four Downtown Boys clustered around him. He was able to watch her, a blonde in a section of town that rarely saw them, walking as if she had every right to be there, exuding a demeanor that would make anyone with any sense think twice before accosting her.

Which explained, he thought wryly, the way his companions began to move, turning to blatantly watch her as she approached.

He should have known she'd turn up. Kit Walker wasn't about to let a simple thing like the fact that the Downtowner known as Choker no longer lived where he had at the time his car was supposedly stolen stop her. Nor that to find out anything about him she was going to have to come to a neighborhood where most men walked with care.

But she slowed, and he guessed she had deduced from their attire and the signature colors that these were Downtown Boys. With anyone else, male or female, he would have questioned the wisdom of walking into four-to-one odds. But he'd seen Kit fight when she had to, and unless they had guns on them, which he was reasonably sure they didn't, they would have a surprise on their hands if they made a move on her. She'd had years of martial arts training. She was tough, quick, and she'd surprise the hell out them.

Not, of course, that he was going to let that happen. If he

let her get much deeper into this without making his presence known, it could get awkward. Besides being a duplication of effort. And he didn't see any point in calling any more attention than necessary to their inquiries.

One of the others made a surprisingly mild comment about the soft, inviting curves of her breasts, and while Miguel couldn't deny that he agreed—just as he couldn't deny the spark of response in his body at the thought—he thought it time to call a halt before things got ugly.

"No tocha," he said sharply. *"Soy mia."*

Claiming her as his woman and telling them hands off was the best way he could see out of this. Kit wouldn't thank him for bailing her out, so it was best if he stopped any trouble before it began.

The others stared at him. One dared to voice disbelief, but shut up when Miguel stood and looked at him coldly.

Kit saw him then. He saw her eyes widen in surprise.

"I've been waiting for you," he said smoothly before she could speak. "My friends here, they have been keeping me company."

He saw her assess the situation and prayed her ever-quick instincts wouldn't fail him.

They didn't. "Sorry I'm late," she said with a shy, fittingly female smile.

"It is all right," he said with an answering smile. "Some things a man does not mind waiting for." He slipped his arm around her possessively, and a little to his surprise, she let him. With an expression he hoped was lurid enough, he began to walk, and Kit instinctively went with him.

The hoots and whistles behind him told him they had bought the story. For all their fierce awareness of their heritage, there was still some lingering trace of instinctive male admiration for one of their own able to claim a beautiful white woman. Miguel hated that it was true, hated the underlying things that made it true, but he knew it was true.

He also knew that they probably thought he'd had her meet him here just to show her off to them. It would appeal to that sense of machismo they cultivated.

As they walked he kept waiting for her to speak, to ask him what the hell he thought he was doing or to at least pull away and demand an explanation. But she didn't. In fact, she seemed to move closer. After a moment he let himself enjoy the feel of her tucked close to his side. Again he noticed how well she fit and that he didn't have to shorten his stride for her to keep up. He took a deep breath, and over the smell of hot asphalt, car exhaust and other unpleasant odors trapped here on the dingy streets, he caught the sweet scent she wore, something rich and heady. Maybe gardenia, he thought, re-membering the white flowers Anna had been forever trying to grow. It was one of those feminine touches that had always reminded him this tough, competent cop was still, and forever would be, a woman.

As if he needed reminding, he thought. The heat that had sparked in him at the almost wistful mention of her soft curves came back with renewed force. It took everything he had not to look at her, at the way the soft white knit of her sweater first clung, then slid over those curves. And the way the jeans hugged her hips, cupped her bottom, making his hands itch to do the same.

God, he had to stop this. If he was going to go into over-drive every time he saw her, he'd have to stay away. It should have seemed silly, heating up over his old friend, but it was painful. And, he realized, hard to hide in the jeans he had put on this morning with a worn white T-shirt with a faded ad-vertisement for a Mexican beer that was popular in the neigh-borhood. If she was at all inclined to look, she'd easily see where his thoughts had wandered.

And for an instant, before his better judgment quashed the idea, he almost wished she would.

Chapter 12

They were well out of sight of their small audience when Kit finally spoke. Miguel was glad when she did, because it made him drag his mind away from the images he found himself battling more and more often. Thoughts he had to keep telling himself he shouldn't be having. Thoughts that weren't paying any attention to what he was telling himself.

"You seemed to fit right in."

Miguel dragged his mind to reality. "I was a street cop down here for a long time. I can still speak the language if I have to."

"What if they'd recognized you? Wasn't that taking a big chance?"

He shrugged. "I gambled that they wouldn't know me on sight, out of context. And none of them were old enough to remember me when I was on the street." He gave her a sideways look. "It was less of a chance than being a hazel-eyed blonde in this part of town."

"I can't stop an investigation just because I don't fit in the neighborhood."

"Nor would I expect you to."

"Then I suppose," she said, returning his sideways look with one of her own, "you have a very good reason for hustling me out of there like that."

She didn't elaborate on "that," for which he supposed he was grateful. He skipped over his concerns for her safety, acknowledging his cowardice in doing so. She hadn't gotten where she was in a tough job in a tough town without being able to take care of herself, and he knew he wouldn't have felt the same concern if it had been a male detective in her place, and that was an issue he'd just as soon avoid. So he cut to the bottom line.

"Because I already have what you were after."

She stopped walking, turned and looked at him. "You do?"

He nodded. "Choker is doing time. For GTA. He got sent up about three years ago."

He saw one corner of her mouth lift at the irony of him being arrested for the same thing they wanted to talk to him about as a supposed victim.

"Well, at least he'll be easy to find," she said.

Miguel let out a breath he hadn't been aware of holding. Apparently she wasn't going to question his hustling her out of there. Whatever her reasons, common sense or not wanting to argue with him, he was glad; he wasn't sure how he would have explained, since he wasn't sure why his reaction had been so immediate and protective. She didn't need—nor would she appreciate, no doubt—him coming to her defense. But neither could he seem to stop the gut-level response. And he didn't like the idea he had his own version of machismo to fight.

He could come up with a simple explanation, that it was a deeply ingrained and quite possibly genetic instinct of the male to guard the female, but he knew it went deeper than that. With Kit, everything seemed more complex, more confusing. Even a simple dinner unexpectedly turned into a morass of emotional entanglement.

"I don't suppose we're so lucky that they knew where?" she asked, coming to a halt.

Her question brought him out of the reverie he found himself slipping into. He realized they were next to her low-slung red coupe, which she'd parked safely several blocks away. He'd left his more recognizable city car well out of the neighborhood. It was another ten-minute walk.

"No," he said, turning back to her question. "But it should be easy enough to find out with a computer check through the Department of Corrections."

She nodded. "I was going to run him today, but Robards has been shadowing my every move."

Miguel's gaze narrowed. "Do you think he suspects something?"

She shook her head. "No. Not about this, anyway."

"Why would he be shadowing you, then?"

Her mouth twisted wryly. "That's his idea of supervision. We all take our turn in the bucket."

He gave her a puzzled look. "The bucket?"

"He sort of takes turns on us. That's why I didn't call about Choker. I was afraid if he was monitoring me, since it seems to be my turn, he might hear and recognize the name."

"Monitoring?"

She nodded. "He'll just be there, hovering, following us around, double-checking everything we do, calling us into his office for status reports, listening in on our phone calls."

He frowned. "That's a bit extreme."

She grimaced. "He says that with a lazy bunch of so-called detectives who couldn't find their ass with a compass, a little micro managing is necessary." Her mouth twisted sourly. "And micro managing, according to him, is the only useful term that's ever come out of all those college boys."

Miguel stared at her. He stifled an oath, then wearily

rubbed a hand over his forehead and down his face. He'd been frowning too damn much lately.

"I didn't realize it had gotten that bad. I should have done something before now."

"Contrary to public opinion, even Miguel de los Reyes can't do it all."

His head came up sharply. She wasn't looking at him as if she'd made a joke, she was looking at him with concern, as if she was worried about him. That warmed him, but there was something else there, something that seemed half-hidden beneath the concern, something that made his pulse speed up and his mind hasten to deny.

"I...my car's farther down," he said, more for something to say to cover his uncharacteristic disconcertment than anything else.

"I'll give you a ride." He hesitated until she prompted him. "It'll look rather odd if any of your friends see us separating so soon, won't it?"

"Good point," he muttered. He didn't think the Downtowners were still around, but everyone knew the gangs had eyes everywhere, and if you were on their turf, you had to assume you were being watched. "But it'll look odd to them if I let you drive, too."

She lifted a delicate brow at him. "That macho thing is alive and well, is that it?"

"Afraid so."

She took it easily, but then Kit had never been one who had to blare her feminism at every turn, he thought. She quietly went about her business in a man's world in that sure, steady, competent way that proved more about her mettle than any verbal claims could.

"Are you sure you just don't want to drive my car as a change from that city boat?" she teased.

He eyed the little coupe appreciatively. He'd admired it more than once since she'd bought it last year and had thought more than once that the little red car and the classy blonde made quite a picture.

"Maybe," he admitted.

She laughed. And tossed the key ring at him. "Feel free to bark the tires if it will add to the image."

He caught the keys and laughed in turn. And he wondered how long it had been since he had laughed like that, easily. A long time. Too long, he thought.

He did bark the tires, but only a little, as they pulled away from the curb. Kit grinned at him, and he laughed again, liking the feel of it.

A mile away, he slowed as they neared where he'd left his car. He found a vacant spot just ahead of it and maneuvered the little coupe into it with an ease that was not lost on him. Maybe next year he'd push for a smaller car. It wasn't all that often he had to cart around dignitaries, although it did happen.

Or maybe he'd do what he'd done this year and take the money that was to go for his car and turn it back to the department. Trinity West could certainly use it. Then he'd buy his own car, one he wanted, and just drive it, forgoing the city car altogether. It wasn't like he had far to drive. If he stayed where he was, of course. He wasn't quite sure if he meant the job or the place that passed for home.

Kit had been quiet on the short drive, and when he glanced at her after parking her car he thought he could read her expression.

"Something else you want to talk about?" he asked. She hesitated, and he was immediately wary.

"We have another problem," she said after a moment.

Something in her tone made him edgy, like he felt when he sensed a flank attack from an entirely new direction.

"Oh, good," he said dryly, "I was running short of problems."

She smiled at his attempt at humor, but it didn't quite reach her eyes, and his tension went up a notch. When she reached into her purse and brought out a small cassette recorder, like many officers carried, he lifted a brow at her.

"When I got in today, Lieutenant Robards was in my office," she said.

Since she'd already told him that Robards didn't suspect the Rivas case hadn't been refiled and forgotten, Miguel knew it couldn't be that. Which meant his feeling had been right—this was something new. She seemed almost embarrassed, which made no sense to him.

"And?" he prompted when she didn't go on.

"I...somebody saw us last night and told Robards."

"Last night?" It hit him then. "At the restaurant?" She nodded. He thought, his brow furrowing as something tugged at his memory. Then he had it. "The big man with the dutiful wife," he said.

A slight smile flickered across her face. "That's what I thought, too. He just looked—"

"Like the kind of guy who would be a buddy of Robards," he said.

"Exactly."

He smiled at her much the same way she'd smiled at him when he'd quickly reached the same conclusion she had. But then he frowned as the possible implications of what she'd said began to run through his mind. He skipped over why the man would have called Robards in the first place—he knew the lieutenant well enough to know his method of choice was spying and acquiring leverage—and cut to what she'd initially said.

"And how," he asked quietly, keeping his seething suspicions at bay for the moment, "is this a problem?"

She took a deep breath. She looked at him, hesitated, and he saw her lips tighten. Whatever this was, it had really upset her.

"Go ahead," he said, his voice a little tight with apprehension as he felt a sinking in his gut along with the growing certainty that he knew exactly what this new problem was.

After a moment she set the recorder on the center console and pushed a button.

He clamped down hard on his reaction as he listened, and it took a little more effort with every second the tape played. Not because of himself, he'd heard this kind of trash more than once, but because it had been said to Kit. He hated to think of her hearing this, of her being put in this position. But at the same time he couldn't help feeling gratified that she had come straight to him with it. That she trusted him enough to do so. And he wasn't sure which feeling was stronger.

When it was finished, when there was nothing coming from the small speaker but the hiss of blank tape, it took even more effort to look at her. His thoughts came back to haunt him.

Had she dared not say no to dinner because of who he was? Had he inadvertently stepped into the sexual harassment ring?

He couldn't believe she would think that way, not Kit, not with all the past between them. She knew him better than that. She knew he would never, ever use his position to force any woman, but most especially her, to be with him if she didn't want to be. She knew. If he couldn't believe that, then he couldn't believe anything in this world.

And then he realized her face was giving him the assurance he needed. She was staring at the recorder as if it was a coiled rattlesnake.

"That man," she said through clenched teeth, "should be fed to sharks. Except they'd probably turn up their noses."

"Do sharks have noses?" he asked mildly. He was surprised at how thoroughly her anger had soothed him, had eased his uncalled for doubts. And she was angry. No, she was furious, he amended when she lifted her gaze and met his eyes.

"How can you joke about that?" She gestured rather wildly at the recorder.

"Kit, I've heard worse, and from better men than Robards."

"Well, *that* part wouldn't be hard," she muttered.

"Rather ironic, isn't it? Support of sexual harassment as an offense, coming from him?"

She grimaced. "Well, he could surely be an expert witness." He chuckled. She looked startled at the sound. "How can you not want to—"

"Oh, I do. I do. But if I get angry, if I let myself be hurt, then he wins. And I refuse to let him win."

"But—"

He held up a hand. "I won't get mad, and I'll go way beyond getting even. He's going to go down, Kit. I promise you that."

She hesitated, looking troubled. "You do know that I would never...that I don't believe—"

"I know," he said softly. "That's why I didn't ask."

She studied him. Then she nodded. And as softly as he had spoken, she said, "He has no idea what kind of man you are. And that's going to cost him."

Her words stirred up a feeling deep inside him that it took him a moment to recognize. Pride. Pride that someone as smart, as good, as sharp as Kit thought that of him.

And there was something in her eyes that warmed him beyond anything he could remember. It was so intense he wanted to look away, but he couldn't. It was as if those hazel eyes held his gaze with some kind odd force. Gold flecks, he noticed rather vaguely. The gold flecks in her eyes were really bright right now, as if—

The sound of her voice filled the car as the tape reached the old section she hadn't recorded over. After giving a start, they both instinctively leaned over to reach for the button to shut it off. Kit hit the button first, but they nearly bumped heads in the process. Both of them looked up, rather sheepish at the unintended physical comedy.

In barely a moment, the atmosphere changed. With their faces barely three inches apart, the sheepish expressions faded into something much more intense. Miguel found himself suddenly very aware of his breathing, aware of the beating of his heart, found himself leaning forward, closing the small distance between them. He saw Kit's eyes widen slightly, but she didn't pull back, didn't blink. His lips parted, and he felt an odd tingling sensation in them. When he realized it was anticipation, the anticipation of feeling her lips beneath his, he tried desperately to pull himself back. But the faint scent of gardenias rose to tickle him, and mixed with the warmth of her body, it was a heady scent that made him unable to heed the warnings that were clamoring in his head.

"Kit," he breathed, knowing he was being a coward, asking her to be the one to say no to this. But he, who had always been in control, who had always made the decision when necessary and carried it out, was beyond this one.

And when Kit answered, a small, breathy sigh that sounded impossibly like *please,* he was lost.

And then his mouth was on hers.

In the unguarded moments he'd thought about this, fantasized about it, he'd thought it would probably feel odd to kiss an old friend like this. But the moment he felt her lips beneath his, any sense of oddity vanished, to be replaced by a stunning sense of utter rightness. A rightness that sent a shock wave of sensation through him, a rightness that generated a heat unlike anything he'd ever known, a rightness that brought his entire body to attention with a speed that left him breathless. Which didn't matter, because he'd forgotten how to breathe, anyway.

It wasn't until he felt the soft, silken strands of her hair threading through his fingers that he realized he'd cupped the back of her head. And it took him a moment to realize the fire searing his chest was radiating from her hands, resting there lightly, her fingertips just below his collarbone. Some vague part of his mind registered that she wasn't pushing him away and that that was good, but any coherent thought beyond that seemed impossible.

Slowly, tentatively, his tongue crept out to flick over her lips. There was a moment of hesitation when he wondered on some level that didn't require thought if she was going to refuse, to retreat. A moment when he knew if she did, he would have to let her go, no matter that it would leave him feeling more cold and alone than he had in a long time.

But in the moment when he began to steel himself for the loss, she decided, and her soft, warm lips parted. As if his body had gotten the message before his hazed mind, he probed forward with his tongue first and felt the shock of it second, the shock of intimacy, the shock of the taste of her.

Unique. She tasted unlike any woman he'd ever kissed, hot, alluring, yet sweet and open. Kit was, above probably all else, honest, and it was there in her kiss. Enough honesty to show the shyness and slight touch of uncertainty that told him he wasn't alone in his tangled feelings about kissing an old friend in a way that went far beyond friendship.

And then, with the same hesitancy, she returned his light caress, and the feel of her tongue stroking over his lips made his body knot fiercely. He shifted restlessly in his seat, too aware of where the ache within him had settled with pulsing urgency.

The blare of a passing car's horn—perhaps in salute or perhaps in protest—made them both jump, and the kiss was broken. For a moment there was the same sense of charged atmosphere as there had been before they'd kissed. Then, inevitably he supposed, the awkwardness set in.

She lowered her gaze, and he couldn't blame her. He felt the same way. He leaned back in the driver's seat, aware of his body's gradual ebb of arousal and of his shock at how quickly and completely it had happened. Yes, it had been a long time, but he'd gone as long before, and he didn't ever remember getting so hot so fast.

He didn't dare look directly at her, but his peripheral vision had always been good, and he could see more than she probably realized. He could see that she was breathing deeply, quickly, as if she was as starved for oxygen as he. He could see that she'd caught her lower lip between her teeth, as if to bite back words. Or, he thought with a shock as he realized he was doing the same thing, to savor any lingering traces of their kiss.

He didn't know what to say. He'd talked a drunk out of suicide, he'd talked an armed suspect into letting his hostages go, he'd talked two gangs out of open warfare on that night years ago. He'd given speeches to groups of officers, chiefs, politicians and unhappy citizens. But he couldn't manage to string two words together for a woman he'd known for fourteen years.

Then her voice came, softly, quietly, echoing his thoughts. "I don't know what to say."

"Maybe—" His voice broke, and he had to swallow and start again. "Maybe we shouldn't say anything."

Out of the corner of his eye he caught her swift nod. "For now," she agreed.

He couldn't deny that eventually they would have to talk about this, but he was glad she was willing to let it wait until they'd both gained some perspective. He, at least, was not seeing anything very clearly at the moment.

Feeling was another matter altogether.

Chapter 13

When she caught herself brushing her fingers over her lips again, Kit nearly swore out loud. Then she silently lectured herself for at least the tenth time this morning to stop. She'd been doing it constantly, unconsciously, ever since—

Ever since Miguel kissed you. That simple phrase, even when only formed in her mind, sent ripples of sensation through her that didn't just make her shiver, but frightened her. It was too intense, too fierce, and no amount of telling herself it was simple overreaction was working. She couldn't forget the feel of him, the incredible warmth of his mouth on hers, the hot, male taste of him and the heady thrill that had shot through her when he'd gently probed her mouth with his tongue.

She wanted to linger over every nuance, every sensation, wanted to relive it again and again, second by second, and she'd never done anything so utterly silly in her life. With Bobby it had been a slow-growing thing. They'd gone through the academy together, they'd forged a bond of deep friendship and utter trust, and it had seemed the thing to do to get married. Their lovemaking had been tender, sweet, even funny sometimes, and she remembered it with a fondness tinged with sorrow because he had died so young.

But it had never been fire. Not like this. Not like Miguel had stirred in her with the slightest of touches, with a single kiss. She didn't dare try to imagine what anything more would be like. What making love with him would be like.

Didn't you learn your lesson? Didn't you swear on Bobby's grave you'd never, ever fall for a cop again?

And the fact that he was the chief only made it worse. If it was anywhere but Trinity West, she could say with some assurance that being chief made him fairly safe. Chiefs of police didn't get shot on a routine basis. But it had happened here, not just to the chief but to Miguel, as well, and he had nearly died.

And even if that wasn't a problem, even if she could accept that as a once-in-a-lifetime fluke and accept that the odds against it ever happening again were astronomical, nothing, no amount of explaining or acceptance, could change the fact that getting involved with her chief would be a career nightmare. For both of them. She knew that, and she knew he had to know that.

And it would be worse for her. In cases like this, albeit grossly unfair, the person of lower rank paid the higher price. If that person also happened to be the female...

She shuddered at the thought. She loved her job, the few remaining men like Robards aside, and she'd worked hard to get where she was, to earn respect from the people who mattered to her. And while her friends might understand, starting a relationship with her highest superior officer could ruin her standing with everyone else.

She'd wondered last night if he might call, might want to get it straight between them that it had been a mistake, that hot, intense kiss. Might want to confirm that she knew it.

Might want to make sure she was retreating as fast as he no doubt was.

And she was. She was sure she was. The fact that she couldn't stop thinking about it, couldn't stop wondering why he'd done it and why she'd not only let him but had participated wholeheartedly, didn't mean she didn't know perfectly well it was impossible.

With an effort, she turned her attention to the report in front of her, telling herself the satisfaction of clearing a missing juvenile case like this one, where Richard Carlisle had come home as a result of her efforts, should fill the empty place in her she'd only recently realized was there.

It didn't.

Miguel leaned back in his chair, frowning at the last batch of statistics he'd read. There had been a sudden surge in burglaries in one particular neighborhood, enough to warrant some attention. A plainclothes team, maybe, if they could find the manpower.

He sighed. It always came back to that, the lack of manpower, lack of money to pay for overtime, which meant any special enforcement such as this took away from the day-to-day protection on the streets. It was a constant high-wire act, and he was getting weary of it. And it made him furious when the city council who insisted their crumbling police units would have to last one more year turned around and spent enough on planting decorative palm trees to buy half a dozen cars. The only dissenting vote on the palm-tree fiasco had been Brubaker, representing the communities on the east side, where surviving was more of a concern than palm trees.

Miguel didn't even like palm trees. Unless they were in Hawaii.

He pressed his lips together as his frown deepened at the thought. And then, abruptly, he was aware of his mouth in a way he'd never been before as he remembered what Kit's had felt like beneath his. Who would have thought his old friend would taste so sweet, like sun-warmed honey? Who would have thought kissing her would cause such instant fire, racing along nerves that had been numb so long he'd thought them dead? Who would have thought he would still be feeling that kiss nearly twenty-four hours later?

Who would have thought he'd ever kiss her at all?

Not him. He never would have thought it. But he'd done it. Without thinking. Perhaps that's why his brain was in such a muddle this morning. It was doing the thinking it should have done before he'd made that stupid move. If he'd done the thinking then, he never would have done the kiss. And he wouldn't be sitting here this morning wondering what the hell he was supposed to do now.

The best thing was to go on as if it hadn't happened, he thought. It didn't seem right, not with the memory clinging so tenaciously to his consciousness, but he didn't know what else to do. Or what to say. And he'd learned the hard way that often the best thing to do when you didn't know what to say was to say nothing. So he should just ignore that vivid memory.

Right, he thought, *and just ignore that elephant sitting on your shoulder, too.*

Besides, Kit hadn't agreed not to say anything at all—she had agreed not to say anything for now. However long that meant.

He let out an audible breath and made himself turn his attention to the report in his hand. He flipped over the last page, scanned it and smiled to see that Cruz Gregerson's suggestion matched his, to run a two-officer graveyard plain-clothes team in the neighborhood suffering the break-ins. Including, Cruz suggested, Max the canine, if Joe Horton, Max's handler, was agreeable. Miguel was sure he would be. Joe was always ready to give his loyal partner the chance to shine. Naturally, Cruz had volunteered to work the shift, and

Miguel knew that was no small sacrifice. He'd seen Cruz and Kelsey together enough to know the felony unit sergeant wouldn't give up nights with his new wife easily.

He'd have to put a time limit on it, Miguel thought, both for fiscal reasons and for Cruz's peace of mind. He scribbled a quick memo recommending Cruz proceed and put it in his out tray. Rosa would pick up the contents of the tray and distribute them before she went to lunch, no doubt lecturing him that she was there to do such memos for him. But he was much happier to do this kind of thing himself and free her up for tasks he detested, like combing the thick binders full of notes about city council meetings for anything he needed to be aware of. Rosa seemed to find the process intriguing, and he was more than happy to hand it over to her. First thing he'd do, if he was ever in a position to, would be to streamline that process. He bet he could cut the paperwork in half if he eliminated the legalese and doublespeak. And if he ever decided to run for office and won, he'd take Rosa with him, if she'd come.

Again he pondered the possibility. A committee of local businesspeople and residents had approached him several times about running for office, and he'd been impressed with their sincerity and enthusiasm. Most of all he'd been impressed by the cross section they represented. They'd come from all areas of Marina Heights, from wealthy Trinity West to the distant east side, from small mom-and-pop businesses to the managers of big shopping centers.

And they had all seemed convinced he was just what the city of Marina Heights needed. Although he'd never thought of himself as a politician—he felt more than a slight distaste for them in general—he did feel the urge to clean things up. He liked this town. It had great potential despite its problems, and it deserved better than it was getting. He didn't have any aspirations beyond the local arena, but trying to deal with the massive and varied problems of just Marina Heights would be a full-time job.

He wasn't sure it would be much tougher than turning around Trinity West. Just different. Maybe, he thought. Maybe.

Mayor de los Reyes has a nice ring to it.

Kit's words echoed in his head, and he smiled. He wasn't sure what at—the words, or that they had come from her. And all of a sudden he was touching his lips with his tongue as if some trace of her lingered.

"Damn," he muttered.

"Problem, sir?" Rosa said from the doorway where she stood. He never closed the door unless he was in a private meeting. His open-door policy was literal as well as figurative.

"Just that I'm going crazy," he said wryly.

"Job requirement," she said blithely as she gathered the things out of the tray. She glanced at the memo on top. Before she could speak, Miguel held up his hand.

"I know, I know. But it was only a few lines."

"I'll forgive you if you get out of here for lunch."

She was always trying to feed him or get him out of the office. She thought he was overworked and too thin. He figured it was a hedge against a good metabolism that was going to start slowing down any day now. He worked out regularly, determined to be in good shape when he hit fifty, a number that made him cringe. He'd never expected to be going on forty-five. He'd never expected to be chief, and he'd certainly never expected to be alone. He and Anna were supposed to grow old together. Now he was doing it by himself and she wouldn't be doing it at all.

Again an image flashed through his mind, of wide hazel eyes beneath thick blond bangs. A man would never get old with Kit around. She was sharp, quick, cracklingly alive, and she'd keep him on his toes every second.

He felt the ugly prod of guilt, as if he was being disloyal

to Anna, but he quashed it. Whatever his feelings, that was not a valid reason for denying them. Anna would have hated it. She had told him, during that Indian summer of well-being that had come just before the end, that he could do nothing worse to her memory than use it as an excuse to sleepwalk through the rest of his life.

"We were happy, Miguel," she'd told him. "But you will be happy again. In time. The sun will shine again for you someday."

He'd been so focused on the fact that she was speaking in the past tense, as if she was already separating herself from this life, that he had barely noticed the sense of her words. But now, all he could think of was the sunny blond of Kit's hair, the brightness of her quick smiles and the glow of her eyes. And Anna's words about the sun shining for him.

"Get," Rosa said rather sharply, and he wondered what he'd betrayed. Rosa had learned as did any good secretary, to read his moods rather well. "You need to eat, do it outside this office. You spend too much time here, anyway."

He felt like saying "Yes, Mother," but knew it would only get her started on her lecture that he indeed needed a mother, since his social life was dead and he wouldn't let anyone into his life to look out for him. He didn't need to hear that now, not when his thoughts kept straying to Kit. And that kiss.

He nodded meekly, wondering how many other bosses were at the mercy of secretaries who had run out of children to mother. But Rosa was the best, and he wasn't about to do anything that might make her want to go somewhere else. That she knew both of those things only made life more interesting.

Seemingly satisfied, Rosa headed out to make her deliveries. Then she paused in the doorway and looked at him. "I almost forgot. The Department of Corrections called while you were on the phone. They said to tell you the prisoner you inquired about is in Chino."

He nodded and thanked her, and she continued on her way.

Chino. Not too far, he thought. And Choker was only in for GTA, so he wasn't in a maximum security lockup. Of course, Miguel amended silently, that only meant he'd been *caught* for GTA. Who knew what else he'd done and gotten away with?

He'd told Kit to let him make the call, rather than her trying to dodge Robards, so he would have to pass this on. He wondered if she was in her office or if she'd gone to lunch. Then he remembered she'd told him she usually stayed in the station when Robards went to lunch so she could get some work done without feeling like he was looking over her shoulder.

He could go by her office before he left for lunch, he thought. It would only take a moment to tell her. And it was silly to avoid her. They worked under the same roof. It was inevitable that they would run into each other, and he wasn't going to get into that kind of habit.

It made perfect sense to him, and he stood up and reached for his suit coat. He'd had a meeting today with the city manager, to discuss the budget farce once again, and he'd donned the suit in deference to that. But the tie had gone the moment the man had left his office, and he wasn't even sure where he'd tossed it.

He gave up the search after a few seconds. He wasn't going anywhere that required a tie, anyway. Probably the café, he thought as he grabbed a couple of reports he needed to read.

He nearly collided with Robards in the hallway. He really was distracted, he thought, if he had missed the smell of stale cigar smoke approaching. And the stogie was there, clenched between teeth yellowed by years of the habit, the end in his mouth already dark, wet and chewed. Miguel looked away from it, wondering if he'd lost his appetite for lunch.

It was, however, unlit. Robards was sticking to that rule, at least, although he didn't have much choice, since the policy was backed up by state law. Had it been his rule only, Miguel was certain the old-school cop would have found a way around it.

Their greeting was more grunts and nods than anything. Neither of them had much to say to the other. And Miguel didn't want that to change, didn't want to do anything to put the man on guard. But he couldn't help glancing at the narrow, muddy brown eyes, wondering if somewhere behind the flatness of them hid a murderer. He couldn't tell. All he could see was the glow of dislike the man didn't bother to hide.

After they passed each other, with more distance than was necessary in the fairly wide hallway, Miguel was aware of the man's stare, felt as if the tiny red laser light from a sniper rifle had settled neatly between his shoulder blades.

He was several steps along, with that spot on his back itching, when he realized Robards could well be watching him for more reason than to be irritating or to vent his considerable spleen. He could be watching to see where Miguel was going, and if he turned to the detective division, who knows what the man would think. Or assume. Or do.

He only had a few feet to make a decision. And while the thought of changing his course because of that man galled him, he realized he wasn't the only one involved here. If Robards was already on Kit's back, if he even began to suspect what was going on and that she was involved, her life would truly become hell.

Another aspect struck him. If the man believed the accusations he'd made on that tape, he'd see this as proof either of their involvement or that he was coercing her. And that could make life even more miserable for her.

He forced himself not to look back. He didn't need to; he could feel the man watching. He wished more than ever that he'd tackled this particular problem before now, but he'd had so many other demands on his time.

Even Miguel de los Reyes can't do it all.

It was good to know that Kit, at least, understood. That

she'd wanted to tell him made him feel even better. He wouldn't pay her back by bringing Robards down on her head, even inadvertently.

He kept walking, past the detective division, not quite sure where he was going but sure he wasn't going to make that turn with Robards's eyes boring into his back.

He was barely past the door when he felt an easing of pressure at the back of his neck. He glanced back. Robards was disappearing through the doorway that led to the outside stairs.

He stopped, more irritated than before. This clown was way out of control. Miguel had wanted to jerk his chain a long time ago. But he'd bided his time, wanting it to be solid, wanting it to be permanent. And it would be. With Kit's help, it would be.

She was in her office. And with Robards's departure, she was the only one in the division at this midday hour. He paused, watching her at her desk through the window beside the door. She was reading a report, her head bent, and he saw the twin sweeps of gold-tipped lashes. So different from Anna's dark eyes, yet no less beautiful.

And oddly, he found himself thinking her intensity, her concentration was as attractive to him as anything else. He'd seen it in so many areas, in her concern for the victims and their families, in her worry over the troubled kids she dealt with every day, even in her attention to routine things like reading that report.

But he'd seen it elsewhere, as well. In the way she'd focused on Anna during that long, awful year. In the way she'd played all out in that softball game. In the way she was always there for her friends. In the way she'd worried about him when he'd been shot.

As it did now and then, his mind went to that time. But it wasn't to the pain, it was to one of the few bright spots in the long, lonely days in the hospital, the times when Kit came, always bringing some little thing to amuse him, from awful jokes to silly cards. But it was her presence, her cheerful, vital presence that had done more for him than anything. More than once he'd thought he should tell her she didn't have to come every day, but he never had. He looked forward to her visits too much.

The sun will shine again for you someday.

He'd known in his heart and gut Anna was wrong. Never again would he risk such pain. He'd loved her so much, it had nearly killed him when she'd died. No way would he risk loving anyone again. He could care for someone, perhaps, but never love. Anna had taken his capacity for that dangerous emotion with her when she'd gone, and he didn't think he'd ever get it back. And anyone he could bring himself to care for wouldn't likely settle for that. They would require—and deserve—what he couldn't, wouldn't give.

Especially Kit. She deserved nothing less than someone who would love her utterly and completely, who would love her enough *not* to die for her, as some seemed to find romantic, but to live for and with her, which he thought was, in the end, a lot more difficult.

As if she'd felt his gaze, Kit raised her head. She saw him through the window and smiled. Instantly, without hesitation, in the manner of one truly glad to see the person she'd discovered there. Warmth kicked through him, and he was seized with the sudden wish to have this all the time, to have Kit Walker look at him with that expression of pure welcome. What scared him was that he was picturing it in all kinds of ways, not just here. He was picturing it despite all the things he'd just thought. He was picturing it outside of the safety of Trinity West. He was picturing her in his life in all sorts of ways.

And for the briefest of moments he pictured her in his bed, and the warmth became a heat that almost staggered him.

She started to get up, and quickly he stepped toward the

door, which put him out of her line of sight. He sucked in a deep breath, barely managing to steady himself before the door swung open.

"Sorry to interrupt," he said, gesturing toward her desk, noting that his voice was steadier than he'd expected.

"It's just routine stuff," she said. "No problem."

He eyed her overflowing in tray. She caught the direction of his gaze and shrugged. "That's the lowest priority stuff. Follow-up phone calls on cold cases."

"I'll get you some help on that."

"I can do it."

"Not even Kit Walker can do it all," he said.

She looked startled, then blushed as he used her words.

"Matching what Gage used to do in addition to my own work is beyond me," she admitted.

"I should hope so," he said. "Somebody else can make the calls, screen them for you, at least, so you only have to deal with the ones where there may be new developments."

She seemed to consider that, then nodded. "That would help."

This was fine, Miguel thought. Nice and businesslike. No mention or reminder of that hot, stolen moment in her car. He could deal with this.

"Did you want something?" she asked.

In an instant, the equilibrium he'd been congratulating himself on vanished, swept away by a flood of vivid images conjured by her innocent words. He wanted something, all right. And he wanted it with her. And no matter how deeply he tried to bury the urge, it seemed determined to surface the moment his guard was down. And sometimes even when it was up. Like now.

"I…" He swallowed and tried again, hoping she'd think he'd forgotten, telling himself she'd never guess what had turned his voice to gravel. "Choker is in Chino."

"Oh." Odd, he thought. She sounded almost as if he'd

said something unexpected. Or as if she'd expected something else. "Guess I'll be driving to Chino."

"I thought I'd go out there on Saturday."

She lifted a brow at him. "Weren't you the one warning me about working weekends?"

He gave her a sheepish look. "Yes, but this is..."

"Different," she finished for him. Then she grinned. "Isn't it always?"

That bright, sunny grin seemed to push aside all his dark thoughts, all the reasons he'd been so sure of, the reasons to forget how she made him feel, forget how much he liked simply touching her and above all forget that kiss. He felt almost drunk on it, that grin, and found himself returning it. Happily.

"Let's go to lunch," he said.

She blinked, looking not quite startled, and it hit him that maybe this was what she'd been thinking he'd say before. He hoped he was right. At least, he did as long as her answer was yes. When she hesitated, when he sensed she was thinking all the dark thoughts her grin had vanquished for him, he fell back on the old safety zone of keeping it work-related.

"We can plan a visit to see Choker," he said.

"We?"

"I told you I'd be there every step of the way." He thought again of Robards's eyes on him in the hallway. "It could get very ugly, and I don't want you taking any of it alone."

"All right," she said after a moment.

He knew she was referring to him going with her to see Choker but chose to react as if she'd said all right to lunch, as well.

"Good. Let's go."

He saw her mouth quirk at one corner, and he knew she realized exactly what he was doing. He also saw the moment when she decided not to dispute it and go along.

They were almost to the outside stairway when he thought to ask, "Any idea where your lieutenant goes to lunch?"

She gave him a sideways look. "Looking to find or avoid him?"

"Avoid," he admitted ruefully.

She shrugged. "Not the café, if that's what you mean. Too many of the new breed go there for his taste."

"Good." His mouth twisted. "I hate letting him have that much control, making me try to dodge him."

"Look at it as an indigestion preventative."

He chuckled at the suggestion, then added, "It's only temporary, anyway."

She nodded. "And probably best to keep a low profile until we have something we can use."

He liked the way she said that *we*. He liked the way she moved beside him. He liked the way her short cap of hair moved whenever she turned her head. He liked the way she could make him laugh.

But he hated the way all that scared him. For the first time he didn't welcome the automatic warning that clamored in his head. And that scared him most of all. He didn't want to be warned away from Kit Walker.

Chapter 14

A prison was a prison was a prison, Miguel thought, and the California State Institution for Men in Chino was no different. He hadn't been to this one in a while. It was fifty miles inland, and despite the view of the mountains—a subtle torture, he supposed, for those stuck here on the flat ground of the facility—it wasn't high on his list of favorite places to visit.

The coils of concertina wire atop the main fence set the mood, he supposed. As they did at most prisons. They might look different on the outside, might be different colors, might be set up differently, but at the core they were all the same. They had the same smell, the same echoing sounds, the same feel—heavy and oppressive.

At least, to him it was oppressive. He knew there were some to whom it was home, people who had somewhere along the way gotten so screwed up they couldn't function on the outside, and if they made it out, they seemed to set themselves up to get sent right back so they'd feel safe again.

He had the stray thought that he was no one to talk disparagingly about wanting to feel safe. He wondered if he wasn't being held in a prison of his own making. He couldn't say he hadn't felt confined on the long drive out here, alone in the car with Kit.

Not that it had been awkward or uncomfortable. Quite the opposite. She'd been herself, the Kit who made him laugh, who made him think, who made him relax. It was that, in fact, that made him edgy. He'd enjoyed her company so much he had to repeatedly remind himself not to get too used to it. It was getting harder and harder to heed his warnings. Lately he'd felt like a kid in front of a shop window, separated from something he desperately wanted by only a pane of glass. He could see it, long for it but couldn't have it. And all the reasons seemed to ring false in his ears on this bright, sunny day with bright, sunny Kit beside him.

The latest of several wolf whistles and rude expressions of appreciation echoed in the visitor's area. Another passing inmate had caught sight of Kit. Snapped out of his musings, Miguel tensed. The guard escorting the man hushed him with a glare and a word, but Kit never turned a hair, never even blinked. She was utterly calm and poised, as if it was all old news to her.

Maybe it was, he thought. He supposed she'd put up with this countless times over the years. But he wished he could be so calm. Instead he found himself getting angrier at each raucous outburst. He wanted to thump the lot of them, imagined the satisfaction of his fist connecting with a couple of smart-ass mouths. He wanted to teach them a lesson, show them they'd better not look at her, better not even think what he had no doubt they were thinking, because she was—

She was what? His? Is that what he was thinking, what all this tension was stemming from, some protective instinct that he didn't think he had anymore, some far too personal reaction to any threat to her, no matter how minor? Was he really more imbued with that machismo attitude than he'd realized? There was no chance in the world any of these guys would even try to get close enough to lay a hand on her, but he was reacting as if they were all armed and there wasn't a guard in sight.

"Are you all right?"

She'd whispered it, and when he glanced at her face he saw that her forehead was creased in concern. She must have sensed his tension, he realized, and was thankful she could have no idea what had caused it. He knew she wouldn't appreciate a caveman, and he was feeling decidedly Neanderthal at the moment. Quickly, he tried to cover his reaction with a bit of the truth, albeit not what had caused his reaction.

"I'm fine. I just feel about these places like I do about hospitals."

"You'd rather walk on hot coals?"

He smiled, and some of his tension ebbed. "Spiked with nails," he confirmed.

"We won't hang around for the afternoon movie, then," she said cheerfully, and this time he chuckled.

"No," he agreed. "It's probably *Escape from Alcatraz* or something, anyway."

She laughed, and the bright sound of it made him think of sunlight again. And in a place like this, sunlight was a precious commodity.

Kit, he thought, *would be a precious commodity anywhere.*

He heard the heavy clank as the door to the cell block opened, and as they looked up a man dressed in the prison's standard-issue short-sleeved jumpsuit walked in. The face was familiar from the mug shots in his extensive record. Not being in for any violent offenses, he wasn't cuffed, Miguel noticed, and he felt an echo of that protective concern. He wouldn't have thought twice had he been alone, but Kit's presence seemed to change everything.

She's a trained officer, so tamp it down, he told himself.

He knew she could handle herself. But he still didn't have to like it. As long as he kept it to himself.

Then he got a close look at Choker and realized he was going to have more than that to keep to himself. He struggled to keep his expression even. It hadn't shown in the stark mug shots, but the self-styled tough-guy convict with the felony record had the face of a choirboy. The angelic cast of his big, doe-soft brown eyes was marred only slightly by the two small tears tattooed beneath the outer corner of the left one. The comparison ended beneath his chin, however, where an intricate, inch-wide tattoo of assorted crudities circled his neck. There was perhaps more than one reason he'd gained his nickname. The eyes might fit Lorenzo, but the neck ring was pure Choker.

Choker eyed Kit up and down, more than a little salaciousness in his gaze, and Miguel tensed again. Choker was more observant than he had expected, for he turned his gaze on Miguel. It was full of challenge.

"She yours?" he asked.

To Miguel's surprise, before he could say anything, Kit answered evenly, "In a manner of speaking."

He knew what she meant, that she worked for him, but for an instant he wished she'd meant it otherwise. And he didn't like that, either. But there wasn't much pleasing him at the moment, so he kept his mouth shut until he had his unruly emotions under control.

Choker turned his gaze to her, and perhaps because of where they were and because he had little choice, he left it at that. "They said you were cops."

She nodded. He looked her up and down again, as if trying to decide if her appearance made up for the fault of her profession.

"I don't talk to cops," he said.

"Even cops who believe you?" Kit asked sweetly.

Choker blinked, then looked from Kit to Miguel and back

again, suspicion obvious on his face. "You believe I didn't steal that car?"

His temper under control, Miguel stifled a grin. Even Choker had the brains to know that was too much to believe. They knew darn well he'd stolen it, despite his claim that he borrowed it from a friend. He'd been caught driving it, had a record of three previous auto thefts, the real owner had never laid eyes on him, and Choker had claimed never to have noticed that the ignition had been punched.

"Not exactly," Kit said.

"But," Miguel said as Choker looked at them with suspicion, "we do believe that your car was stolen five years ago."

That startled him.

"Why don't we sit down and talk about it?" Kit asked, gesturing toward the gray metal table beside them. Choker hesitated, and Kit moved first, pulling one of the unpadded chairs out from the table and sitting in it. Miguel shifted his weight and sat on the edge of the table, keeping a foot on the floor, on some level aware that he wanted to be free to move fast if he had to.

At last Choker grabbed a chair, pulled it around and straddled it, keeping the back of the chair between himself and them.

"Cops didn't believe anything I told them then. You sayin' you do now?"

Kit nodded, and went on with what they'd planned to say. "We think it happened just like you said, that your car was stolen and you had nothing to do with shooting El Tigre."

"I didn't," Choker said vehemently. "Thought about it, offin' that *pendejo*. But I didn't."

Miguel hoped Kit wouldn't ask for a translation. It didn't have any real equivalent, but *bastard* was the nicest of the possibilities. But perhaps she already knew that. Her expression was contemplative, and he wondered if she was thinking, as he was, that Choker was very adamant about something that had happened so long ago and that hadn't landed him here. And it wasn't like gang members were averse to claiming their kills. They usually did so loudly and proudly.

"Would you tell us again what happened that night?" Kit asked, her voice quiet and encouraging. Miguel wouldn't have thought it would work with a hard-core guy like Choker, but he answered her.

"Told you all back then, nobody believed me. You all think I did it. Cops are always ready to hang anything they can on a Downtown Boy. That's all they're good for, that and shaking down homies. So why should I talk to you?"

"Because we'll listen," she said.

Choker seemed as startled by that as he had been by the statement that they believed him. Miguel grimaced inwardly, wondering how many of these gangsters had started out as normal, trusting kids. He felt frustrated at what made them turn to gangs as their only salvation.

"Why should I care? You couldn't prove nothin' on me, anyway."

"Wouldn't you like to have the cops have to publicly admit they were wrong, that they couldn't prove it because you were innocent?"

Something flashed in Choker's eyes, some flicker of response, and Miguel silently congratulated Kit for her acuity. But after a long moment, Choker shook his head.

"Downtowners don't help cops with nothing."

"Even when one of your own is accused and you can clear him?" Kit asked.

"Couldn't prove nothin' against me," he repeated. "That's good enough."

"No, they couldn't prove it, but you know every cop in Marina Heights thinks you did it. And they hassled you because of it, right?"

That clearly struck a chord. "Yeah. But they didn't need

no excuse. Shake us down for no reason all the time, just 'cuz they got the juice to do it.''

"What if we had to tell them to back off because you didn't do it? That'd make you a pretty big man, having all those cops have to leave you alone when you get out. Ought to be worth something, talking up on the street.''

She was exaggerating, but if it worked, Miguel was all for it.

"And it's not like you're selling out one of your homies,'' Miguel put in. "Just the opposite. We think we can prove no Downtown Boy was involved.''

They waited while the tattooed young man seemed to be weighing his options. At last, arriving at his personal bottom line, he asked, "What's in it for me?''

Kit glanced at Miguel, tacitly turning it over as agreed.

"You're up for parole soon, aren't you?'' he asked.

"Yeah,'' Choker said cautiously, eyeing Miguel with much more wariness than he had Kit, although, to Miguel's relief he had stopped ogling her.

"I could talk to the parole board. A good word from your hometown chief of police about how you cooperated couldn't hurt any.''

Choker's eyes widened. "The chief? You?'' Miguel nodded. "I heard some homies offed the head heat a while back,'' he said, clearly suspicious.

"I was there,'' Miguel said. Then, remembering what store most gang members put on survival, with surviving knife and gunshot wounds at the top of the list, he added, "Took a couple of those rounds myself.''

Choker's eyes widened. "You got shot, too?''

"Guess the city council figured if I was tough enough to survive that, I was tough enough to be chief.''

Choker considered this, then shook his head. "Nah, no white council like that would make you police chief.''

Silently, Miguel reached into his pocket and took out his

leather ID folder. He flipped it open and held it out so Choker could see the badge and his ID card. Choker's eyes went wide again, and he glanced at Kit.

"He's really the chief? Like, boss of all those cops?"

"He is."

Choker leaned back in his chair as if he needed support to absorb this. When he looked at Miguel, there was a tinge of respect in his gaze.

"You'll put in a good word for me when I come up in a couple months?"

Miguel nodded. "You help us with this, I'll help you with that. No promises, though. If you don't watch yourself, whatever I say won't make any difference. But I'll talk to them."

"I been cool," Choker said, and the flaring of hope in those choirboy eyes was something to see. Miguel would be glad if he wasn't so sure the guy would end up back here sooner rather than later.

"Then you've got a chance."

There was another hesitation, then Choker let out a long breath. "What do you wanna know?"

"Tell us everything that happened that night," Kit said. "Even if it doesn't seem to have anything to do with your car being stolen."

He shrugged. "Me and my homies, we were watching Monday night football, you know, with the rowdy friends song? We were all at Little Ricky's place, just kicking. He's got the best TV, you know?"

They did know. This had all been in Cruz's follow-up report. Choker had insisted that's where he'd been, and so had a crowd of witnesses. Biased witnesses, yes, but witnesses nevertheless. It was why they'd had to drop him as a suspect. It would have been impossible to break his alibi. Homies didn't give each other up.

And Cruz had noted in his thorough analysis that the stories were consistent in content and different enough in the telling

that he tended to believe them. They didn't sound like a re-
hearsed cover-up. That was another reason they were here—
both trusted Cruz and his instincts implicitly.

And now Choker told them essentially the same story
again. He'd driven to his fellow Downtowner's house to
watch the game and down a few *cervezas*—none of that sissy
light beer, but the real stuff. They'd partied after the game
and seen or heard no one, although Choker admitted they'd
been making a lot of noise and couldn't have heard much of
anything from outside. When he'd gone out, his car, his precious, lowered and finely painted car, was gone.

"But you got it back," Miguel said.

He nodded. "Those fancy beach cops found it." He
snorted loudly. "Didn't want a home boy's car in their pretty
town, so I got it back in a hurry."

Miguel had to smother a smile and saw Kit's mouth tighten
slightly, as if she was having to do the same. That mouth,
those soft, warm lips that had felt so...

He yanked himself off that dangerous path. "Anything
missing from the car?"

Choker made a face, his grimace moving the two inked
tears. "All my stuff was there, except—"

He broke off, eyeing them warily. "We read the report,"
Kit told him dryly. "We know they booked a weapon and a
gram of cocaine."

And they hadn't been able to pin those on Choker, either.
He claimed they weren't his, that both must have been planted
by whoever stole his car. The gun was clean of prints, and
the paper bindle of coke hadn't yielded any, either, so Choker
had walked on that, as well. But now he had nearly incrim-
inated himself with his own words. And was about to clam
up entirely, Miguel could sense it.

"Probably something silly like a road map or something,
right?" Miguel suggested.

Slowly, Choker nodded. "Yeah, that was it. My map of Beverly Hills."

The kid had a sense of humor, he'd have to give him that, Miguel thought. They asked him a few more questions but got nothing more than Cruz had at the time. And he was wary after that stumble. Maybe this had been a wasted trip. He hadn't told them anything they hadn't already known.

Well, not wasted, he amended silently as Kit probed. He'd had a morning with her away from Trinity West. And he realized he'd have gone a lot farther for less for that. That realization spawned another, the realization of just how far gone he was.

It was impossible, he told himself for what had to be the hundredth time. For so many reasons, both professional and personal. And even if they could work out the problems that would arise out of him being her boss at Trinity West, that still left the biggest problem of all, the simple fact that he knew he could never, ever survive what he'd gone through with Anna again. She'd had so much more courage than he. She'd faced her impending death with grace and dignity, while he had wanted nothing more than to run and hide from it, crying like a child to make it go away.

He heard Kit's voice without really hearing what she was saying. He looked at her. Even here the intensity showed in her concentration on Choker. He saw the determined set of her jaw, the softness of her lips, the silken cap of pale hair that bared her delicate nape.

He thought of something happening to her, some accident or illness, and felt the same nausea inside him he'd felt when Anna had been diagnosed. A chill swept him, and he felt sweat break out on his skin.

Abruptly, almost involuntarily, he stood up. Kit didn't seem startled by his sudden motion, so he guessed she must have been about finished with her questions anyway. He wondered what he'd missed while lost in that painful reverie. He tried to focus, but something was hovering on the edges of his mind, something he couldn't pin down but sensed was a revelation he wasn't going to like.

"Who's got your car now?" Kit asked Choker.

Choker scowled. "Sold it to my cousin Leonardo. He always wanted it, you know? He got it cheap, too. Said it wasn't worth as much anymore with those burn marks on the leather. Really pissed me off."

Kit started to nod, then stopped, looking at the young man with renewed intensity. "The report mentioned those marks. You mean they weren't there before?"

"Hell, no, I told 'em that. I take care of my wheels. *Nobody* drops ash on my seat covers, you know?"

She made him assert again that the burn marks hadn't been there before. Then, at last, she stood up. Miguel was grateful. He wanted out of here, although as long as she was within sight, he had a feeling this foggy sensation wasn't going to leave. He felt like some part of him had arrived at a momentous conclusion, but his brain hadn't gotten the message yet.

They didn't speak as they cleared security and headed toward his car. It was a clear, sunny day, and a lot hotter inland than it was on the coast. The heat felt good beating down on his back, drying that odd film of sweat that had come over him inside. He'd probably be sweating normally by the time they reached the car, but he could handle that. What he couldn't handle was that sick kind of sweat that came with nausea, that reaction to the thought of Kit suffering or dying. Of going through it all over again.

And in that instant, his brain finally got the message. Shock nearly took him down. Fortunately they were at the car, and he was able to lean on it and stay upright.

"Got another piece," Kit was saying.

He heard as if through a fog and had to fight his way back to the moment. "What?"

"We've got another piece," she repeated. "A little one, but it fits."

"I..." He shook his head sharply, trying to shove aside what had just hit him. It didn't want to shove.

Kit gave him a curious glance. "Are you all right?" she asked for the second time today.

No, he said silently, *I'm not. God, I'm not.*

"Is it your stomach again?"

Mutely, he shook his head, barely able to manage that.

"It's hot," she said. "Maybe we should get in and turn on the air before we start back."

Her voice was full of concern, and it only made the knot in his churning stomach tighten more.

It's too late, too late, too late...

The words roiled in his mind like a mantra gone haywire. He'd been so on his guard for years, never letting himself care, let alone anything else, and now...

Numbly, he opened the driver's door and flipped the lock on the passenger side. He should have, would have walked around to open it for her, but he wasn't sure he could move. And when he collapsed as much as sat in the driver's seat, he knew he'd made the right choice. He would never have made it.

"That's better," she said a few minutes later when the car had cooled to a comfortable temperature.

Desperately, trying to focus, he tried again. "What fits?"

"The burn marks," she said. When he didn't respond she added, "On Choker's upholstery."

"Oh."

He supposed he must have sounded blank, because she gave him another curious look and elaborated. "If they weren't there before the car was stolen but were there after, it's a good bet the thief left them there."

That made sense, he told himself, pleased that things seemed to be settling. "Yes," he agreed.

She seemed to be waiting for more from him. When it didn't come, she asked quietly, "Have you ever seen Lieutenant Robards's car?"

It hit him then. "Cigar burns," he said.

She nodded. "All over the front seat."

The police-trained part of his mind took over. He nodded slowly. "It's not hard evidence," he warned, although every instinct he had was saying it meant just what they thought it meant.

"No," she agreed, "but it's another pointer showing we're on the right track."

They were. He sensed it just as she did. He was as sure of it as she was. They were in complete agreement, total accord on this case.

It was elsewhere they were out of synch. Completely. Totally. The realization that had struck him like a blow had made that undeniably clear. It had finally gotten through to his stubborn brain that his reaction to the thought of Kit hurt or sick or dying had its basis in a fact he'd refused to recognize until it became impossible not to.

What he'd felt then was as fierce as what he'd felt when Anna had been ill. And there was only one thing that could evoke that kind of response. The very thing he'd sworn never to fall victim to again in his life. The very thing he'd fought for so long. The very thing he'd declared off limits, kept so carefully at a safe distance.

Love.

The very thing he'd warned himself against when he began having these unexpected thoughts about Kit. He'd warned himself repeatedly that it was impossible, that it was unwanted and unsought.

But he realized it had all been for nothing, that on some buried level his heart had ignored the warnings and forged ahead. His heart, the part of him that should have known all the dangers, had left him with only one piece of bitter knowledge.

It's too late, too late, too late...

Chapter 15

Kit stole a discreet glance at Miguel, admitting to herself she was concerned.

No, be honest, you're downright worried, she told herself. He'd been acting very odd since before they left the visiting room. She thought it was the prison—it certainly wasn't her favorite place to be, either—and had kept an eye on him as they'd gone through security.

Then she thought maybe he was ill. He looked rather pale. Perhaps there was more to his buying that milk shake yesterday than he admitted to. Perhaps he really was having stomach problems. Lord knew his job was enough to give anyone an ulcer.

The thought of him hurting made her hurt inside. It was far too easy for her to call up the memory of him looking haggard and strained and pale in a hospital bed. Odd, but the memory upset her now as much as the reality had then. She felt that same clenching pain, that same urge to shout at the unfairness of it. She frowned. She'd thought herself past that.

She'd remembered before without this fierce feeling, so why was it kicking up now, when he was alive and safe?

She glanced at him. The traffic was fairly heavy on this Saturday afternoon, and he was focused on the road. And he seemed all right. Maybe it had been the surroundings. He insisted he was all right, and once they got to his car and he had the blast of the air-conditioner in his face, he seemed to recover.

Physically, at least. He hadn't said two words the entire drive. She thought he might relax when they cleared the gates, but he seemed as tightly wound as he had been inside. And it had continued as they headed west.

She didn't want to ask him again if he was all right. Clearly he wasn't, and equally clearly he didn't want to talk about it. So she tried to concentrate on the case, tried to take the fragments they had and put them together into some kind of pattern, unable to rid herself of the idea that there was something there, if only she could see it.

She dug out her notebook and flipped through the pages, her notes on Carmela Rivas and her surviving son, Martin, Robards's behavior, extreme even from him, the encounter with Mako, the interview with the happily retired Welton, all the tiny bits and pieces, and now the interview with Choker.

I know he did it, she thought fiercely. *And if I can't prove it, it's going to really make me crazy.*

"What it will do is eat you alive."

Miguel's quiet observation was her first hint that she had spoken. "I didn't mean to say that out loud. Sorry for disturbing you."

He gave a low halfhearted chuckle that had an undertone she couldn't put a name to. "You don't know the half of it," he muttered.

She had no idea what that was supposed to mean, and something about his expression made it difficult to ask. So she said nothing, just stared out the window. After a moment he spoke again, his tone normal.

"You can't let it do that to you. We knew going in we probably wouldn't be able to take him down as hard as we'd like."

"I know." She rubbed her forehead, feeling a tightness she hadn't noticed until now. "It's just hard to accept that he could go on with his life while Carmela Rivas weeps at her son's grave."

"They're out there, Kit, the people like that. And you'll never change them. You might shut them up by making speaking of or acting on their hate a crime. You might make them keep it to themselves, but they'll find others like them, the way flies find a corpse. And they'll believe what they believe and tell themselves they're right."

"I know," she said wearily. "And that's what I hate."

She heard him let out a long breath and glanced at him. He wore an odd expression, almost wistful. "That's one of the things I admire most about you. You've never lost that righteous anger at injustice, at unfairness. After all you've seen and been through, you can still find the energy to go out and fight one more day."

She was gratified by the admiration he expressed but not sure about the rest. "You make me sound like a naive idealist."

He shook his head. "You're something more rare, more precious, Kit. A realist, someone who knows it's probably hopeless but goes out and fights the battle anyway, someone who believes the little victories may not seem like much, but when you add a bunch of them together, you find you've made a difference."

"That's the point, isn't it? It's what you've done at Trinity West, made a difference."

"Trinity West I can deal with," he muttered.

She eyed him, wondering if that was one of those comments better left unexplored. But she didn't want him to slip back into that tense silence, either, even though the ride was almost over. She pondered and decided she'd rather risk it than let it go and forever wonder what he'd meant. She took a breath, then took the plunge.

"So what is it you can't deal with?"

She saw his hands tighten on the wheel. "Sorry. My turn. I didn't mean to say that out loud."

The thought occurred to her that Miguel never wasted words, never said anything he didn't mean. If those words had slipped out, it was because he had wanted them to. Maybe not consciously, but on some level. Perhaps he *wanted* her to question him.

"Didn't you?" she asked quietly.

He gave her a startled glance that turned thoughtful, then almost rueful before he turned his eyes to the road.

"Maybe I did," he admitted.

"So what is it you can't deal with?"

His mouth twisted as he let out an ironic sigh. Then, looking much like she felt, balanced on an edge and about to plunge over, he said simply, "You."

With one word, he took her breath away. She fought the surge of emotions that wanted to well inside her—shock, amazement, fear. And, she realized, one thing more powerful than any of those—joy. She fought that hardest of all, telling herself he couldn't mean what it sounded like, that it was wishful thinking on her part.

While she was struggling with that, he surprised her by continuing past Marina Heights and heading toward the coast. But she couldn't spare much attention. She didn't want this conversation to come to a halt, didn't want to be left hanging because they'd arrived at her house, where he'd picked her up for the trip this morning.

"What do you mean?" she asked finally, careful to keep

her voice even, trying desperately to hide any sign of her reaction.

"If I have to explain," Miguel said as he turned onto Pacific Coast Highway, "then I must be way out of line."

Kit's heart began to hammer in her chest. She said nothing, could think of no words, as he pulled into the parking lot of the coastal state park south of Marina del Mar. Miraculously, on this Saturday afternoon, he found a spot to one side, overlooking the water, and parked. He shifted in his seat and turned to look at her.

She could see this wasn't coming easily to him. The ever calm Miguel de los Reyes had one hand curled into a fist on his long-muscled thigh. He'd worn jeans today, and Kit had decided the moment she'd seen him this morning that they should only be sold to men who could wear them and look like this.

It took him a moment to speak. "Is it really just me, Kit? Is it just one way?"

"Miguel," she said on a harsh breath.

"It can't be, can it? Not when you can say my name—" he looked away and his voice dropped "—like that."

Oh, God. Kit realized she was trembling, tried to stop it, then gave up.

"No," she whispered. "It's not one way."

He let out a long breath, and his head lolled against the door frame, as if he'd been relieved of some great burden. "I didn't think it could be. Not us."

Something in the way he said it made her ask, "Us?"

His head came upright again. "We're too wary, aren't we? We wouldn't be even talking about this if the signals weren't going both ways. We'd be talking like a couple of old friends with a common goal."

He was right, she realized. With so much stacked against them, obstacles, past pain and sorrow, with two battered hearts locked away, it would have taken some pretty strong

mutual signals to get them this far. She thought of the courage
it had taken for him to be the first to open the door.

"It's ironic, isn't it?" he asked. "We both swore never to
care about anyone again, but—"

"But neither one of us is capable of getting involved with
anyone we don't care about," she finished when he faltered.
"I've been trying to deny it. Hide it. Think of all the reasons
it was impossible. Tell myself you would never—"

She broke off as the belated realization struck her that he
had, in essence, said that he did, indeed, want her. That he
had admitted he'd been wrestling as she had been. And then
he took her breath away again, as if he'd read her mind.

"Oh, I do, lady," he said with wry emphasis. "I've spent
more nights lately lying awake considering the merits of cold
showers than I care to think about."

Kit blushed furiously.

"I kept telling myself it wasn't what it was," he said.
"That all I was feeling was…I mean, you're my friend,
Anna's best friend—"

He stopped when her gaze shot to his face. She felt the
color in her cheeks drain away.

"Don't," he said. "I didn't mean that…that way. I don't
feel like… This is not…"

He stopped, clearly angry with himself and the fact that his
usual articulateness was failing him.

"I'm not neurotic about this," he finally blurted. "I don't
think this is a betrayal of her or something. But I loved her,
and in a way I always will."

"So will I," Kit said gently.

"But she's been dead a long time now. Even her folks told
me I'd been alone too long."

"They did?" Kit asked, startled.

He nodded. "They told me it was time to move on, that
Anna would hate it if I never let myself care for anybody
again." He grimaced. "As it turned out, I didn't let myself

at all. It just happened. I was busy telling myself it couldn't, then turned around and there it was.''

''It?'' she asked, thinking that for all his honesty, he was sure using a lot of unspecific pronouns.

''I never intended this.'' His expression turned rueful, and he shook his head. ''I found myself using this Robards thing as a reason to be with you, and at the same time a...''

''Buffer?'' she suggested, recalling her thoughts.

''Exactly. A way to convince myself it was only business.'' He sat up straight, turning to face the windshield, staring at the Pacific, beautifully blue on this sunny day. ''But in there today, I kept thinking about the risks you take just by being a cop—hell, just being alive—and how I'd feel if something happened to you.''

''Nothing's going to happen—''

''Stop it,'' he snapped, and his hands went to the steering wheel, clenching it until his knuckles were white. ''That's what Anna said. 'Nothing will ever happen to me, you'll be stuck with me until we're both old and gray,' she used to say.''

Kit felt moisture begin to well in her eyes and blinked rapidly. The last thing she wanted to do was cry. She watched as Miguel stared at his hands, then loosened them from the wheel.

''I didn't want this.'' He ground the words out. ''I didn't want to ever care enough to get hurt like that again. And then I thought about it happening to you, and I realized it was too late, that I already did.''

It was a raw, painful, amazing admission, and it shook Kit to the core. As much as she sometimes wished for this, she had never really thought about this aspect. She'd been too caught up in the impossibilities of their respective positions and too busy trying to convince herself it couldn't happen because of that to think about what it would mean on a personal level if it did happen. And as impossible as it seemed, it apparently had. The moment he'd admitted he felt it, too, her walls of self-protection had crumbled, and the feelings she'd been trying to keep barricaded behind them rushed out. At this moment, all the reasons this couldn't be didn't matter. What mattered was this man, his pain and his courage.

When she spoke, she chose her words very carefully, sensing what might depend on them.

"After Bobby was killed, I wanted to quit. To give up everything. To run and hide some safe place where the worst thing a cop had to do was direct traffic. But when Anna died, I realized that civilian life was just as cruel, that there were no safe places, not really. Life is a risk, Miguel. Living it is the biggest risk of all."

There was a long, silent moment when he did nothing but stare at the ocean. Then, softly, he said, "You're so much braver than I am, Kit. You faced reality. You went out and tried again, which is more than I ever had the guts to do. I hid from it."

"No," she said emphatically. "It wasn't bravery. I just had no place to hide. Oh, my work kept me occupied, but it wasn't consuming. It wasn't anything like trying to save Trinity West. If I'd had that to deal with, I would have welcomed it. Welcomed the chance to bury myself in it so deeply that I couldn't be found. And I'm not sure I'd have ever come out."

He looked at her, his gray eyes soft with wonder and something more, something warm that conversely made her shiver.

"You're young to be so wise."

She grimaced. "Who was it who said it's easier to be wise for someone else than for yourself?"

He smiled, and she felt pleased at that small victory. She sensed some of the tension leaving him, and hers eased a little.

"I'm not sure either of us is particularly wise to be thinking about this," he said.

"It is," Kit agreed, "one of the larger cans of worms I've ever seen."

"I'd hate to lose your friendship," he said.

She was touched that, of all the problems they faced, that was of first importance to him. "That's mutual," she said softly.

"I've been hiding behind my work for a long time," he said. "You're the only woman who's ever made me want to change that."

"Thank you," she said, so moved by the depth of the compliment she couldn't think of any more to say.

He tapped a finger on the steering wheel. "So now what?"

She sighed. "We're both too old to go blundering into this blindly without even talking about it, like a couple of kids, pretending we don't know the consequences."

"So I guess we have two choices. We walk away from this and go on as before, or we..."

"Keep our eyes open and jump into the fire?"

He closed his eyes and leaned his head back, and she thought she saw a shudder sweep through him. "It is that, isn't it? Pure fire."

His words, the simple admission he felt it as she did, hot and intense and urgent, caused a rush of reaction in Kit unlike anything she'd ever felt. She closed her eyes, as if that could hold it back. It was futile. Sensation burst within her, hot and cold at the same time, careening around until it pooled low and deep and filled her with a hollow ache. This was a hunger that was new to her, a hunger she'd never known herself capable of.

Until Miguel de los Reyes had kissed her and changed her world.

She heard him move and opened her eyes. He'd turned toward her and was looking at her with an intensity that told her what was showing in her face—no doubt every feeling that had just flooded her.

He reached for her. She moved instantly, instinctively, sparing a fraction of a second to be grateful his car had a bench seat. And then she was in his arms, and they were strong and tight around her, but they were nothing compared to the feel of his mouth on hers, hungry, tasting, probing as if she was the last meal of a dying man.

Or the first of a man come back to life.

It was her last coherent thought as pure fire enveloped her. She gripped his shoulders, not to hold him off but to pull herself closer. When he probed past her lips she met him welcomingly, eagerly. And when he shuddered as their tongues brushed, she rejoiced. She reveled in the low groan of pleasure she dragged from him and barely recognized the faint whimper she heard as her own. She tasted him as deeply as he tasted her, moved against him in the same instant he slid one arm around her to hold her more tightly. Her breasts pressed against the solid wall of his chest while her nipples tightened and rose, and she helplessly moved against him to ease the ache.

She heard him make a sound that was half groan, half gasp. And then, without realizing quite how it had happened, she was stretched out on the seat with his heavy, welcome weight atop her. He cupped her face, moved her head slightly so he could deepen the kiss until she felt nothing but him, until he was her only anchor in a world threatening to rapidly spin away.

She reached for him, felt the heavy, dark silk of his hair sliding over her fingers. She traced the strong, uncompromising line of his jaw, then the high, aristocratic cheekbones. As she did, her fingers brushed his ear, and she felt him shiver. She did it again, lightly, following the curve. He moved sharply, almost convulsively, grasping her shoulders as if to hang on while he pressed himself into her.

She felt the rigid proof of everything he'd confessed to digging into her belly. He was hot and hard and hungry, and she exulted in knowing it was for her. All the warnings she'd been chanting for days were charred to ash by his heat and the fire he set in her.

His hand slipped down to cup her breast, and she lifted herself to him, longing for that touch. She'd been so cold inside for so long, and she hadn't realized it until he'd given her his heat. She whispered a silent prayer that it was the same for him, that this heat was melting the ice that had encased his heart. And then she couldn't think at all as his thumb rubbed over the taut peak of her breast and she cried out as fire shot through her again.

She arched her hips, loving the feel of him against her, full and erect. She wanted to feel more, wanted to be rid of the barriers between them, wanted to touch him, to caress the rigid length of him. She wanted to feel him sliding into her, filling her, filling that empty place, wanted it as desperately as if she knew only he could end that hollow ache.

She moved her hands down his back, encountered the shocking heat of bare skin and realized his shirt had pulled free of his jeans. She tugged at it, wanting nothing more than to feel that skin, to stroke the sleek smoothness of it. The cloth came free and she moved quickly, urgently.

At the first sliding caress of her hands over his back, he arched into her and gave a low, guttural sound. She took the sound into her mouth as if it was tangible, some sweet, palpable evidence that he was as lost in this as she was, that she hadn't been crazy to think of this all this time, that he'd been right, the signals had been mutual.

When her stroking fingers reached a circular ridge of raised tissue and she realized it was a scar from when he'd been shot, she wanted to hold him closer, to treasure the fact that he'd survived, that he was alive and in her arms.

Miguel went suddenly still. And he broke off the kiss, as if her touching the scar reminded him of everything they'd both put out of their heads in these mindless moments.

Slowly he sat up, his normal grace hampered by the confines of the car. Kit smothered the whimper that rose to her lips, knowing it would come out sounding pathetically bereft. He shifted his long legs restlessly, as if he couldn't find the right place for them. It had been so long for her that it took her a moment to realize why he was uncomfortable. The moment she did, a shaft of heat arrowed through her anew as she remembered how fully aroused he'd been.

"I'm too old—and too tall—for this," he muttered, staring at the bright orange sun as it began its journey to the horizon.

Glad his first words hadn't been regrets or some reference to how crazy this was, Kit made an effort to match his wry humor. "Not to mention it's still light out, and we're in a very public place."

He cringed, and she hoped it was exaggerated for effect. "Don't remind me."

"Maybe we should go somewhere else," she said. "We could stop at the market and I could fix dinner or something."

He looked at her. "If we go to your place right now," he said slowly, "there's every chance we'll skip dinner and go straight to the *or something*."

Kit's heart leaped in her chest. She took a deep breath before saying softly, "I know."

"Do you also know how insane this is?"

"Yes. I also know how rare this is."

His jaw tightened before he said, "So do I. Why do you think it's so damned hard to walk away, even though every ounce of common sense I have is screaming at me to do just that?"

"Are you going to? Walk away?"

"Maybe I should be asking you that."

"My common sense is screaming, too. I'll bet there isn't a reason you've thought of for why this is insane that I haven't thought of, too. More, probably, given that some peo-

ple will think I'm trying to sleep my way up the ranks, while
you—''

"While my reputation is enhanced in some quarters? I
know that, Kit. I hate it, but I know it's true. Just like I know
historically it's the woman who pays the higher price.''

They sat looking at each other, all the reasons they both
knew hanging tacitly between them. But what filled the small
space of his car was the memory of the kiss, the heat of it,
the sweetness of it, like the joy of coming home at last after
a long, painful trip over a lonely sea.

"Do we risk it?'' Miguel asked quietly. "Is it worth it,
Kit? To you?''

He said it as if his answer to the question was a given, and
that made a little thrill shoot through her. For a long moment
she looked at him, realizing how different this was. She'd
loved Bobby, but he'd been barely more than a boy when
they'd gotten engaged. Miguel was a man, a man who knew
the cost of caring for someone, a man with the wisdom to
know this was not something they could easily toss aside if
it didn't work. Miguel de los Reyes would never be swept
away by his own wants. He would always be aware there
were someone else's feelings and emotions to consider. He
was one of the strongest men Kit had ever known, and it was
that strength that let him be gentle when it was called for,
gentle and caring the way only a truly strong man can be.

"I know all the reasons I should say no,'' she said softly.
"I've been living with them twenty-four hours a day. But
now maybe I should look at all the reasons to say yes.''

He swallowed and said tightly, "Such as?''

"The man you are. How I feel about you. The fact that I
know you would walk away if I said no.''

He looked moved by her first words, but his eyes narrowed,
in the way of a man who has just been reminded some of his
brother males don't always play by the rules that should be

inviolate. Kit saw the look, acknowledged it and went on with her list, feeling somehow it needed to be said.

"That we've both been alone so very long. How amazing it is that this has happened at all, considering who and where we are. But most of all because it feels too strong, too right to just throw away."

Miguel uttered an oath, low and heartfelt, and pulled her into his arms. "Thank God," he whispered against her hair. "I thought you were going to talk us both out of it."

"We may wish I had."

"I have a feeling we'd regret it more."

Kit agreed.

"So where's that market?" he asked.

Kit blinked, startled. "I... You want dinner after all?"

He gave her a sideways look that could have melted stone. "Just after," he said.

Kit felt color flaring in her cheeks. But eagerness flashed along her nerves, and when he started the car she hoped he was in as big a hurry as she was.

He was.

Chapter 16

"You are," Kit said frankly, "the most beautiful man I've ever seen."

"With all these scars?" The golden bronze of his skin usually protected him from visible blushing, but she was pleased to see color tinge his cheeks. "I'll get you a subscription to one of those women's magazines so you'll know better."

"The scars are probably the most beautiful, because they're a badge of honor, of survival. And I know perfectly well. I'm a trained observer, remember?"

"So am I," he said softly. "And I've never observed anything more beautiful than you."

She supposed the words were typical for a first time, but that it was she and Miguel made them ring heartfelt and true. That's what happened when it was for real, she thought. It made standing naked together for the first time not awkward but intense, made her tremble with the knowledge of what was to come, that soon this beautiful, masculine body would become part of her in a way that would leave her forever changed.

She felt a last-minute frisson of anxiety, wondering if perhaps the risk truly was too great. But then Miguel touched her, and she knew this was worth any risk.

To her surprise he cupped her face rather than touching her body. When he looked at her, the intensity of his gaze made her tremble.

"You'll have to help me, Kit. Show me what you want, what you like. I'm a bit…rusty."

"We'll learn together," she said.

"And your arm. I'll be careful—"

"I barely feel it anymore. And when you touch me it doesn't hurt at all."

Then she took his hand and put it to her breast. His eyes closed, he rocked backward slightly and an audible breath escaped him. Then his fingers flexed, just barely, as if he wanted more but was uncertain. She pressed herself into his hand to urge him to take what he wanted.

He cupped her soft flesh, lifting and gently squeezing. Then he moved his other hand to her other breast to do the same, and she moaned softly with the pleasure of his hands on her. She glanced at his face and saw that his eyes had opened, that he was staring. She followed the direction of his gaze, and the sight of his hands, of his long, strong fingers dark against her pale skin, sent a shiver of delight through her that she didn't try to hide.

He whispered her name, and her gaze shifted to his face. She stared at those thickly lashed light gray eyes, hoping he truly could see her soul, because right now her entire being was focused on him and the fire he was kindling in her.

And then his fingers moved, his thumbs slipping up to rub her already taut nipples. Sensation, hot and jolting, shot through her, and she cried out. He caught the flesh he'd aroused between his fingers and plucked gently, then harder when she arched her back.

She wasn't sure how they got to the bed. Maybe they'd

both simply fallen. She could believe that—she'd never felt so weak in the knees. Nor had she ever felt so ready, and when he continued to slowly stroke and caress her, she wanted to scream at him to hurry.

"Please," she finally whispered, unable to form more than the one coherent word.

"Not yet," he said. "Because once I'm inside you, I can't promise I'll be able to last."

"I won't last if you don't, now," she urged.

But he wouldn't be hurried, even when his fingers probed the nest of golden curls between her thighs and found her wet and slick and ready. Instead he began to caress her there, slowly, gently. Her hips moved involuntarily, and he increased the pressure, as if he'd been testing to see how much she wanted.

Kit reached for him, hungry to touch what she'd only seen. Her hands slid down his rib cage, over the scars on his back, then the one on his thigh, caressing, showing him with a loving touch what she thought of those marks of honor. Then she moved her hand to his hip, but there she hesitated. He moved slightly, to tilt his body to give her access, a silent encouragement she understood and welcomed joyously. He shivered as her hand slid over his lower belly and groaned when her fingers curled around hot, erect flesh.

She nearly groaned. He was so smooth, so beautiful, more than she'd ever expected, and she was going to take that heavy, hard maleness deep inside her until he would never be fully gone from her again.

A harsh breath escaped him as she stroked his length. His hands continued to move on her, and he changed the caress to a circular movement that was gradually more intense, until she cried out at the sudden convulsion that rippled through her, making her body undulate helplessly.

Only then did he give her respite, and only long enough to fumble with one of the foil packets he'd dumped on the nightstand. She nearly sobbed at even that short absence, and when he came back to her, easing himself between her legs, she lifted them and enclosed him.

He groaned as the movement brought her heated flesh in contact with his. She stroked herself against him needily, and he groaned again, a louder, more helpless sound that made her a little dizzy with a sense of feminine power she'd never experienced before.

If it was not Miguel, she would not feel this, she realized. He was so much man, he'd been through so much, had been forced to be stronger than any other man she knew in so many ways. That was what made this precious, the fact that he would entrust himself to her like this, that he would let himself become so vulnerable in her arms.

And when he at last moved to join them, she gave a tiny cry of joy. It had been so long, and she had never expected to want like this, need like this, and had never, ever expected to find the answer to those wants and needs with this man.

He slid into her, his way eased by her readiness, yet he stretched her until she was moaning at the exquisite fullness. Then he was in her to the hilt, and she heard him say her name as if it had been torn from him, as if it was the only word he could think of to say what he was feeling.

And then he was moving, and she had no choice but to move with him. Their rhythm was not practiced or smooth, but it was urgent and swift and deep, and it didn't matter. He groaned at the depth of each stroke, and she gasped each time he withdrew and plunged into her again.

She knew he'd been afraid he would be too quick for her, after all that time. She didn't care. This was enough, more than enough, for now. Then she felt him go rigid, heard him cry out her name in a voice she'd never heard, never thought to hear from him, a voice tinged with wonder and awe.

His body arched, driving him hard into her, and he threw his head back as he shuddered. Kit stared at him, at the muscles standing out in stark relief, at the beauty of his body, aristocratic features drawn taut with passion. In that moment nothing existed in her world but him, and when he shuddered again, and she felt the pulse of him hot and deep within her, it hit her unexpectedly. Her body clenched suddenly, violently, and an explosion of sensation clawed at her. She clawed at him in turn, felt his arms come around her, holding her tight and close as she spasmed, until she felt only him and the harsh pant of his gasping breaths against her skin.

Miguel slept well past his normal waking time, although since that was usually four o'clock, it was still early for a Sunday. What surprised him was how natural it felt, awakening slowly, feeling Kit's soft warmth beside him. Even that he was in a different place didn't seem odd or disconcerting. It was Kit's bed, her home, and he felt utterly welcome in both.

Almost as welcome as he'd felt in her body, he thought, suppressing a shudder as heat rushed through him at the thought. In one passionate night, she'd seared away all the long, lonely years, and the change from the empty sameness he'd awakened to for all that time to this sated, drowsy contentment seemed nothing less than a miracle.

He watched her sleep, snuggled close, and felt a tenderness he'd thought himself incapable of feeling anymore. And when he looked at the bandages that covered the healing slice on her arm, he felt a qualm of fear for her. On some deep level it still scared him, but he couldn't find it in him to care. Not this morning, not as he lay here utterly satiated, not after the night they'd spent.

It had been, he thought, a unique experience. Neither of them had been kids fumbling blindly, but it had been so long for both of them it had seemed new and special and inordinately right, and while he knew they'd face huge problems eventually, right now he was happier than he could remember being in a very long time.

Not to mention drained, he thought, smiling into the morning light. He tried to avoid comparisons, but he supposed they were inevitable. Anna had been quietly, almost shyly giving and loving in all areas of her life, including bed. Kit was…Kit. She was vital, alive, determined and by turns generous and demanding. Once they'd decided, she wasn't shy about showing him she wanted him, and he'd found that more arousing than he would have thought; he'd never been so out of control as he'd been with her.

Time and again they'd come together, and each time there was something new and different. Anna had always wanted gentleness. Kit wanted it, too, but there were times when she wanted a little wildness, as well, and that realization had cut loose some tight restraint deep within him, and he'd responded so fiercely, and she had answered his need so perfectly, he was amazed they weren't both carrying marks.

Maybe we are, he thought ruefully.

Kit stirred in his arms, then raised her head. Her lashes lifted, and she gave him a sleepy-eyed smile that made his chest tighten.

"Hi," she said simply.

"Hi."

"Mmm," she murmured, snuggling closer. "This feels good."

"Everything since we hit your front door has felt good," he said.

Kit smiled and hugged him, and he wondered if she, too, was remembering the trail of discarded clothes they'd left across her living room, pausing only long enough to set down the groceries they'd bought. He'd barely remembered to grab the small bag from the drug store and take it into the bedroom. It had taken him nearly as long to make his purchase as it had taken her to buy food. The last time he'd bought condoms there weren't nearly so many choices.

Her stomach growled, a decidedly unladylike declaration of hunger. She looked startled, then laughed. That was Kit, too, he thought, laughing where others might be embarrassed.

"We never did have dinner, did we?" he said.

"Did you miss it?"

"Hardly," he retorted, seeing her teasing for what it was. He grabbed her and rolled over, settling himself on top of her. She shifted to make it easier for him, and that little sign of welcome nearly broke loose the flood of tenderness he'd been feeling.

This time, in the soft light of morning, it was slow and sweet and gentle, a dance of slight moves and tiny sighs, of slow rocking and a gradual building, until they were clinging tightly together, moving as one, when the rising swell of pleasure took them both.

And afterward, when she smiled at him, Miguel thought he'd never seen anything so beautiful. And when she rather plaintively asked if they could eat *now,* he burst out laughing. This was new to him, such lightheartedness in bed, and he found he liked it very much.

"I suppose you do need feeding," he said.

"I do," she confirmed, another growl of her stomach perfectly timed for emphasis. "Otherwise I could end up nibbling on you."

It was a moment before he could get past the images that comment brought to mind. "Now that idea has potential."

She didn't blush, and he knew when she winked at him that he'd walked right into her trap. He didn't care. The idea of her following up on the promise of that wink was making him heat up again. Then she sat up, the covers falling away, baring the soft, full curves of her breasts, and the sight chased everything else out of his mind.

"Food," she insisted, and he guessed his thoughts were showing clearly in his face.

"Okay, food. First."

"Is this bribery?" she teased.

"It'll be extortion soon," he warned, "if you don't put something on."

She laughed, and from a clothes tree at the foot of the bed grabbed a silky-looking robe that he didn't think was going to help much.

She was halfway through the door, and he had sat up and reached for his jeans, when she stopped dead.

"Extortion," he heard her whisper.

"What?" he asked as he pulled his jeans on, not bothering to snap them.

She turned, and he saw that her eyes were wide with a look that told him she was onto something.

"Extortion," she said again.

"I was only joking," he said, uncertain what she meant.

"No, it's not that—"

She stopped suddenly, and Miguel crossed the room to her. "Then what?"

She shook her head. "I need to think about this. It could be nothing. Let's eat first."

She moved off without a backward glance, and after a moment Miguel followed her to the kitchen. He supposed this was part of the price of her intensity and focus. Sometimes she just…went away. A small price when it meant he was sometimes the recipient of that intensity. Like last night, he thought as he watched the movement of her body beneath the silken fabric of the robe.

Although neither of them had any problem with the idea of dinner for breakfast—both had spent enough time working graveyard that their concept of time had become very fluid— they decided that the menu they'd worked out was a bit much to face at seven. So the steak and trimmings became smaller portions of steak and eggs.

It wasn't until they'd finished that Kit gave him a grateful look. "Thanks for just letting me work through this."

He nodded. "So is it nothing? Or something?"

"I think it's something. Maybe a big something."

He trusted her instincts and knew she wouldn't say that lightly. He stood, gathered the plates and carried them to the sink. On his way back he picked up the coffeepot, filled both their cups, returned the pot to the brewer and sat.

"Okay, let's have it."

"Let me do it step by step."

He nodded.

"When I went to see Jaime's brother at the honor ranch, he said something in passing. I didn't think anything of it, since it's the kind of thing we hear all the time from kids in trouble."

"Said what?"

"That cops just like to beat on people, beat them or rip them off."

"Yeah," Miguel agreed, "there's nothing new there. Choker was spouting the same old song."

"Exactly. What did he say? That cops shake them down for no reason all the time just because they've got the power?"

"Pretty much." Miguel took a sip of hot coffee, thinking he could get used to this, drinkable coffee in the morning, across the table from Kit, with her hair still tousled from his hands and her mouth still swollen from his kisses. "It's the standard gang defense, you know that."

"Yes, it is. Mako said something like that, too, that the cops were always hassling him or shaking him down. But it occurred to me that there's more than one meaning to the phrase 'shakedown.' That in addition to stopping and searching somebody, it also means—"

It hit him then. He set down his mug abruptly, making the coffee slosh. "Extortion?"

She nodded.

"Kit," he began, giving a half shake of his head.

"I know, I know. But when you said that this morning, I remembered something one of the kids with Mako said. I was so focused on Mako I didn't think of it until now, but he asked me if I was going to take over the racket now."

Miguel drew back slightly. "The racket?"

"That's the word he used. Among other less charming epithets."

He could imagine, and again felt the churning of his stomach at the thought of her in danger. He barely restrained himself from looking at her forearm, at the cut she'd gotten in her tussle with Mako. He made himself go on.

"So," he began slowly, "you think Robards was...is shaking these gang kids down for money?"

"I know it's a stretch, a big jump. It sounds crazy, and there isn't any real evidence. And I'd never believe it of anybody else, but..."

"It sounds just like Robards."

She nodded. "And my gut is yelling about this. It keeps coming up. Martin, Mako, Mako's pal, Choker. Maybe I was listening but not really hearing."

He had a great deal of respect for Kit Walker's gut feelings. But he also knew there was no profit in ignoring the reality of life. "Finding proof could be difficult."

"It could be impossible," she said flatly. "If he's got those gangsters, most of whom don't even go to the bathroom without a piece, intimidated enough to be calling him boss and paying him off, they're not likely to roll over on him."

"Especially if he killed Jaime Rivas to make his point."

Her eyes widened, and he realized she hadn't yet made that jump. "My God," she whispered.

"It would have been the perfect setup. He picks somebody

who doesn't belong to a gang so that when he kills him, he doesn't have the homies coming after him.''

"But they still all know it could happen to them if they don't pay up," she said, sounding stunned. He guessed she'd only thought she'd found a way to help take Robards down, not that she might have come across the answer to the Rivas case, as well. "So it's really true?" she asked, looking across the table at him.

"It all fits. We can't prove anything, maybe won't ever be able to, but it all fits.''

"Then he killed El Tigre, too, because he saw him kill Jaime. Those burns really were from him.''

"Stands to reason. If the rest is true, then Robards is our fatheaded killer in the ski mask.''

They'd been heading toward this revelation for days, but it was still a shock. And they didn't have a shred of solid proof that would stand up in court. All they had was supposition and hearsay.

"So now what?" she asked.

He took his mug and took a long, deep swallow, willing the caffeine to hit hard and fast.

"I want him out, and I want him out now," he said flatly.

"But we don't have anything concrete.''

"I know. But with what Choker gave us, I have enough to give me some leverage. I'll bluff a bit if I have to. And if he won't go quietly, I'll start an internal investigation the likes of which Trinity West has never seen.''

"Maybe you should wait, give me a chance to look into this shakedown thing. Maybe I can find somebody who'll talk. Maybe somebody already has and I can find who they talked to and backtrack.''

"Even if you could, it wouldn't be a lock. He's picked the perfect extortion victims, gang members who aren't about to file a complaint.''

She grimaced, then reluctantly agreed. "And probably wouldn't be believed if they did."

"Exactly." He shook his head. "I'm surprised they haven't taken him out themselves."

"That's why he sticks to the young ones, the ones he can intimidate," Kit said. "And he's got about an even chance they won't survive to grow up."

It was, Miguel knew, painfully true. "But the ones that do, why haven't they gone after him?"

She gave him a long, considering look. "I think you're underestimating the reputation of Trinity West. Since you turned things around, not even the adults want to risk the heat killing a cop would bring down on them."

The simple declaration warmed him more than the coffee could.

"Especially after The Pack went down," Kit added. "Quisto tells me the word on the street is that if the Pack couldn't stand up to Trinity West, the rest of them better walk carefully."

"Thank Ryan for that, then. He did it."

"But him going in deep cover like that was your idea."

"And I regretted it a hundred times," he said wryly. "We almost lost him."

"But we didn't. He came through, and he brought down Alarico and his henchmen. And the ripples from that have reached even to the street kids."

"So in effect we've made it possible for Robards to run this little operation of his by making the gangsters afraid to take him out," Miguel said wearily. "Talk about a mixed blessing."

"Only because Robards is around."

"Yes." He shook off the weariness any discussion of the man seemed to bring on in him. "That's why I want him gone now. We'll keep looking for more, but I'm not going to put it off any longer. It's time to confront the devil."

"All right. We'll just have to lay it out for him—"

"*We* won't be doing anything. *I* will."

"What?"

"I'm the chief. It's my responsibility. And it's me he's after in the end, so it's up to me to stop him."

"But I—"

"No, Kit. I don't want you there. I may have to say some things I'd rather you didn't hear. And I don't want you having to testify later, if it should come to that."

He also didn't want her there to draw any of Robards's fire, although he knew he couldn't tell her that. And he was afraid of what he might do. If he lost it and clobbered the guy, he didn't want her there to witness it.

"I have to do this alone, Kit," he said when he saw she was still looking doubtful. "I'm not trying to keep you out of this just for your sake, but mine, too."

She didn't look happy, but she nodded. "But I'll be close at hand," she insisted.

He smiled and gave her a small nod. "Like I said, you're the best backup around."

Her mouth twisted, then softened with concern. "Maybe you should do it today," she said. "At least he wouldn't have any backup of his own handy on a Sunday."

"That's just why I can't," he said. "I don't want him to have that to throw at me, that I didn't have the guts to face him except alone, that I'm afraid of all the support he has at Trinity West. He's threatened more than once to mutiny, in effect."

She drew back slightly. "You don't believe that, do you? That he has enough support to really challenge you?"

"He's got enough to make it damn ugly," Miguel said sourly. "And they all know their parts, everything from accusations of incompetence to favoritism to age discrimination. For them it would be like storming the Bastille."

"They've already come to you?"

He nodded. "At one time or another since I took over. I wondered if maybe they weren't laying the groundwork. To get rid of the greaser, as Robards so eloquently put it."

"Bastard," Kit said, the epithet made more potent by the soft but fierce voice she used and the fact that she so rarely swore.

"Thank you," he said quietly, meaning it. Her instant, passionate summation meant a great deal to him.

"It's the truth," she said. "So. Monday?"

He nodded, then drained the last of his coffee. "Monday. I've got a meeting first thing, but definitely before lunch."

"All right. That gives me today to look into this. I'll just clean up the dishes first."

His gaze shot to her face, and she stopped in the act of getting to her feet. "I was hoping we could find...something else to do today."

She sank into her chair, her eyes widening, and a second later her lips parted, as if she suddenly couldn't get enough air. He knew the feeling.

"We'll do that first," she finally whispered.

The dishes didn't get done until much later.

Chapter 17

Ugly hadn't been a strong enough word, Miguel thought. Robards had been on a roll since he'd strolled into the office in that swaggering waddle of his. And he'd taken his sweet time getting here, one of his usual ploys to show he wasn't impressed by Miguel or his rank.

Miguel been restless all morning, since he'd sent the message to Robards that he wanted to see him before noon. His mind kept bouncing between sweet, hot memories of Kit and thoughts of the upcoming confrontation. The roller coaster ride had been wearing, at best.

He knew there were things he and Kit needed to talk about, things they needed to settle, things they had to decide how to deal with, but neither of them could get past this thing hanging over them. By tacit agreement they'd concentrated on this alone, with him outlining his battle plan while Kit was out pounding the pavement again, looking for anything to support the extortion theory, the only slim chance they had to nail Robards on a criminal charge.

Rosa had been watching Miguel closely, as if she sensed something was up, but she was nothing if not discreet, and she held back any questions.

After Robards's arrival Miguel had gone to close the office door and leaned out to tell Rosa to hold any calls except from Detective Walker. Rosa had smiled at the mention of Kit's name, making Miguel wonder if she knew something. Then her quick, alert eyes had darted from Robards, his bulky figure lolling with studied casualness in a chair opposite his desk, to Miguel. Her brows rose, and her eyes lit up.

"Finally," he heard her mutter.

It was the last supportive word he'd heard. Robards was building up a real head of steam.

"You think you can accuse me—*me*—of murder and get away with it? Not on your miserable life!"

Miguel leaned back and watched the heavy jowls redden as Robards's fury rose. Maybe he'd have a stroke and keel over right here, putting an end to it all. It wouldn't be the first time hatred had turned on a man like this.

"Interesting," he observed mildly, knowing nothing infuriated a man like Robards more than the target of his anger remaining calm and unimpressed. "I don't recall anyone accusing you. Why would you assume that's what I meant when I asked what happened between you and Jaime Rivas that night?"

"You can take your fancy words, twisting what a man says, and your college degree and shove them. I knew something was up, should have figured you were behind it."

Robards spat out the words, and tobacco-stained saliva sprayed out. Miguel reached into his pocket, took out a handkerchief and, with a distaste he didn't bother to hide, wiped the glass on his desk. The action, as he had intended, added fuel to the flame.

"You're done for here, I'll see to that! And don't think I

can't do it. There's a whole lot of us who are sick of you and your foreign ways.''

"Last time I looked, that degree on the wall said UCLA," Miguel observed, "and that's still in California, I believe."

Robards swore, low and crude. "Uppity smart ass, that's all you ever were." He got to his feet. "I'm getting out of here."

"Sit down."

"Go to hell. And if you're recording me, I'll say it louder."

"No recording. This is—for now—off the record."

"Because you don't know anything and you can't prove anything."

"I know more than you can imagine, Kenneth," he said, knowing his use of the man's first name would infuriate him further, maybe push him closer to an incautious statement or two. "For instance, I know you've orchestrated the string of complaints from your cronies with an eye toward my dismissal. Unfortunately for you, the mayor and city manager know it, too. And they're not putting much credence in what are clearly groundless charges."

Anger flickered in the flat brown eyes. "We'll see how a hearing goes on that."

"You may try, of course. It is your right to a public hearing. But then, naturally, the Rivas case will have to come out."

"You'd never do that. You haven't got enough guts to go after a real man."

He has no idea what kind of man you are. And that's going to cost him. Kit's words, soft and fervent, came to Miguel, and he smiled. It seemed to infuriate Robards, and his voice rose.

"Even if you did," he declared, "not only can you not prove a damned thing, but the *real* cops on the force will desert you in droves. I'll propose a vote of no confidence, and they'll back me to a man."

Miguel didn't react. If he didn't have the backing of his people by now, he never would. Instead he leaned back in his chair as if this was no more than a friendly conversation.

"Sit down," he said again, "while I run through a list."

Warily, and clearly unwillingly, Robards took his seat once more. Miguel was certain it was only to find out how much he knew.

"Carmela Rivas," Miguel began, "who will provide proof her son was never a gang member. Martin Rivas, who will not only verify his brother wasn't in a gang, but will swear that he was murdered by a cop. A kid named Mako, who saw you a block away right before Jaime was murdered—"

"You think any sane jury would take the word of—"

"Shut up," Miguel snapped, and Robards blinked in surprise and subsided. "A witness who saw you beat an unarmed, innocent kid to death, then was conveniently murdered himself. But not before he told his story."

"Hearsay, and from a gang member," Robards snarled. "You aren't going to get far with that, Mex."

"Cuban, actually," Miguel said smoothly, then went on as if the interruption had never happened. "And then there's the matter of the missing supplemental filed by Officer Welton."

For the first time concern flickered in Robards's reddened face. But he hid it quickly. "Don't know a thing about any missing report, so I guess it's your word against mine."

"No, it's your word against Welton's. Who, by the way, is now nicely out of your reach and will be more than happy to testify about that night, including how you told him to keep his mouth shut and never bothered to call the paramedics. How do you think that will go over? Of course, you already knew he was dead because you'd made sure of it. Just like you made sure you handled the scene yourself and wrote all the reports so nothing could point to anything but a gang hit."

"You're full of it." The chair creaked as Robards shifted

his weight, and Miguel knew he was getting nervous. He pressed the advantage.

"For that matter, isn't it coincidental that the entire Rivas file seems to be missing, when you were the last one with it?"

"That bitch!" Fury flashed in the flat brown eyes again. "I knew she started this! So she did run to you. She spreading her legs for you? Is that what this is all about?"

Miguel stared at the man. He kept his hands pressed to his desktop, ordering himself not to lose contact with it, knowing it was the only way he could keep himself from wrapping his fingers around the pudgy throat and squeezing until Robards's face matched his spotted blue tie. He almost shook with the rage that filled him, and it took every bit of self-mastery he'd ever learned in an unfair world to keep it from showing.

"I suggest," he said carefully, "that in your precarious position, you refrain from personal attacks on anyone."

Perhaps he hadn't been entirely successful in concealing his wrath, because Robards abandoned that tack.

"I don't know what you're talking about," he said. "Must have been misfiled. You know how those girls in records are, too busy filing their nails to pay attention to their jobs."

"Isn't it just convenient, then, that Detective Walker made a copy of every page of that report before it was…lost."

Robards swore, crudely, viciously. He owed, Miguel thought grimly, an apology to everybody in Trinity West for not ridding them of this evil affliction sooner. He was in control and went on as if the detour hadn't occurred.

"And then there's the car, which was stolen to perpetrate that second murder and was conveniently marked by the thief. Marked with burns from his disgusting cigars." Robards's teeth clenched on the stub between his yellowed teeth. "You know, they found some ash residue in the car that night. It's on its way to be analyzed. Want to bet it will match those stogies of yours?"

"Circumstantial," Robards blurted, but he was truly nervous, Miguel could smell it. And apparently, Robards couldn't smell a bluff. The Marina del Mar officer who'd found Choker's car hadn't been at all interested in those burn marks, other than noting them on his report. But Miguel was betting Robards didn't know that.

"Perhaps," Miguel said, knowing it was time to take the gloves off. Time to let off some of that pressure. The words came out like machine-gun fire. "But it's more than enough to open an internal investigation that will make your life a living hell. That's your choice, Robards. Retire gracefully while you have the chance or face every dark, evil corner of your twisted mind being dragged into the sun for the world to see."

"Who the *hell* do you think you are? I was a cop when you were still dancing around a sombrero—"

"I'm the man who's going to take you down, who's going to expose you for the vicious, bigoted, racist, misogynistic slime you are, unless you make the choice you don't deserve to get."

"You'll never get away with this! I've got thirty years on this force. Nobody will ever take the word of a bunch of street punks and Mexicans over mine."

"Don't count on it. Carmela Rivas alone will make a powerful witness. And I'll call in every favor owed to me to make sure your name and face are splattered over every paper in the state, along with a full list of the charges against you."

Robards sputtered. Miguel ignored him.

"Even if you're exonerated for lack of evidence, you'll never wash it away. You'll be like a child molester, looking for a place to hide and never finding it. You'll never work in law enforcement again, and if you try to get a private cop job, I'll do my damnedest to stop you. And you'll find my damnedest is pretty damn good."

Robards turned so red-faced Miguel wondered if that stroke

wasn't a very real possibility. He swore, a long string of crude words and slurs that lost their impact after the first few. Miguel leaned forward.

"It's over, Robards. There's no room for your methods and attitudes at Trinity West. There's no room for you."

"You stinking *bastard!*" Robards leaped to his feet.

"Is that your choice?"

"You're damned right it is! I'll fight you to the end, and you'll be the one left in the dirt, where your kind belongs."

"Last chance," Miguel said. "Take the retirement and run."

Robards spat intentionally, then walked over and yanked open the office door. "I'll have your fucking badge for this, you spic bastard!"

If I lose this fight, you're welcome to it, Miguel thought.

Still looking at him, Robards roared on. "I'll have that vote of no confidence done before you can—"

"Not at Trinity West, you won't."

The voice cutting Robards off came from his anteroom. And he knew that voice, knew it so well. He'd heard it bright with laughter, he'd heard it solemn with sorrow, he'd heard it husky with passion.

And now he heard it deadly with intent. Kit.

Robards stopped dead in the doorway, staring into the other room as if poleaxed. Miguel got to his feet, brow furrowing.

"You think you've won, don't you, bitch?" Robards shouted. Miguel moved from behind his desk in a rush.

"It's over, Lieutenant."

Cruz's voice, strong and clear. Miguel crossed his office in two long strides as Ryan Buckhart's voice rang out, heavy with the menace he could project so well.

"Two can play your game, white man. The only mutiny that's going to happen at Trinity West is against you. My wife will love the chance to tell the world the truth about you and what happened the night we took the Pack down."

Robards sputtered, for once too furious for words. Miguel stared into his anteroom. Not only Kit, Cruz and Ryan, but the entire detective division was there. Along with plain-clothes personnel and civilians. There was Betty, and near the front Rosa, pride beaming from her face. And there were uniforms sprinkled among them, Quisto Romero and several other patrol officers. In fact, it looked like almost the entire day watch was crammed into the crowded room.

The unprecedented show of total support stunned him. For a moment he had to look away, blinking rapidly. He didn't care if his people saw how moved he was, but he'd be damned if he'd let Robards see he'd ever doubted their support for a moment. He knew perfectly well who had pulled this all together, and he'd carry the image of Kit leading her small army to his rescue with him until the day he died.

"There's not a real cop in this whole damn room," Robards snarled. "You can all go straight to hell."

"I don't think so," Kit said. "But you'll be going straight to jail."

Robards laughed, and Miguel knew he wasn't imagining the agitated, almost frantic undertone. The man was on a crumbling edge. And then the sense of Kit's words hit him, and his gaze shot to her face. To his amazement, she winked at him. He knew she'd found something.

"You can't prove I ever touched that Rivas kid, and you know it. All you've got is hearsay and circumstantial, and I'll sue for false arrest and slander and own all of you."

"We know you killed him," Kit said with steady certainty. There was a stir among the ranks. She apparently hadn't had time to give them all the details when she'd gathered them to come here, no doubt guessing how the confrontation was going to go. "And we'll make sure the public knows what we know. But it isn't that that's going to take you down. It's that little racket of yours, your little shakedown scam."

Robards went very still.

"Funny thing. When all of us—" she gestured widely at the room full of officers "—pooled our knowledge, we had an amazing amount of information on somebody who'd been running shakedowns on young street kids for years. Must have been quite a nice living you were making off those kids in return for leaving them alone. How many burglaries and robberies do you suppose you caused, since that's the only way they had to make enough to keep you off their backs?"

"You can't prove any of this!"

"I think any jury will doubt that when we parade witness after witness through court, all of them identifying you."

"You think they're going to believe a bunch of—"

"Teachers?" Kit suggested. "We've got a couple of those. Counselors? One of those. How about a guy who runs his own construction business now?"

How had she done it? Miguel wondered. In just a few hours she'd scoured this up?

"And one," Kit went on almost gleefully, "who's about to graduate law school, inspired by you. He wants to wipe slime like you off the planet." Robards gaped at her. "You see, that's where you really messed up, with your tunnel vision. Some of these kids survive. And some of them make something of themselves. But they *all* remember you, and they'd all like nothing better than to put you where you put so many of their friends."

She had had, Miguel thought in amazement, a very busy morning. She was the most amazing woman he'd ever known.

"I wouldn't bet a nickel on you making a year inside," Cruz said cheerfully.

"Six months," Ryan countered, equally cheerful.

"How fitting that you're going to be defeated by your own prejudices," Kit said with a grimly satisfied smile. "You figured because you didn't care about one Hispanic kid, no one else would, either. But you were wrong. Again."

Kit smiled, her eyes alight with the fierce energy he'd always envied her. The odd thing was that, in this moment, with their gazes locked, it was as if she was giving some of that energy to him. He could almost feel it coursing through him.

"And I," Miguel said slowly, looking at Kit rather than the walruslike man before him, "can think of at least one very angry young man in a CYA camp who would be happy to spread the word that the cop who killed his brother for no reason other than to scare kids into paying up is inside now."

"And if you so much as try and wiggle out of this with that no-confidence vote," Kit said, her voice so sweet Miguel made a mental note to be wary if she ever turned that tone on him, "I'll help Ryan scalp you and all your dinosaur buddies."

Laughter rang out in the room. And being laughed at so publicly, by so many, was the last straw for Ken Robards. He moved sharply, his hand streaking to his side. To the plainclothes holster he wore.

The room erupted into action the instant he moved. Robards fumbled trying to get his small revolver from his too-tight belt. He was too late. A split second later, there were at least twenty weapons, including Kit's, cocked and aimed at him, and Ryan Buckhart's big knife was at his throat.

"To hell with all of you!" he screamed. "That kid was nothing but a punk Mexican, too smart for his own good, thinking he was something special. I won't take disrespect from street scum like that."

"And El Tigre?" Miguel said softly, very softly. Every trigger finger in the room had tensed when Robards had begun to scream. They'd all dealt with men who had snapped, and they were ready to jump whatever way necessary to keep this one under control. The cops of Trinity West were the best, he thought. And he was damn glad they were on his side.

"Another punk Mexican."

"And you knew he'd seen you kill Jaime, so you had to kill him." There was a stir in the room, but Miguel didn't alter his carefully soft tone.

"Somebody would have, sooner or later, anyway. I just did a little advance pest control."

The rustling in the room grew, and Miguel knew the others were realizing how far gone the man was to have confessed to two murders in front of a roomful of his colleagues. Robards seemed to realize it, as well. His bluster vanished, and his flat brown eyes looked vacant as he swayed slightly on his feet.

Miguel looked at them, the cops of Trinity West, and saw the varying degrees of shock and distaste on their faces. But one thing was the same from one officer to the next. They flicked quick glances at him, waiting for his orders. Gratification filled him, washing away the abhorrence he always felt when a cop went bad.

He looked at the roomful of his people. He looked at Cruz, whose bright blue eyes were full of support. He looked at Ryan, whose usually unreadable face was warm with approval. When their gazes locked the big man nodded. Even Quisto Romero, the newest of the Trinity West family, was smiling.

Miguel looked at all of them, at the best of Trinity West, all there because Kit had probably told them he might need some help.

"Thank you," he said, his throat tight. "All of you."

His gaze went to Kit as a murmur of acknowledgment rose from the group. He knew he didn't dare say what he was feeling, not in front of them all. But then she looked at him and smiled, that slow, sleepy smile she'd awakened with that morning, after a second night spent in the kind of passion he'd never really believed in before. And he knew he didn't have to say it at all.

So instead he looked at the roomful of cops again. "Anybody got some handcuffs?" he asked mildly.

Laughter broke out again. A dozen sets of cuffs were dangling in front of him within ten seconds. With a grin he grabbed one and slapped them on the broken Robards. Then he turned to face the room again.

"So," he drawled in mock severity, "who's minding the store?"

Laughter again, followed by a few snappy shouts of, "Yes, sir!" And he knew Trinity West would survive.

But when every single one of them paused to salute him as they left the room, he wasn't sure he'd survive the next minute without bawling like a baby.

Chapter 18

Kit sighed. She'd thought she would be glad when it was over. But while she was glad that Robards would pay, and it had done her a world of good to be able to go to Carmela Rivas and tell her the murderer of her son had been found and would be punished, it left an evil taste in her mouth that the slime had done his dirty work under cover of the badge, making all cops everywhere have to work harder for the trust they had to have to do their jobs.

But there was more to her unsettled feeling than that, and she knew it. In the week since Robards had snapped, Miguel had been caught up in an endless round of meetings, hearings and briefings with city officials and the press. He was, she was glad to see, coming off once more as the hero. Rightfully so, she thought. It had taken guts to do what he had done, to face alone a man whose hatred and unbalanced mental state could have easily made him draw that gun when they were alone in Miguel's office.

But the whirlwind had left them little time together. He

came here at night—after she'd seen the small, stark apartment he'd been living in she was glad to have him out of it—but usually it was so late, and he was so exhausted, long talks were out of the question.

This left her far too much time to sit alone and think. And she had finally had to face the simple fact that she was in love with Miguel de los Reyes. And that their situation was just as impossible now as it had always been. He was still the chief, and she was still his subordinate. The problems that entailed were huge, maybe insurmountable.

She sipped slowly at her glass of wine. At nine she'd given up on any kind of early night. By eleven she'd undressed and put on her robe, curling up in the big, overstuffed chair in her darkened living room and wishing she was in his arms instead. But the past three days had gotten more chaotic, and they'd barely seen each other at all.

And she kept thinking. Was this really her only choice? she wondered dismally. Was it really her job or Miguel?

She had never thought anything would tempt her away from the work she loved. She couldn't conceive of doing anything else. But the thought of not having Miguel in her life was crushing. The thought of having to work with him but not have him, to see him each day but no more, was unbearable.

And she knew that if it came to that, she would leave. She could live without Trinity West before she could live without him, and she'd never thought she'd say that, never in a million years.

No wonder they warned you about fishing in the company pond, she thought sadly.

She heard the sound of a motor, then a car turning into her drive. She recognized the sound of it and set down her wineglass. The car drove along the side of the house, then stopped in front of the garage, in the parking spot that was out of view from the street, one of the precautions they'd taken until they had time to decide what they were going to do. Or not do.

Kit got to her feet and walked quickly through the kitchen to the back door. She'd given him a key to the house, but this door had only a dead bolt. She turned it quickly and pulled the door open just as he was getting out of his car.

She noticed he was wearing the bright red tie she'd bought him on impulse, saying he needed some color in his life instead of his usual black and gray. He'd accepted it, even agreed with her, but told her that it wasn't a problem anymore. He had more light and color in his life than he'd ever thought to have again. Still, he was wearing it, and she sensed it was a bigger step than he perhaps realized.

Then he looked up, and the back porch light she'd left on illuminated his face. He looked weary. The strain of the past week was showing in his eyes. And he looked physically tired. He was moving more slowly than usual. But he still looked beautiful to her. Sometimes in the night she would wake up and simply look at him, feeling nothing short of awe at this man who had been through the fire so many times, this man who could be both the gentlest of souls and the harshest of opponents. This man who wasn't afraid to be kind, nor to be strong when it was needed. This man she loved, totally and irrevocably.

"You keep looking at me like that," he said when he got to the doorway, "and it's going to be morning before we get around to 'How was your day?'"

"You have a problem with that?" Kit asked, her voice husky.

He dropped his briefcase and the jacket he had tossed over his shoulder. "No problem at all," he said gruffly, reaching for her.

It hit them in a rush. All the need they'd suppressed in the past days of chaos bubbled up at once. When he saw she had nothing on under the silky robe, he growled her name in a voice she'd never heard from him before. His hands slipped under the fabric and over her bare shoulders, and he backed her against the tiled bar, then held her there with his body. She felt the rigid press of male flesh and realized he was already fully aroused. His mouth came down on hers with all the fierceness of a striking raptor, but she welcomed the attack and returned it with her own, probing quickly and deeply with her tongue, wanting the hot, male taste of him.

Her eagerness seemed to unleash something in him. He stripped the robe from her, leaving her naked before him. She found it unexpectedly erotic and shivered, not from cold but from heat as his eyes swept over her, eyes that had gone dark gray with urgent need. Want rippled through her, and a tiny cry broke from her lips.

"Kit," he breathed, and in the hoarse tone of it she read his question.

"Yes," she said, "right now, right here. Hurry."

He muttered a harsh, grateful oath. His hands slid down her back to her waist. He grasped her, and Kit felt the novel sensation of being lifted as if she was tiny.

Then she felt the cold tile of the bar under her buttocks as Miguel set her down. She shivered again, wondering what he was going to do, at the same time trembling with anticipation, wishing he would do it now.

He did. He spread her legs and stood between them. He urged her back until she was resting on her elbows, then he leaned forward and, without preamble, suckled deep and hard on her nipples. She cried out at the sudden shock of fierce sensation. Her head lolled back, and her body arched. She had the thought that she was offering herself to him as if she were a meal served on this counter. And then he took up that offer, his mouth sliding over her belly, his hands parting her thighs, his gentle fingers opening the most intimate part of her.

Kit moaned, knowing, waiting, helpless.

And then his mouth was on her, his tongue stroking her with a wet heat that seared her to the core. He found that little knot of nerves and flicked it again and again, until she was crying out with every touch. She shuddered, her body on the verge.

And then he was gone. But before she could cry out at her loss, before she could lift her head, he was back, lowering his head once more to her breasts. She felt the hot, blunt probe of his body and lifted her hips to urge him home. He sheathed himself in one swift, driving stroke, burying his length in her, stretching her with his thickness. It was all her ready body needed, and she convulsed around him violently, crying out his name in shock as her body surprised her yet again.

"That's what I wanted," he whispered against her ear. "I wanted you to explode the minute I was inside you. I wanted to feel every sweet ripple, every hot, tight second of it."

His erotic words made her shudder anew and cling to him, gasping. Her legs were wrapped around him. She was only vaguely aware of the feel of cloth, telling her he was still dressed. She didn't care. If anything it aroused her even more to know he couldn't wait to get undressed before he had to be inside her. She wanted to reverse that sometime, she thought, the image of him naked while she teased and tormented him giving her the kind of pleasure she thought he must be feeling.

Her body clenched again as an aftershock of pleasure shot through her. He groaned and began to move, as if those deep muscles made it impossible to hold still. He slipped his hands under her back and curled them over her shoulders to hold her steady for his long, steady, driving strokes. He was tall enough to drive in and down, to the very heart of her, and to her surprise she felt her body responding again, when she'd thought herself beyond it, exhausted.

He lowered his head to her breasts, sucking hard, biting with just enough pressure to make her writhe as reborn flames raced through her. He groaned her name like a litany, increasing his pace, driving harder, faster.

When the explosion came it took them both, shattered them and left them drifting slowly in each other's arms, trembling, shaking, clinging.

They never got around to "How was your day?"

Miguel sat at Kit's desk, reading what he'd written. He'd apparently lost what slight ability he'd ever had to sleep late, at least with Kit in his arms. But since they'd spent most of the night doing just about everything but sleeping, he'd slipped out of bed quietly and left her to rest.

He shook his head in amazement. Even thinking about it was having an effect on him, his body tightening eagerly. He was forty-four years old, for God's sake, not some horny teenager. So why did just thinking about making love with her make him ready to do it again?

So stop thinking about it and worry about how you're going to make sure you get to keep doing it.

It was a while later when Kit padded out of the bedroom on bare feet, wearing only his white dress shirt from yesterday. It barely covered the essentials on her tall, slender body, and the length of leg it bared ought to be criminal, he thought, and probably was in some states.

"What're you doing?" she asked sleepily, shoving her tangled blond bangs out of her eyes. He wanted to scoop her up and take her right back to bed.

"You're just in time," he said softly. "You can help me."

"Help you what?"

"Write my annual state of the department speech."

Kit blinked at his mention of the annual speech he gave to all the personnel of Trinity West, congratulating them on a job well done and outlining plans for the future.

"Isn't it a little early for that?"

"I know I usually do it in December, but circumstances seem to dictate it needs to be early this time."

"Oh. Robards?"

"Not really. It's something else I need help with. From you."

She laughed, more awake. "Me? That's a hoot. I'm no speech writer. At least, not the kind of speech where you convert everybody in the audience who isn't on your side already."

"Actually, this part only you can help me with."

"What part?"

"The part where I'd like to announce to everybody that I'm getting married."

Kit stared at him. "Married?" she whispered.

He nodded and reached for the small box he'd set to one side on her desk. He flipped it open and held it out to her. Her stare became a gape as she stared at the ring.

"It's beautiful," she said, still sounding shell-shocked.

"I love you, Kit. I never thought I'd say that to a woman again. But it seems very, very right to say it to you. I highly recommend falling in love with your best friend."

"So do I," she whispered, looking at him at last. Then, as if belatedly realizing she'd not said the actual words, she added, "I love you, too."

He smiled at her. "I think I figured that out when you rounded up the cavalry for me."

She colored slightly and lowered her eyes.

"I thought for a long time about the stone," he said, a little nervous at her lack of an answer. "Then I saw this peridot, set with all those tiny gold bits around it, like the gold flecks in your eyes. And your eyes are that color sometimes. But if you'd rather have a diamond, of course—"

"No."

He held his breath. Then he made himself ask, "Was that to the diamond or the proposal?"

Her gaze shot to his face. "Miguel, you know there are so many problems, things we need to—"

She stopped when he slowly shook his head. "It's all right, Kit. It will all be all right."

"But—"

"That meeting last night? It was with a citizen's committee that's approached me to run for mayor. They were pushing for an answer. I gave them one."

Kit's eyes widened. "You're going to run? Now? I mean, this election?"

He nodded. "In June. That's why they wanted an answer now."

"Oh." She looked stunned all over again.

"I think the ring's distinctive enough for a mayor's wife, don't you?"

For a moment her expression was troubled. "Miguel, this isn't because—"

He stopped her with a sharp shake of his head. "Don't even think that. You know I've been thinking about this for a long time."

"But leaving Trinity West..."

"It wasn't an easy decision," he admitted. "But I'm at the point now where I think I can do more from the outside. Where I can pound some sense into people who buy palm trees instead of fixing potholes or making neighborhoods safer."

"Trinity West's loss will be Marina Heights's gain," she said softly.

"So sure I'll win?"

"Positive. They'd be crazy not to grab you."

"What about you, Kit?"

She smiled at him, a bright, sunny smile that could have banished a hurricane.

"I'm not crazy," she said. Relief flooded him. But before

he could say anything, she added warningly, "I'm incapable of being a typical politician's wife."

He grinned at her. "Fine with me. I'm incapable of being a typical politician."

"Thank God," she said.

"So, was there a yes in there somewhere?"

"Yes. Oh, yes," she said, throwing her arms around him.

This time they ended up in her big, overstuffed chair, an awkward but joyous lovemaking that left them both spent and laughing. And both of them knew what a miracle it was, that two battered, wary souls had found such happiness, that two old friends had found love together.

And both of them knew Trinity West was going to see its biggest wedding yet.

* * * * *

Clay Yeager. This elusive loner has been missing in action for far too long. So don't miss the next installment in the TRINITY STREET WEST *series as Justine Davis delivers Clay's compelling story— only in Intimate Moments.*

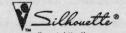

Take 2 bestselling love stories FREE
Plus get a FREE surprise gift!

Special Limited-Time Offer

Mail to Silhouette Reader Service™

P.O. Box 609
Fort Erie, Ontario
L2A 5X3

YES! Please send me 2 free Silhouette Intimate Moments® novels and my free surprise gift. Then send me 6 brand-new novels every month, which I will receive months before they appear in bookstores. Bill me at the low price of $3.96 each plus 25¢ delivery and GST*. That's the complete price, and a saving of over 10% off the cover prices—quite a bargain! I understand that accepting the books and gift places me under no obligation ever to buy any books. I can always return a shipment and cancel at any time. Even if I never buy another book from Silhouette, the 2 free books and the surprise gift are mine to keep forever.

345 SEN CH7Z

Name	(PLEASE PRINT)
Address	Apt. No.
City	Province Postal Code

This offer is limited to one order per household and not valid to present Silhouette Intimate Moments® subscribers. *Terms and prices are subject to change without notice.
Canadian residents will be charged applicable provincial taxes and GST.

CIM-98   ©1990 Harlequin Enterprises Limited

MATERNITY LEAVE

Coming September 1998

Three delightful stories about the blessings
and surprises of "Labor" Day.

TABLOID BABY by Candace Camp

She was whisked to the hospital in the nick of time....

THE NINE-MONTH KNIGHT
by Cait London

A down-on-her-luck secretary is experiencing
odd little midnight cravings....

THE PATERNITY TEST by Sherryl Woods

The stick turned blue before her
biological clock struck twelve....

*These three special women are very pregnant...and very
single, although they won't be either for too much longer,
because baby—and Daddy—are on their way!*

Available at your favorite retail outlet.

**Available September 1998
from Silhouette Books...**

World's Most
Eligible Bachelors

THE CATCH
OF CONARD COUNTY
by Rachel Lee

Rancher Jeff Cumberland: long, lean, sexy as sin. He's eluded every marriage-minded female in the county. Until a mysterious woman breezes into town and brings her fierce passion to his bed. Will this steamy Conard County courtship take September's hottest bachelor off of the singles market?

Each month, Silhouette Books brings you an irresistible bachelor in these all-new, original stories. Find out how the sexiest, most sought-after men are finally caught...

Available at your favorite retail outlet.

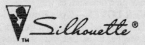

Silhouette ®

COMING NEXT MONTH